W9-BSV-663

DEAD, WITHOUT A STONE TO TELL IT

DEAD, WITHOUT A STONE TO TELL IT

JEN J. DANNA
WITH ANN VANDERLAAN

FIVE STAR
A part of Gale, Cengage Learning

GALE
CENGAGE Learning·

Detroit • New York • San Francisco • New Haven, Conn • Waterville, Maine • London

GALE
CENGAGE Learning

LIBRARY OF CONGRESS CATALOGING-IN-PUBLICATION DATA

Danna, Jen J.
    Dead, without a stone to tell it / by Jen J. Danna ; with Ann Vanderlaan. — First edition.
        pages cm
    ISBN 978-1-4328-2695-6 (hardcover) — ISBN 1-4328-2695-6 (hardcover)
    1. Policewomen—Fiction. 2. Serial murder investigation—Fiction. 3. Forensic anthropologists—Fiction. 4. Mystery fiction. I. Vanderlaan, Ann. II. Title.
PR9199.4.D365D43 2013
813'.6—dc23   2012051188

Find us on Facebook– https://www.facebook.com/FiveStarCengage
Visit our website– http://www.gale.cengage.com/fivestar/
Contact Five Star™ Publishing at FiveStar@cengage.com

Printed in Mexico
3 4 5 6 7 17 16 15 14 13

AUTHOR'S NOTE

The title of this novel comes from the poem "Across the Lines," written by the American poet Ethel Lynn Eliot Beers. Composed during the American Civil War, the poem tells of a Union soldier, fallen on the battlefield and on the brink of death, who fears being buried in an unmarked grave without a headstone to tell the world of his passing.

> *Dead? and here—where yonder banner*
> *Flaunts its scanty group of stars,*
> *And that rebel emblem binds me*
> *Close within those bloody bars.*
> *Dead? without a stone to tell it,*
> *Nor a flower above my breast!*
> *Dead? where none will whisper softly,*
> *"Here a brave man lies at rest!"*

ACKNOWLEDGMENTS

It takes many hands to help write a book that contains a large amount of factual research. We've been fortunate to have been assisted by a group of extremely knowledgeable experts and we're very thankful for their contributions: Reverend Stephen Ayers, for his personal tour of the crypts below Boston's Old North Church and for sharing current research on the crypts and the columbarium. Massachusetts State Police Detective Lieutenant Norman Zuk, for details concerning the Essex Detective Unit and his willingness to answer any and all questions concerning law enforcement. Essex District Attorney Jonathan Blodgett and Steve O'Connell, Director of Communications, Essex District Attorney's Office, for sharing their knowledge of law enforcement in Essex County. Ellie Reese, for assistance on legal details. Dr. Tara Moore, for providing information on Boston University's forensic anthropology labs and graduate program. Dr. Donald Siwek and retired FBI agent Gary Reinecke, for a tour of Boston University's anthropology labs and an enlightening discussion on forensic cases and classes. The assistance we received from these experts has been invaluable in firmly basing our story in realism; any mistakes after their contributions are ours alone.

From a writing standpoint, we owe thanks to many others: Our agent and number one cheerleader, Nicole Resciniti, for believing in us and this novel, and for working so hard alongside us to get it published. Our editor, Gordon Aalborg, who showed us that working with a professional editor is actually a great experience and not one to be feared. Our beta readers and first test audience—Kelly McMillen, Anna Dymarsky, Catherine Albano, Micki Sellers, Jessica Newton, and Rick Newton. And, last, but definitely not least, our fantastic critique team—Margaret McMullen, Sharon Taylor, Jenny Lidstrom, and Lisa Giblin—for their willingness to always be available at a moment's notice and for constantly challenging us to be better writers.

J.J.D. and A.V.

My personal thanks to those who offered support and encouragement during the plotting, writing, and editing of this manuscript: My son, Paul, and his wife, Shelly (who is the best daughter-in-law a mother could ever have) supported my decision to leave the 8 to 5 rat race and do something that I really enjoyed—there is no shortage of faith, sympathetic ears, or cell phone minutes in their home. My neighbors Don and Margaret Newman helped keep my daily life on track after an accident knocked me off my feet for several months. Angel Thundertail, an alumnus of Love-A-Bull Pit Bull rescue in Austin, Texas, greets me every morning with a big pittie smile and a somewhat restrained wiggle. His fur brother, Spike, a deaf dog from the same rescue, taught me that you don't have to shout to make yourself heard.

A.V.

My sincere thanks to those who walked beside me on the path to publication: My fellow writing partners-in-crime—Marianne Harden, Amanda Flower, Amanda Carlson, Melissa Landers, Lea Nolan, Cecy Robson, and Marisa Cleveland—for all the encouragement, understanding, and commiseration; it's been a pleasure taking this journey with you. My mother, who instilled in me a lifelong love of reading and introduced me to the mystery classics. And my family—Rick, Jessica, and Jordan—for believing in me and allowing me the time and space to follow a dream.

J.J.D.

PROLOGUE

Three years earlier
Essex Bay Coast, Massachusetts

The night is never silent. Even in its darkest hour, it has many sounds: the mournful sigh of the wind as it whispers through graceful stems waving silver in the moonlight; the musical rush of water on its inevitable journey to spill into the sea; the furtive scurry of night creatures foraging for food; cunning hunters, stalking their prey before sunrise.

Sounds of the cycle of life.

Until a life ends . . .

The shovel scattered loose soil into the gaping tear in the earth. Clumps of dirt spread over tangled limbs and ragged flesh; the dark earth shading deathly white skin streaked with vivid splashes of red.

The man looked down into the grave, his heart filled with satisfaction and victory. He had held life in his hands until it slipped through his fingers. Gone forever.

Ashes to ashes. Dust to dust. The silent earth reclaiming its own. The dead feeding new life as the cycle continues.

He felt a twinge of sadness at the completion of this challenge, but welling up through the melancholy was an overwhelming anticipation.

This round was over.

But there was always another round to play.

The cycle would continue . . .

CHAPTER ONE:
MARSH WREN NEST

Marsh Wren Nest: a hollow, ball-shaped structure woven from marsh grass and sedges by the short-billed marsh wren (*Cistothorus platensis*); it is attached to the stems of marsh grasses a few feet above the high water mark.

Monday, 10:57 A.M.
The Old North Church
Boston, Massachusetts

The heels of the woman's boots rapped sharply against worn wood as she descended the centuries-old staircase. Not many ventured from the sun-streaked upper reaches of the church into the oppressive stillness of the dark, damp basement below. Only those who would commune with the dead.

She was one of those people.

She stopped at the bottom of the stairs, the large area under the church sanctuary spreading before her. Through the doorway opposite, a long corridor stretched away into the gloom that shaded the far reaches of the space, dimly lit by the few exposed light bulbs that hung from the ceiling. There, long held safe in the quiet darkness and forgotten by all but a scarce few, were the oldest crypts in Boston.

Standing in the nearly silent basement, with only the creaks from the floorboards overhead betraying the presence of the funeral mourners, the centuries of history entombed in this building surrounded her, just like the dead sleeping inside the aged brick walls.

The vicar's words rang in her head. *I'm sorry I can't take you down, but the funeral is about to start. You'll find him if you go down the stairs and turn right into the columbarium.*

The atmosphere changed the moment she stepped over the threshold. The basement and the crypts were cold and damp, but even surrounded by walls of modern burial niches, the columbarium seemed warm and inviting. A space where the living could feel closer to the dead who had gone before them.

Mournful music filtered through the floorboards into this quiet room of remembrance.

It felt . . . peaceful.

The peace was abruptly shattered by the clatter of something solid falling to the floor followed by a soft curse.

There he is.

On the far side of the room, a door opened into a small chamber. A doorway was cut into one of the whitewashed chamber walls, bright russet clay revealed at the entrance. Moving to stand in the gap, she looked into the tomb, staring in shock at the chaos within while breathing air musty with centuries of undisturbed stillness.

Rotting wooden boxes of different shapes and sizes were stacked haphazardly along the walls. Many of the boxes had collapsed, their lids loosened and their contents spilled out over other boxes and across the floor. Bones of every size and description lay in tangled piles, mixed with funeral ornaments and remnants of moldering cloth. A solitary skull grinned up at her from where it lay tipped against the cracked side of a crumpled box.

A movement to her left drew her attention and her gaze shifted to the man kneeling with his back partially turned to her. He bent over the pile of debris, freeing a single bone before transferring it carefully in his gloved hands to a clear plastic tub on the floor beside him.

The small ball of tangled nerves in her stomach clenched tighter. So much was riding on this case and she had so much to prove—

She jerked her thoughts back into the present. *That's water under the bridge now. You have to do this right. And to succeed, you need* him.

Her eyes sharply assessed the man kneeling before her. *Mid-thirties, medium build, about 190 pounds, brown hair.*

What surprised her most was how much he'd changed since her single encounter with him years before. In her memory, while tall, he had a slight build, like a man who spent all his time with his nose in a book or bent over bones in the lab.

Not anymore.

He'd filled out considerably in the intervening years. His hunter green, crew-necked shirt stretched taut across his wide shoulders and muscled back as he bent over his work, and his biceps stretched and bunched as he picked up another bone.

As he placed the bone into the container, his overlong hair fell over his eyes. He raised a latex-gloved hand and pushed it back with his wrist.

For a brief moment, the scar was revealed by the bright spotlight—a thick furrow of twisted skin that started on his temple near his right eyebrow and disappeared into his hairline. Leigh stared at it in surprise—how had she missed it before? Whatever caused that scar had struck dangerously close to home. Any closer, he wouldn't be kneeling in a dusty church basement, and she wouldn't be here asking for his help.

She must have made a tiny involuntary sound because he suddenly twisted to face her. His hazel eyes widened in surprise as they met hers, and he gave a small jerk of his head, sending his hair tumbling back over his forehead.

"Dr. Lowell?" Her words seemed jarringly loud in the silence.

His gaze slid down her body. Unlike many men, his stare wasn't predatory; rather it was a critical examination, as if cataloging her features. "I'm Matthew Lowell." He rolled to his feet, pulling himself up to stand several inches taller than she.

He's aged well, she thought. The only signs were the tiny lines around his eyes that gave his face character.

She pulled back the edge of her jacket to reveal a gold shield, bright against the black leather oval. "Trooper First Class Leigh Abbott, Massachusetts State Police, out of the Essex Detective Unit."

His face clouded with confusion. "Essex? I haven't been up there for probably two or three years."

"Essex is my jurisdiction, but it's what you can do here in Boston that interests me. When I was told you were out in the field, I asked whomever I talked to at the university to let you know I was coming."

His expression grew wary. "I guess the message never made it through." Planting his feet firmly, he crossed his arms over his chest. "What is it you think I can do for you?"

Leigh noted his sudden move to a defensive posture with a small spurt of alarm. "I'm looking to consult with a forensic anthropologist on a case. I would like to retain your services for—"

"No thanks. Not interested."

Leigh drew up short, staring at him in stunned disbelief, dread starting to slowly pool in her stomach. This wasn't the easygoing professor she remembered. "You haven't even heard my proposal, Dr. Lowell. How can you make that decision?"

"I don't need to hear it. The answer is 'no.' "

Anger started to build, swamping the dread. She forced herself to calm down and try a different tack. "I'm familiar with your skills and you're exactly what I need to help me solve this case. If you'll just let me explain—"

"Don't bother. I've worked with you before. I don't need to hear the details."

Leigh stepped closer, drawing herself up to her full height. This was familiar ground; she worked with bigger egos than his on a daily basis in her own department. "I can assure you, Dr. Lowell, we have *never* worked together."

He didn't retreat. Instead, he simply stared down at her from only inches away. "Not you personally, Trooper. Your kind." His tone was thick with disdain.

"My *kind?* Do you mean women? Or cops?"

"Cops. You come in, you make demands, and you expect results. You don't care how, or why, you just want answers and you want them *now.* And you're willing to bully and threaten to get them. So . . . no thanks." He pushed past her, carefully skirting the debris on the floor and stepping back into the small prep area.

Leigh followed him, her eyes narrowed on his stony profile. She had one last weapon in her arsenal and she wasn't above using it—his own words from years ago, overheard as he spoke to a Boston detective after class: *If you think Sharpe is the expert, then you deal with him. Personally, I don't like his style and I have serious doubts about his methods and some of his conclusions. I wouldn't send a student I disliked to work with him.* "Thank you for your time, Dr. Lowell," she said with stiff formality. Turning away, she paused in the doorway to speak into the empty columbarium beyond. "You're clearly a very busy man, so I'll take my request to Dr. Sharpe at Harvard. He may be interested in a case like this. I'm told he likes—"

"Wait." The single word was clipped short with banked irritation.

Standing with her back to him, Leigh allowed a very brief smile of triumph to curve her lips. *Gotcha, you arrogant bastard.*

17

But when she turned back to face him, her features were schooled into polite interest. "Yes?"

She glimpsed the battle warring within him by the way the muscles in his jaw bunched and his hazel eyes simmered with frustration. When he spoke, his voice was resigned. "What is it you need, Trooper Abbott?"

Relief flooded through Leigh. "I have a bone I need examined."

"*A* bone?" His dark brows drew together. "Singular?"

"Singular," she confirmed. "It was found by a man out walking his dog near the town of Essex. The dog ran off and the owner caught up with it at a beaver pond. That's when he noticed the bone protruding from the dam."

"It was *in* the dam?"

"Yes. The beaver built it right into the dam. Having only one bone tells us nothing except that there's a body. Dr. Edward Rowe, Medical Examiner for the State of Massachusetts, has declined the case at this point due to the lack of evidence recovered at the scene. But he suggested having a forensic anthropologist take a look to see if anything could be learned from examining the bone itself."

"I know who Rowe is. Why doesn't he use his own anthropologist for this?"

"He doesn't have one anymore," Leigh said. "Budget cuts. The person who used to be on staff took a position out of state, so we need a new consultant on a case-by-case basis. One with the appropriate qualifications to serve as an expert witness in court if the case comes to trial."

"I've worked at two body farms during my training and have run my own lab for years. It's my reputation on the line if I give faulty testimony in court, so I wouldn't do this if my qualifications, knowledge, and experience didn't stand up. But you already know they will or you wouldn't be here in the first place." His eyes narrowed on her in speculation. "Why me?"

"Sorry?"

"Why did you come to me? There are other forensic anthropologists in the area. Trevor Sharpe, as you noted, being one."

"You taught one of the murder school classes I took."

" 'Murder school'?" He looked vaguely confused.

"That's what we call the course troopers take when they transfer from Field Services to the Detective Unit. You taught my class on skeletal recovery and identification." He scanned her face as if searching for some memory of her features. She gave him a twisted smile at the lack of recognition in his eyes, pushing away the small twinge of pain at being overlooked by the men in her professional life once again. "I guess I'm not that memorable."

He flushed slightly. "I teach a lot of students, so I don't always remember someone in particular unless I've had some personal interaction with them."

"To be fair, it was about three years ago and there were a lot of us in the class. I'd have been impressed if you'd remembered my face out of all those strangers."

"If it was three years ago, I was also brand-new on campus, so everyone was a stranger." He pushed back his sleeve to check the time. "I can meet you at my lab at one o'clock to examine your bone. I need to close down the site for the day since I might not be back this afternoon."

"That will be your call depending on what the evidence tells you." Leigh moved past him to stand in the doorway of the tomb. The smell of mustiness and disuse struck her again, as well as the shock of so many remains in such a small space. Her gaze traveled over the contents, picking out small details: ivory bones, scattered and piled haphazardly; a narrow, plain gold band winking dully in the light; a small bottle-green medicine vial lying on its side; a bonnet, so tiny it could only belong to a child.

A shiver ran up her spine. So many dead, reduced to nothing but bones, their most precious possessions now simply a few misplaced trinkets. Unbidden, her mind flashed to her father, dead now four years. What would be left of him? A rib cage with his police force Medal of Honor pinned to a rotting uniform, or his shield lying atop a pile of dry, splintered bones? She closed her eyes briefly on a sudden wave of grief; she simply couldn't bear to think of that dynamic, vibrant man reduced to so little.

"It's kind of a mess, isn't it?" Lowell brushed against her back as he came to stand behind her, and suddenly the cold mustiness of the tomb was overlaid with warm hints of citrus and sandalwood. "But out of chaos comes order. That's my job. To sort through the remains in this charnel house and to reassemble the dead. To identify them. And, if possible, to return their grave goods to them."

"What do you do with the remains once they're identified?"

"We bring them home."

Startled, Leigh swiveled to look at him sharply. He'd unconsciously echoed her own feelings about the victims she stood over so often. Some had faces and identities, but for those without, it was a constant struggle to unite the dead with their families and to give the survivors both closure and justice. It struck her abruptly that they shared a similar goal. The only difference between them was simply how long the dead in their care had been lost.

"We contact the families if we can track them down. We haven't found a family yet that didn't want their long-lost relatives back." He moved away to step back into the prep room.

Leigh started toward the doorway as Lowell snapped off the bright spotlights and made some final notes in the notebook on the small table. But as she stepped into the columbarium, her head jerked up as his earlier words finally sank in. "Hold on, did you say that you wanted to examine the bone *in your lab?*"

Lowell set the book down and neatly laid the pen on its smooth burgundy surface. "Sure. I'll be able to tell you more there and—"

She cut him off with a raised hand. "The sample needs to be examined and then stored in the M.E.'s lab space. That's protocol."

Irritation flitted over Lowell's face. "I really need to examine it in my lab. All the equipment I'll need is there."

"We can't do that. Legal chain of evidence requires that it be maintained in a secure location. You'll have to work at the M.E.'s facility. Trust me, it's the best the state has to offer. If you're missing something, you can just bring it in. No one will mind."

His jaw tightened. "That's not the best way to do this. Do you want accurate answers or not? If so, we need to do it my way."

Leigh felt their brief connection evaporate. "Are you always this stubborn? Do you always have to get your way or you just pick up your ball and go home?"

Irritation segued smoothly into temper. "Let's get one thing straight, Trooper Abbott. If you want my help, you'll have to give me some leeway. I'm taking time away from my own research. If you want to make it easier for me to do so, then you have to meet me halfway. If not, I'm out and you can ask Dr. Sharpe for help."

She refrained from snapping at him by taking a deep breath while she weighed his response. *Stuck between a rock and a hard place. You have nothing to base this case on without him. If Sharpe's not trustworthy, then Lowell's your only choice.* "Then let me make this crystal clear, Dr. Lowell. If we're going to break protocol

21

and use your lab instead of the state facilities, then you have to guarantee me a credible chain of evidence and complete security at your site."

"Chain of evidence is no problem. And we're just across the road from the M.E.'s office so if something needs to be stored there long term after we've examined it in the lab, we can easily move it. Our building has both security in the lobby and keycard-only access, but if that's not good enough for you, then you can arrange for additional security with campus police. I'm going to be busy with your remains. *You* can take care of security."

They stubbornly stood toe-to-toe until Leigh forced herself to take a step back. "Fine. But until it's set up, I stay with the remains."

"Fine," he snapped back. "One other thing. Me and my lab includes my grad students. We're a team and they'll be helping on this." Leigh opened her mouth but Lowell held up an index finger an inch from her lips. "That's the deal. I'm a teacher and there's no better way for them to learn than through hands-on experience. Trust me when I say that you'll be glad to have them. Each one brings something of value to the table."

Leigh nearly ground her teeth in frustration. "All right. In return, I want access to your lab at my convenience and that means starting now. If we're meeting in the middle, then you have to come halfway."

"We'll do our best, but some of us do have prior commitments."

"This could be murder, Dr. Lowell. That takes priority."

"It could also be a hiker lost in the woods who died from an accidental fall. Murder remains to be seen. But," he conceded, "if it's murder, then, yes, it takes priority."

"Then we need to determine what we're dealing with."

"Agreed. Give me time to gather my students and we'll meet

you at one o'clock." He rattled off a south Boston address. "We're in room ten-seventeen. Bring maps of the area where the bone was found and the bone itself. Then we'll see what we can do for you, Trooper Abbott."

"Very well, Dr. Lowell." She turned sharply and strode from the columbarium, quickly climbing the vestry steps to re-emerge into the light.

He's on board. He may be a stubborn son of a bitch, but he's on board. Now to see what he and his team can do.

She reached for her cell phone to report in with her sergeant.

Matt listened to the hollow thud of her footsteps as she climbed the wooden staircase, followed by the sound of the door slamming behind her.

"Damn it!" He blew out a heavy breath and ran a hand through his hair.

Very smooth, Matt. The lady comes looking for help and first you refuse, then you snarl at her when she tries to follow protocol. Well done.

With a muttered curse, he sprang for the stairs, taking them two at a time. At the top of the staircase, he pushed through the fire door and burst into the Third Lantern Garden, a peaceful oasis of sprawling, sun-splashed flowers and shrubs surrounding a redbrick patio.

She had already climbed the garden steps and was briskly striding toward the front of the church. "Trooper Abbott," he called, his eyes narrowing on her retreating form when she ignored him. "Trooper!"

She turned around and he saw the phone pressed to her ear. She held up a finger, signaling him to wait. He wandered to the far side of the small garden and sat down on the wall of the gurgling circular fountain that graced one corner.

As he waited, Matt found himself staring at the woman standing at the top of the steps, taking in the honey-colored hair coiled neatly at the nape of her neck, crisp white shirt, and conservative charcoal-gray blazer and tailored pants. She was slim but the lines under her clothes spoke of a sleek, muscular build. The only jewelry she wore was a pair of discreet gold studs and a simple dial watch on a plain leather strap.

She dresses like a man and ties her hair back to downplay her looks. His eyes passed over her again and since she was partially turned away, he allowed his gaze to linger appreciatively on the curves she tried to hide. *Is it expected in her profession . . . or is she purposely trying not to stand out?*

A gust of wind ruffled his hair and metallic musical chimes shivered through the air. He recognized the sound as the breeze blowing through the thousands of dog tags suspended in the Memorial Garden at the back of the church, a memorial dedicated to the men and women of the Armed Forces lost in Afghanistan and Iraq. Unconsciously, his hand rose to rub the scar at his temple.

So many lost. Kirkpatrick. Rogers. Dutton. Williams. Boddington. Too many lost.

"Dr. Lowell?"

Her voice broke through his thoughts. She stood on the stairs, one hand resting lightly on the wrought iron railing.

"Did I forget something, Dr. Lowell?" Her tone was crisp.

He climbed to his feet. "No. Look, I think we got off on the wrong foot in there." He strode across the sun-warmed patio and abruptly stuck out his hand.

Her eyes flicked from his hand back up to his face, her brow wrinkled in confusion. "Are we . . . starting over?"

"We are. And please, stop calling me Dr. Lowell. Not even my grad students call me that. Most academic research labs are pretty casual and everyone is on a first-name basis. If we're working together, it's going to be weird if you keep calling me

'Dr. Lowell.' " He thrust his hand out further. "Hi, I'm Matt."

She stared at his hand briefly before sliding her hand into his. "Then it should go both ways." Matt's warm hand closed around hers and she returned his firm grip. "Hi, I'm Leigh."

"Nice to meet you, Leigh. Again." He released her hand. "I feel like I owe you an apology. I'm not usually this hard to work with, but I've been burned working with the police before."

"You've worked a forensics case with the local police?"

"No, it was back when I was at Texas State, finishing my doctorate. My advisor was asked to assist on a case and, as his senior student, I was also involved. We worked with a detective from the San Marcos P.D. He was . . ." Matt's eyes narrowed briefly in memory. ". . . very difficult to work with."

"Some officers . . ." Leigh paused as if choosing her words carefully. "Some officers, especially those set in their ways, find new techniques and new procedures to be a challenge. And sometimes, when an officer is ordered to work with outsiders, it doesn't always go smoothly."

"You can say that again," Matt muttered quietly.

"I'm not one of those people. You have knowledge and expertise I don't. There's a family out there who's lost a loved one. They deserve to know what happened, and that lost victim deserves justice. To do that, I need your help."

"I can help you with your evidence. You'd be surprised how even one bone can help narrow your search. Depending, of course, on the condition of the bone."

"Which you'll see shortly." She glanced at her watch. "But not if I don't get on the road. Thank you for agreeing to help. I'll see you at one o'clock." She strode from the garden and disappeared around the front of the church.

Matt pulled his cell phone from his pocket, speed dialing a familiar number. "Hey, it's me. I need you all back in the lab by no later than one. We've been asked by the police to consult on a case . . . It could be murder."

CHAPTER TWO:
BITTERN

Bittern: any of twelve species of solitary marsh birds in the same Family as herons. Bitterns are camouflaged by their streaked brown and buff plumage, which lets them hide in plain sight among the reeds and marsh grasses by standing upright with their bills pointed toward the sky.

Monday, 11:59 A.M.
Essex Detective Unit
Salem, Massachusetts

The maze of corridors and rooms that made up the Salem office of the Massachusetts State Police buzzed with activity as Leigh strode down the hallway. She carefully cradled the bone, securely sealed in a clear plastic evidence bag. She passed the door of the long, narrow conference room, glancing in to scan the homicide board at the head of the table and quickly categorized the seven current homicides—four ready to go to court and three currently under investigation. Her own name was associated with "John/Jane Doe" at the bottom of the list.

The hallway opened into the Detective Unit bullpen. The small, cramped room was lined on both sides with an identical trio of short-walled cubicles, their fabric dividers a dull generic beige to match the walls. Every spare foot of available wall space was jammed with filing cabinets or bookcases of binders detailing protocols or holding forms for the endless river of paperwork.

There were two officers in the bullpen, both dressed in soft clothes. Trooper Brad Riley, the squad rookie, sprawled at his desk, tipped back in his chair. He grinned up at Trooper First Class Len Morrison, one of the senior members of the squad, who leaned casually in the doorway of Riley's cube. Morrison made a rude hand gesture and both men burst out laughing.

Morrison fell silent as Leigh entered the room, his cold eyes flicking toward her. For a brief moment, her steps slowed as his insolent gaze ran up and down her body, but there was nothing seductive or appreciative about his perusal. His lip curled in a sneer, and he deliberately turned his back to her, stepping further into the cubicle to block her view of Riley with his shoulder as if to shield the younger officer.

Eyes fixed straight ahead and her face a blank mask, Leigh marched purposefully past him, leaving as much space between them as the narrow corridor allowed. She slipped inside her own cubicle in the back corner, sinking into her chair. Only then did she let her neutral expression crumple. She closed her eyes, concentrating on pushing back the anger and hurt from Morrison's deliberate snub. It was the second time today she'd been checked out by a man, but at least Matt Lowell's perusal hadn't left her feeling less than a woman. Her eyes shot open as she heard Morrison murmur something to Riley, followed by Riley's answering laugh.

Unconsciously, her right hand clenched into a tight fist. Morrison's exclusion was blatantly meant to hurt, but she would cut out her own heart before she ever let him know how effective it was.

Morrison had made it clear from the beginning that he had it out for her. The daughter of the former Unit Sergeant, she'd been brought in from Field Troop A after only three years on the job, compared to Morrison's five. His resentment of what he saw as special treatment had been obvious from the moment she set foot in the bullpen. And that resentment was painfully obvious whenever a senior officer wasn't in the room.

The camaraderie between the men in the department was strong, but even after three years in the Detective Unit, Leigh found the men either weren't sure what to make of the only woman in the room or were openly antagonistic. Riley was still learning the ropes, but he was taking his cues from the men around him. She knew the unspoken rule—if she hoped to make it in the Unit, then she had to put her head down and take it. But she didn't have to like it.

She tucked the bone into the messenger bag on her desk, closing and securing the flap.

Sitting back in her chair, she scanned her desk. Like every other officer in the bullpen, she had a huge amount of paperwork to deal with. But unlike the men's desks, which were strewn with forms and notes, her paperwork was organized into folders and neatly stacked, leaving the desktop mostly clear.

She gave a small sigh. Her cubicle was a testament to how she fit into the department. Neat. Organized. Sterile. *Like a square peg in a round hole.* There was almost nothing personal on her desk. The men in the Unit plastered the walls of their cubicles with mementos of their lives—hand-drawn pictures from their kids, photos of their wives and lovers, competition ribbons, ball caps and other sports memorabilia. The Red Sox were sacred in this room and every man proudly displayed his team loyalty.

She was the exception. She had no children, so there were no pictures drawn with more love than skill. She didn't watch sports, which in itself set her apart from the men. And the lack of a lover was a gaping hole in her life.

The only personal memento in her office was the framed

photo behind her mouse pad. Tucked neatly into the corner, it couldn't be seen from the doorway of the cubicle; it was only visible from her chair. Reaching out, she rubbed her thumb along the lower edge of the frame as one might caress a touchstone while she studied the well-loved face.

It was her father's last formal departmental picture. In it, he wore his smoky-blue dress uniform jacket, matching dress shirt, and navy tie tacked down with the State Police insignia. His salt and pepper hair was cut short under his uniform cap and his face was set in serious lines. It was the face he had typically shown the department, but she fondly remembered the man who had shouldered the lonely job of raising a devastated little girl by himself even as he mourned his young wife's death. It had been just the two of them against the world, until the world had taken him away too, leaving her devastated and alone.

I miss you, Dad.

She rubbed her thumb over the frame one more time as if to draw strength from the spirit of the man who had gone before her. Then, sitting back in her chair, she glanced at the time. She needed to get on the road if she hoped to meet Matt and his team at one P.M. Standing, she found the room deserted. Riley and Morrison had slipped out while she was lost in thought.

She squared her shoulders and picked up her messenger bag. She had a job to do. And even if she was on her own, she'd damn well get it done.

Head high, she strode from the bullpen.

CHAPTER THREE:
ESTUARY

Estuary: a partially enclosed body of water where fresh river water mixes with salty ocean water in a coastal transition zone.

Monday, 12:50 P.M.
Boston University, School of Medicine
Boston, Massachusetts

Leigh paused in the open doorway to peer into the large lab, brightly lit by banks of overhead fluorescent lights. She scanned the lab—racks of chrome shelving holding trays of pale bones, a whiteboard splashed with anatomical sketches, desks strewn with personal items, and miles of countertops holding equipment and instruments—before finding Matt Lowell on the far side of the room.

Leigh allowed herself a moment to watch him interact with the three students grouped around him. They watched him with rapt attention, freely jumping in to comment or question. She sensed the comfort level and closeness between them; even to a stranger across the room, they felt like a unit.

She knocked quietly on the doorframe.

Matt's head came up sharply and the corner of his lips curved in a welcoming smile. "Excuse me for a minute, guys." He crossed the room toward her in long strides. "Come in." He indicated the messenger bag tucked under her arm. "Is that it?"

"Yes. I also brought the maps you requested."

"Great. Come meet my students."

They turned to face the students across the room, who stared at them with undisguised curiosity. At a quick glance, Leigh placed each of the two men and one woman to be in their mid-twenties.

Matt took her arm, pulling her into the group. "Guys, I'd like you to meet Trooper Abbott. Leigh, these are my grad students. They'll be working with us on this case." He motioned first to the only female in the group, a tall, slender woman of Japanese descent with an athletic build. She wore her jet-black hair in a loose bun pierced with two artfully placed decorative sticks. "This is my senior grad student, Akiko Niigata. Kiko, this is Trooper Leigh Abbott."

Kiko smiled and extended her hand. "Hi." Her features were beautifully exotic, but her confident voice was born-and-bred American.

"And this is Paul Layne." Matt indicated a tall, lanky young man with slightly spiky dark-blond hair wearing a red hoodie and worn jeans.

Paul's clear blue eyes fixed on her with blatant interest, and there was a glint of humor in them as he abruptly stuck out his hand. "Hey."

She smiled back at him as she shook his hand. "Hey."

"And Juka Petrović," Matt continued.

Leigh turned to the last student who stood silently a half pace behind the others, a stocky young man with a swarthy complexion and dark eyes and hair.

"It's very nice to meet you." His soft-spoken, slightly formal greeting carried a hint of Eastern Europe.

"Let's take a look at what we have here," Matt suggested. "Paul, get the door, please. All of this has to stay confidential. And we're going to be handling evidence, so lab coats and gloves on." He glanced at Leigh. "I've already filled them in on the background details and the security requirements."

They gathered around a stainless steel table that was large enough to hold a complete set of remains. Reaching inside her messenger bag, Leigh withdrew the evidence bag and handed it to Matt.

He pulled out the long, thin bone, cradling it carefully in both hands, turning it over as he examined it.

What remained of the small ball of nerves in Leigh's stomach loosened as she noted the care he took with the evidence. "What can you tell me about our victim?"

"I can't tell you race or sex, not from this particular skeletal component, but there are still details I can give you. How much do you remember from class?"

Leigh flushed. "You covered a lot of ground in a short period of time. And some of it's kind of fuzzy for me three years later."

"So not much, in other words. That's okay; that's why you've got us." He turned to his students. "I want you to each examine the bone, then we'll discuss it." He handed the bone to Kiko.

Leigh shifted restlessly, wanting to jump in to speed the discussion along, but Matt caught her eye, something in his expression asking her to wait. She reluctantly swallowed her impatience, watching Kiko as she cradled the bone carefully in both hands, staring at it silently.

"Everything okay?" Matt asked his student when she remained silent and motionless.

"Yes. It's just . . ." Kiko rotated the bone, examining the underside as she spoke. "This isn't a research specimen from some old man who died in his sleep at ninety and donated his body to science. This isn't from someone who lived centuries ago . . ." She paused and met Matt's eyes. "Although you know seeing a child's tiny bones gets me every time. This is someone who was alive within the past few years. Someone I could have met on the street." Her gaze dropped to the bone and she turned it over in her hands again. "Someone who died young, maybe even the same age as me. It's just . . ."

"A little freaky," Paul finished for her. "Yeah, we feel it too."

Leigh studied the students as they grouped together around the table. Her concern about involving Matt's students started to diminish; these kids might work out fine after all.

Kiko passed the bone to Paul. Juka then examined it before handing it back to Matt. "Okay, tell me what we're looking at," Matt said. "I know this is different from anything you've done before, but put emotion aside for a few minutes and simply look at the evidence. This is how we can do the most good."

"It's a radius," Paul stated. "More specifically, a left radius." He held out his left arm toward Leigh, running his index finger from his inner elbow to his wrist, ending at the base of his thumb.

"It's from someone likely in their late teens or early twenties based on epiphyseal fusion," Kiko added.

When Juka remained silent, Matt simply looked at him expectantly. "The bone shows signs of being buried," Juka said. "Possibly for a prolonged period of time. It also shows signs of scavenging. Probably rats. Maybe opossums."

"And that's on top of the beaver." Matt straightened and stepped back from the table, turning to Leigh. "That's a very fast macroscopic examination. To be able to give you an opinion that you could use in court we'd need to do a microscopic examination, which takes a little more time."

Leigh's brows drew together as she studied the bone. "Why didn't you comment on the cut mark on the bone?"

Matt's face clouded briefly. "Cut mark?"

She pointed to one end of the bone—a wedge-shaped indentation was clearly visible where the flared end met the shaft. "That was made by a weapon, right? Possibly giving us cause of death?"

Matt shook his head. "No, there are no tool marks—or, as we call them, kerf marks—on this bone. If you look closely, you can see that there are no sharp margins in the defect. That mark is actually a remnant of normal maturation. It's where cartilage once lay at the growth plate before being converted to bone."

"Really?" Leigh leaned in to examine the defect more closely. Matt was right; the sides and margins of the notch were smooth and rounded, not sharply defined like a cut from a blade. "Damn. I thought we had something there."

"We do, just not what you think."

Straightening, Leigh pulled a small spiral-bound notepad and pen from her inside breast pocket. Flipping it open, she made a few quick notes.

"You don't have to write this down," Matt said, tapping her notepad with an index finger. "I'm not expecting you to remember every detail or make notes to cover all of it. I'll give you a full report."

She glanced up. "Yes, you will." She bent over her notepad again, but not before catching the expression of incredulity that flashed across Matt's face, and Paul's quick amused grin at her blunt expectation of a report. "But I'd like to get some of this information down now. My sergeant will want an update later today. So, that mark. You're saying there was soft tissue there that decomposed after death, leaving that gap?"

"Exactly. It's one way that we're estimating the victim's age. Now, we can be a lot more accurate when we've got the full remains and we can consider dentition, cranial suture fusion, and pubic symphysis modification."

"Fair enough. Can you estimate how long it's been buried to narrow down my missing persons search?"

"That's a little harder to do from just this one piece of evidence. Buried bones tend to absorb minerals and take on the color of the soil around them, given full skeletonization and enough time. This bone has started this process so it's been buried for at least a couple of years. Except that it didn't stay buried. Somehow scavengers got to it."

"Considering that this bone was removed from the burial site, is it safe to assume that we're going to be missing other pieces of the remains?" Leigh asked.

"It's doubtful that it was the only bone taken."

Her lips a tight line, Leigh met Matt's eyes. "So it doesn't bode well for recovery or identification of this victim."

"Maybe. We need to move fast on this because if the remains are only partially exposed, we might be able to recover the majority of the victim. Perhaps only one arm was exposed and removed."

Leigh's eyes narrowed. "Why were the remains exposed? That could be very important for locating the actual burial site."

"It could," Matt allowed. "Let's get out the maps. I think this bone will be able to tell us enough to give you a good idea of where to start looking."

Matt watched Leigh pull a well-used, highly detailed map from her messenger bag and lay it out on the table. "The beaver dam where the bone was found is here." She indicated an area of the northern Essex coast, just west of Cape Ann, the small, eastern-most peninsula in Essex County.

"Essex Bay," Kiko murmured. "Was the dam right on the river?"

"No, it's on one of the smaller branches west of the river, just north of the Essex Marina," Leigh replied.

"So, north of Route 133." When Leigh looked up in surprise, Kiko said, "Local girl. I grew up in Gloucester."

"Good to know."

Matt carefully studied the map, noting the network of channels that drained into Essex Bay. "That's pretty close to both the town and the marina. I'm assuming you've already done a detailed search of the area?"

"We came up empty. We worked in conjunction with the Essex Police Force because it's their jurisdiction. They're only a fourteen-man force, but they were a huge help because they really know their district." Leigh tapped the span of Essex Bay with her index finger. "Part of what makes the search for the rest of the remains difficult is the terrain."

"Makes it tough when part of your search area is under water twice a day," Kiko stated.

"Exactly."

"Wait. You're talking about the tide?" Matt asked.

"Yes. You said earlier that you haven't been to Essex County since you first came to Massachusetts," Leigh said. "How much time did you spend on the coast?"

He shrugged. "Almost none. I've been down to the wharves in town and to a beach or two, but most of my water time is on the Charles. I row."

Leigh's gaze suddenly skimmed downwards, over his chest and arms, and he felt a small spurt of heat when her eyebrow unconsciously cocked in appreciation. Then Kiko spoke, drawing them both back into the conversation.

"Spending time on the wharves here in town would only count in this discussion if you did it two hundred years ago," she said. "Back when Boston was a tiny peninsula surrounded by swampland before they filled in those areas to allow the town to grow. But that's the kind of area you still find along the Essex coast. It's a huge, complex ecosystem."

"And this here—" Paul tapped the section of coast Leigh had indicated was the site of the discovery of the bone. "It's a swamp?"

"Salt marsh, actually." Leigh indicated a shaded portion on the map. "Basically, it's a large area of low-lying wetland, with no roads or houses inside the actual marsh."

"You obviously didn't find a full set of remains when you did the search," Matt stated. "Where did you look?"

Leigh used the end of her pen as a pointer, circling a large area of coast. "We covered west of the Essex River and north of Route 133. We even checked the Spring Street Cemetery because someone suggested the bone might have been removed from a grave there."

"Worth checking out considering the proximity," Matt agreed. "It didn't pan out though, obviously."

"No, there was no disturbance in the cemetery and there was no sign of other human remains anywhere. We also dragged the river."

"It's not in the river," Juka reminded her. "The color of the bone tells us that it was buried."

"I know that now. But at the time, considering the bone was found in the beaver dam, checking the river was a logical next step."

"What's the soil like there?" Paul asked.

"Assuming it's the same as Gloucester, the soil is very loamy with a high sand component so it usually has good drainage," said Kiko.

Matt glanced back at the radius. "That would explain the brown tinge to the bone. Clearly it's been buried in well-drained, dry soil."

"What makes you think that?" Leigh interrupted.

"It's a guess," Matt explained, "based mostly off the minimal scavenging marks on the bone, but I think these remains went through putrefaction and full decomposition while still buried."

"The lack of adipocere substantiates your assessment," Kiko said, then looked at Leigh. "You probably know adipocere as 'grave wax.' "

"I've heard that term," Leigh said. "But I don't know much about it."

"Adipocere is a thick, waxy substance that's sometimes found on bodies when fatty tissue decomposes in the presence of moisture and bacteria and without oxygen," Matt explained. "It's significant because it slows the normal process of putrefaction to a crawl."

"But you know this didn't happen because the bone was found without flesh, right?" Leigh asked. "So that gives you more information about where the body was buried."

Matt was pleasantly surprised; she'd been paying attention. "That's right. And we know from the types of scavenger tooth marks on the bone that decomposition had already gone to completion before they had access to it."

Leigh straightened. "So what does all of this really tell us?"

"It means we won't find the remains in the intertidal zone," Kiko said. "There's simply too much moisture. The area within the intertidal zone is flooded with seawater at high tide. Even if it's only a couple of inches deep, the ground is still saturated twice a day. A body buried in that area would almost certainly have adipocere." She whistled. "That's a huge area to take out of the search."

"It's going to make our job much easier." Matt bent over the map and drew a large circle with his index finger around the marsh that surrounded the Essex River. "You can cut this area way down. Any area that's in the intertidal zone is very unlikely to hold the missing remains."

Leigh's mouth dropped open in surprise. "Cut it all out? Are you sure?"

"That's what you wanted us for," Matt pointed out. "To locate your remains and determine what happened to your victim. This is just the first step."

Leigh gave a surprised half-laugh. "Well, yes, I knew from

your class that you'd be good, but I didn't think when I brought you one bone that you'd be able to tell me this much this fast."

"It's simply a matter of reading the evidence you've given us. The next thing to think about is why was this bone recovered? We know the body was buried, but why was it just found by scavengers after all this time?"

"So you mean something like reports of digging that uncovered something unusual or a sand dune that collapsed revealing something beneath it?" Kiko asked.

"Exactly. What else?"

"Heavy rains?" Paul asked.

"What about high coastal winds?" Leigh suggested.

The missing puzzle piece suddenly clicked into place in Matt's head and he snapped fully upright. "Idiot!"

Leigh straightened abruptly in surprise. "Excuse me?" she asked icily.

Matt shook his head at her distractedly. "No, no. Not you. Me. I should have thought of it sooner. I know exactly why your body has just surfaced. You just said it—heavy rains and high coastal winds."

Kiko gave a small jerk. "Of course!" She leaned forward over the table. "Let me see that map."

Matt pulled the map toward them and they bent over it together.

"Hold on, hold on . . ." Leigh slapped both palms down on the map. "You lost me. What just happened?"

Matt looked up to meet her eyes. "Hurricane Claire."

Leigh gave a small gasp as she suddenly understood the implications of his theory.

Hurricane Claire, a Category 2 storm that struck Massachusetts two weeks earlier, had first devastated Nantucket and then made landfall on Cape Cod. The eye of the storm transected the Cape before thundering across Cape Cod Bay and Boston Harbor. After making landfall one last time at Manchester, it had moved up the Essex coast and into New Hampshire.

"The damage from the storm," she breathed. "Essex County was hit *hard*."

"Yes, it was." Reaching over to a nearby bench, he picked up a curved pair of forceps. "The path of the storm went like this." Matt dragged the tip of the forceps from the open ocean, over the triangular form of Nantucket Island, over the center of Cape Cod, and then out into open water again. "The final landfall was in Manchester, right?" He glanced at Leigh, who nodded. "The eye then stayed parallel to the coast inland by about five miles before moving into New Hampshire. What category was it when it hit Manchester?"

"It was still Category 2 strength," Leigh answered. "Do you think the wind and rain uncovered the remains?"

"I'm actually thinking more along the lines of the storm surge—the wall of seawater hurricane force winds push onto land. We know the storm hit here at Manchester." He circled the small town on the south side of Cape Ann. "But because hurricane winds move in a counterclockwise direction in this hemisphere, the winds would have circled around the Cape to blow southwest . . . directly into Essex Bay and right up the Essex River."

"But if the southwest winds are driving the storm surge," Kiko murmured, her eyes locked on the map, "that means the remains came from upstream of the dam. From here." She pulled a pencil from her pocket and drew a circle on the map around the coast and a section of the salt marsh. "Northeast from where the bone was found."

Matt stepped back far enough to lean against a bench top. "It makes sense, doesn't it? Hurricane Claire blows through two weeks ago, generating a storm surge driven by hurricane force winds. The storm surge strips the soil from over the grave, or at least from part of it, uncovering a burial that's remained hidden for several years. The surge then carries parts of those newly revealed remains inland. Travel backwards from the end point of the surge and you get a potential area for the burial site." He glanced at Leigh to find her green eyes focused sharply on him. "You were searching in the wrong place, and certainly on the wrong side of the Essex River. The burial site could easily be a mile or more away from the beaver dam."

Leigh made another note in her notebook. "We need to confirm a storm surge happened in that area."

"If it did, the National Hurricane Center will know, but other areas along the coast experienced a storm surge, so I'd be surprised if this area was left untouched." He tapped the map with the forceps. "This is a rough estimate. But it's enough for us to get started."

With a quick flip, Leigh closed her notebook. "I agree." She glanced at her watch. "We have a little over six hours of daylight left."

"We can be ready to roll in about twenty minutes." Matt addressed his students. "You'll each need a full field kit with a complete set of brushes and probes. Juka, Paul—make sure we have a couple of shovels and small spades and Tyvek suits for each of us. We'll also need a couple of body bags and several tarps in case we find something this afternoon and need to secure the scene overnight." He turned to Leigh. "Your guys will take care of sample collection at the site? We're also going to need to thoroughly document the scene before we break ground and then throughout the process since the excavation will destroy the scene."

"If we are lucky enough to find the remains, I'll get Crime Scene Services out to take samples and photos."

"We'll take our own set of photos so we've got them on hand

in case we need to refer to them during reconstruction. Kiko, pack your sketch pads and all the camera equipment. And make sure you're all dressed appropriately. This is going to be messy. We're going to be aiming for dry ground, but it sounds like we're going to have to go through muddy ground to get there, so wear appropriate footwear." He glanced at Leigh. "You're coming with us?"

"After what we just figured out? You've got to be kidding. I wouldn't miss it."

His gaze skimmed over her tailored suit. He was looking forward to seeing her in something more flattering. He also wouldn't object to something more form fitting. "You'll need to change. You go out in that and you'll ruin your suit."

"Don't worry about me." She turned to Kiko. "Do you know the seafood restaurant just east of the Essex main strip? Across from the marina on Route 133?"

Kiko grinned. "Do I ever. Best fried clams on the North Shore."

"Let's meet in the parking lot there at three P.M. That should give you enough time to get your equipment together and to drive up. I'll stop in Salem to report to my sergeant and change clothes, then I'll meet you there."

"That works." Matt glanced down at the map one last time, his eyes fixed on the land contained within the circle Kiko had drawn over their new search area. "Let's see if we can find those remains."

CHAPTER FOUR:
BARRIER BEACH

Barrier Beach: a protective sand barrier that runs roughly parallel to the coastline and shelters a coastal area from severe wind and waves; it allows for the formation of shielded environments such as a salt marsh.

Monday, 2:53 P.M.
Town of Essex, Massachusetts

There was no mistaking when Leigh pulled into the parking lot; the midnight blue Crown Victoria practically screamed "cop car." Matt rested his arm on the sill of the open driver's window of his own vehicle, and lifted his hand in a wave as she got out.

He much preferred her current outfit to her business attire—she wore an athletic T, hiking boots, and jeans, with her firearm in a cross-draw holster at her hip. She sported a high ponytail, revealing the gold and caramel highlights in her hair, and dark glasses hid her eyes in the late afternoon sun.

She approached the open window. "You made good time. You still want to stay east of the Essex River?"

"I think that's the best plan for now. We've always got the option of making a secondary search area."

"Then let's get started. Stay with me." She returned to her car and when she pulled into traffic on Route 133, Matt was right behind her.

They drove quickly through the small town and then they

were into the salt marsh. On their left, the countryside opened into flat expanses of grass and sedge. Tall salt grasses rippled in the gusting breeze and brilliant sunlight glinted off serpentine swathes of open water. In the distance, hills covered with dark trees rose out of the flat plain of the landscape.

As he drove, Matt kept one arm propped on the sill, enjoying the fresh air. The breeze was surprisingly warm for this time of year, and smelled of sea creatures, salt, and marsh life. He tuned out his students as they discussed the merits of a new indie band they'd just discovered, turning his attention instead to the woman he followed. Back at the church, she'd seemed nearly desperate for his help. What choices had she made in life to bring her to this intersection where her needs and his skills combined with their joint desire to bring home the dead?

They drove through dense forest, turning north at Harlow Street, and then finally onto Conomo Point Road. They broke clear of the forest, crossing over a narrow neck of land and onto Conomo Point. Leigh eased off the road at the northernmost point of the peninsula and Matt pulled in behind her. He and the students poured out of the SUV to gather in the space between the two vehicles, silently taking in their surroundings.

They were at the mouth of the Essex River, where the water finally spilled free beyond the confines of land and marsh and flowed into the ocean. A clutch of sailboats and motorboats were anchored offshore, well clear of the low-lying marsh plants and the dangerously rocky shoreline.

Leigh unfolded her map and struggled to lay it out on the hood of Matt's SUV. The wind pulled at the edges of the map, trying to snatch it away with playful fingers.

"Let me help." Reaching around her, Matt grabbed the bottom corner of the map with his left hand as his right hand came down over hers. She raised her head and he found himself looking into her green eyes over the top of her sunglasses as he held her between his body and the warm hood of his car.

She gave him a quick smile, sliding her fingers out from under his as she slipped under his arm. "Thanks. It's pretty windy out here."

"It is." He looked over his shoulder. "Paul! Give us a hand here." He jerked his head toward the map.

Paul immediately jogged over to help hold the map. Juka and Kiko grouped around them.

"Okay, we're right here." Matt pressed one forearm along the edge of the map to hold down the flapping corner and used his free index finger to circle the tip of the peninsula. "We'll start here and move southwest toward the marsh."

"You were right, by the way," Leigh interjected. "I made a few calls on my way up here and there was a storm surge in this area. I have someone getting the specifics for me and we should have that later this afternoon. But I think your theory is solid."

Kiko's faraway gaze suddenly caught Matt's eye. "Kiko?"

"What about Cross Island?" Kiko pointed north of where they stood. "The remains could be buried out there. That would have been right in the path of the storm surge."

Matt studied the land mass that lay a few hundred feet across the channel. Weathered cedar shingle and clapboard houses hugged its rocky shore, nestled in the trees that crept down the hill toward the water's edge. Further along the shore were the ruins of an earlier home. All that remained now was the charred fieldstone foundation and a lone chimney that rose into the air, an eerie reminder of the fragility of life.

The island would have been directly in the path of the storm surge, and it was exposed enough to have borne the brunt of the storm's force.

"How do you get out there?" Matt asked. "Is there a bridge?"

Kiko shook her head. "No, only boat access."

Matt looked over at Leigh. "If we don't find anything today,

I'd like to see about arranging to get out there. Kiko's right; the remains could be there."

"I can arrange for a boat from the Essex Police," Leigh offered.

"Let's keep it in mind." Matt pointed to the area bordering the salt marsh that led directly to Essex and the discovery site. "This is the area I'm really interested in. But we need to work our way down there first and we've only got about four and a half hours of daylight left. Keep your eyes peeled for depressions from dirt settling as the body decomposed, disturbed ground, exposed bones, signs of digging, anything like that. Let's cover it all the first time." He proceeded to outline a search protocol for the group, assigning positions to each member. Then he turned to his students. "Let's take all the equipment. If we find the remains, we won't have time to come back to get it."

"What can I carry?" Leigh asked. "There's no reason you and your students should carry everything."

Matt grinned. "Oh, don't worry. I have a pack for you too." He briefly scanned down her body to her booted feet and then back up again. "You look like you can manage it."

"Thanks." She turned to the students. "Let's move. We're wasting daylight."

Monday, 5:12 P.M.
Essex Bay Coast, Massachusetts

"Let's take five."

Grimacing, Matt pushed his sweaty hair out of his eyes. "We should keep going," he argued. "We're going to run out of light soon."

"Five minutes won't make a difference. We've been at it for almost two hours straight and everyone is tired. Take a break," Leigh insisted.

He fought the urge to argue with her, part of him realizing she was right. "Fine. Hey, guys!" he shouted. "Come on back for a minute. We're going to take a short break."

The sound of fallen branches snapping underfoot signaled the students making their way toward them. While Leigh settled on a wide patch of springy moss, Matt swung his backpack off his shoulders and leaned a hip against the large boulder that pierced the forest floor, a craggy mass of bedrock thrust free from the earth's hold.

"Check your pack," Matt called, unzipping his own and pulling a bottle of water from inside to wave it in Leigh's direction. "I put water in yours too."

Surprise flashed across her face. "I didn't expect you to pack for me. Thanks."

Matt drank half of his water in a continuous series of swallows before lowering it and wiping the back of his hand across his mouth. He pulled in a deep breath of salt air, forcing himself to take a minute to relax.

He was recapping his water bottle when Kiko pushed her way through the bushes. The younger woman shrugged off her backpack and dropped to the ground. "Thanks. I needed that."

"You're the athlete in the crowd," Matt said, pointing his water bottle at her accusingly. "Shouldn't you be the one with the most stamina?"

Kiko laughed and opened her pack, retrieving her own bottle. "Kendo teaches concentration, coordination, and agility. It also teaches how to knock your opponent on his ass. What it does not teach is hiking endurance. Besides, you're the rower with the cardiovascular stamina." She sipped her water. "We're getting nowhere. We've covered almost all the land we thought would be the most likely location for the burial and we've come up empty."

She paused as Juka and Paul came through the trees together, dropping their shovels and shedding their packs to sprawl on the ground beside her. Paul made a half-hearted attempt to snatch Kiko's water bottle from her fingers but she easily slapped his hand away. "Get your own."

Matt gave the men a moment to quench their thirst. "Anything, guys?"

"Nothing," Juka said, discouragement in his voice.

"And we've nearly covered the whole area that we set out to search," Paul added.

Matt fell silent, absently tapping his fist against his thigh, as he turned over his search strategy in his head again. *This is taking too long and we're nearly done with this area. You must have miscalculated.* Setting his water bottle beside his pack, he started to pace the forest floor, mentally re-examining the bone for some other clue.

Leigh's voice broke into his thoughts. "I can look into getting us out to that island tomorrow," she offered. "Maybe that's where the remains are."

Matt's head jerked up and it took him a moment to focus on her face. "Yeah, I think we're going to have to. We're running out of areas that make any sense down here." He frowned and distractedly ran his hand through his hair. "The real question is how far did the storm surge carry that bone? I'm betting not that far. But if I'm wrong on that, then maybe I have us searching in the wrong spot."

"So we keep looking."

He stopped pacing and just stared at her.

"Welcome to police work," she said. "It's not nearly as exciting as they make it seem on TV. It's asking a lot of questions and going over the same ground again and again until something pops. It's searching a forest until you find what you're looking for, even if it means revising your search area or covering the same ground twice. Contrary to what you see on TV, we're not going to be solving this mystery in exactly forty-two and a half minutes."

The corners of Matt's lips twitched. "We wouldn't be able to solve it in forty-two and a half minutes just from the science end of things. Do you know how unrealistic those shows are? Sexual identification from just a quick glance at a scattering of bones. Mass spec profiles in three minutes or less. PCR results in ten."

Leigh let out a cynical laugh. "Oh trust me, I know. It can take anywhere from six months to two years to get DNA results back from the state lab simply because they're overworked and understaffed. The problem is those shows make us look bad because people now have unrealistic expectations." She took another long pull from her water bottle before screwing on the cap to slide it back into her pack. Climbing to her feet, she bent forward at the waist to stretch out her back muscles before linking her arms behind her hips to stretch out her shoulders and chest. The fluid way her body moved drove all thoughts of human remains and search patterns from Matt's mind. Then she straightened and his face heated as she caught him staring. "What's wrong?"

Reality slammed back into place, bringing with it their current dilemma. "I'm wondering if I've given you unrealistic expectations."

Leigh stare at him, befuddled. "Why would you think that?"

"I thought I had it nailed and that we'd find something today. Looks like I was wrong." He jammed his hands into the pockets of his jeans, hunching his shoulders.

"You think you've let me down?"

"Well, you did come to me so that I could help you find these remains."

"Do you always take this much on yourself?"

His head snapped up. "What?"

"Is it perfection or nothing at all for you? Every detail has to line up or you're not satisfied? Once you're on board, it's your responsibility to get the job done?"

"I'm used to taking care of things on my own. If you want the job done right, do it yourself. That way, no one else can let you down."

"I don't let people down," she said shortly. "And it's not your responsibility. It's mine as the responding officer. I'm thrilled with how far we've come today. When I found you this morning, I never dreamed I'd be out in the field this fast. What you do in the lab may be an exact science, but police work isn't. Loose ends don't always get tied up and we don't get all the answers we want. Sometimes the crime remains unsolved and nothing frustrates a cop more than a cold case. But with your help, I don't think that's going to happen here. The remains have to be here somewhere." At her words, Matt relaxed fractionally and the tightness in his chest eased. "I'm happy you've come on board and that you're taking this so seriously. But I don't want *you* to have unrealistic expectations." She quickly checked her watch. "There's maybe two and a half hours of daylight left, probably less in the trees where the light level is lower. What do you want to do?"

"We've covered almost all the way down to Harlow Street and back on this side of Conomo Point Road. We can always go east of Conomo Point Road. There's quite a bit more forest over there but I still think that area is much less likely." His eyes scanned the thick forest around them. "You know, I really thought cutting out the salt marsh would improve our chances of finding the remains." He paced to the edge of the clearing and pushed back some of the branches that blocked his view of the marsh beyond.

A foot or more below, the salt marsh was a huge expanse of open land and waving grasses just starting to yellow with autumn's cooling temperatures, the landscape stretching out in an unending flatland toward the ocean. Except for . . .

"Damn it, that wasn't on the map."

Leigh was on her feet, striding toward him. "What wasn't on the map?"

"That upland area out there." He pulled the branches down a little lower for her. "Can you see it?"

"No, it's too high. All I can see is marsh. Hold on." She set her foot on a nearby fallen trunk and, bracing her hand on his shoulder, she boosted herself up so she now stood several inches taller than Matt. Leaning her weight on him, she peered through the small gap in the branches.

He knew she'd spotted it when she went absolutely still.

About a quarter mile from where they stood, situated close to one of the major branches of the Essex River, was what appeared to be an island in the salt marsh—an upland area perhaps two or three hundred feet across and covered with trees. Another area, about a quarter of the size, stood due north of it.

"We didn't look at that area because it's in the salt marsh," Leigh stated. "But that's not marshland, is it?"

"No, that's going to be upland forest, just like where we're standing now." He stared intently at the small parcel of land. "But think about it. A storm surge moves ahead of the hurricane. We've been looking for land that would be close to the salt marsh because it would be more exposed. Nothing is going to be more exposed than an area in the *middle* of the open marsh. How high do you think that is, maybe ten feet above the marsh? Maybe twelve feet max above sea level at the highest point?"

Leigh leaned forward, squinting. "Maybe. It's hard to tell from here, especially since there's so much tree cover."

"I know you're checking on the storm surge and what the

51

height might have been, but if it was thirteen or fourteen feet high, that would be enough to swamp that entire upland area. Even a smaller surge would still scour the outer edges." He glanced sideways at her, still leaning in close and braced against his shoulder. "We need to go out there."

Suddenly a head popped between them. "What are we looking at?" Paul asked.

Leigh jerked backward in surprise at Paul's abrupt appearance, the sudden shift in her weight causing her foot to slip on the mossy bark of the trunk. With a small gasp, she started to fall backward. Reaching out, she grasped handfuls of Matt's shirt, desperately trying to anchor herself.

One moment she was falling, the next he was pulling her against him to slide down his body before setting her smoothly on the ground, his hands firmly holding her waist. He held her steady as she regained her balance, turning to glare at his grad student. "*What?*"

Paul's face had gone beet red right up to his hairline, his alarmed eyes wide. "Uh . . . you seemed pretty interested in something out there, so I came over to find out what was going on . . . and . . . uh . . ." He trailed off, his horrified gaze darting from Matt's angry expression to Leigh's look of baffled surprise. "How about I wait over here until we're ready to start again?" He turned and fled.

"Always the smart ass. He needs to learn a little of Juka's discretion." Matt loosened his grip on her waist, but didn't release her. "You okay?"

The only sound she made was a strangled half-laugh against his shoulder as she slowly released her death grip on his T-shirt. She awkwardly smoothed the material against his chest as if embarrassed by the wrinkles she'd put there, her eyes downcast so she missed his raised brows at her stroking. "Yeah, thanks." She abruptly stepped back, pulling against the hands that still held her and he instantly released her. "Almost ended up on my ass," she said, as she busied herself straightening her shirt and weapon. "That wouldn't have been very graceful."

"No problem. But try not to fall out here. You might get a bit heavy if I have to carry you all the way back to the car because you fractured your lateral malleolus after supination with external rotation." He looked at her pointedly, but with a half-smile so she'd know he was joking. "On the other hand, if Paul caused it, *he* can carry you."

She laughed at that. "Do you always sweet talk women like this? I assume that was geek-speak for me breaking my ankle after gracelessly falling on my ass?"

"Got it in one," he shot back.

"I try to be a quick study," she quipped.

He turned away, calling to his students that the search would continue in a new location.

Hope pushed away exhaustion.

They had a new area to search.

Chapter Five:
Marsh Border

Marsh Border: the upland edge of the marsh above the level of the normal high tide; an area flooded only during extreme tides and storms.

Monday, 6:35 P.M.
Essex Bay Coast, Massachusetts

The team picked their way across the marsh. They waded through the saltmeadow cordgrass, its slender stems parting easily before them only to be flattened by wind and water into tangled mats further into the marsh. As they made their way deeper into the intertidal zone, more drainage channels snaked through the marsh, forcing them to alter their course.

"When's high tide today?" Matt called to Kiko. He glanced down at his watch before scanning the distance for the goal that never seemed to get any closer.

"Not for a few hours yet, but it's coming in," she called back. "We're going to get caught in it on the way back if we stay out too long."

"Great," Matt muttered.

As they approached one of the meandering drainage channels snaking through the marsh, the grasses around them changed, becoming thicker, coarser, and taller. Juka and Paul swung their shovels over their shoulders and the group had to part the chest-high, dense grasses in front of them to push through.

The beauty of the marsh belied its danger. Crickets chirped, hidden deep in the grasses, and occasionally grasshoppers would fly into the air to protest the disturbance as the group passed by. The plaintive, slurred *tlee-oo-whee* of a migratory golden plover in flight, wings gracefully outstretched as it soared on the breeze, drew their eyes upward. In the distance, a great blue heron could be seen fishing in one of the offshoots of the river. It stood motionless in the water, waiting for prey to swim within reach of its great pointed bill.

A chill slithered down Matt's spine as a stronger gust of wind blew through the open area of the swamp. The heat generated while hiking through the protected forest was disappearing, the sweat on his skin chilling rapidly in the cooling ocean breeze as the day eased gradually toward evening.

Finally, after hiking across the width of the marsh, they left the brightness of the open flats and moved into the shadow of the trees, stepping up onto solid ground at last. Matt climbed up first and then, bracing one foot, he held out a hand to Leigh and then to Kiko. Paul and Juka scrambled up from the marsh side-by-side.

Hands braced on his hips, Matt surveyed the small, forested area. "We're at the south end of this island and it looks to me as if it expands outward from this point. We'll fan out from here in parallel. Anyone sees anything, yell. We should all be able to hear one another, or send a message down the chain. Let's go."

They broke apart, each heading at a different angle, carefully picking their way over fallen trees and around thick bushes and scrub. All eyes fixed downward, sweeping back and forth, closely examining every square foot of land. The forest floor was different here, with more fallen branches and downed trees. Smaller and lighter debris like leaves and needles had been swept away— all signs of the storm that had roared through, holding this small land mass in its fierce grip for a short period of time.

The silence and solitude of the search gave Matt time to turn over the events of the day.

If someone had told him this morning that he'd be putting aside his own research to help a cop with a murder investigation, he'd have laughed in their face. And yet, here he was. He didn't think that Leigh had any idea when she'd mentioned Trevor Sharpe earlier that it was like waving a red cape in front of a bull. After years of competition between them and one incident of suspected academic dishonesty, Matt would practically sell his soul to avoid giving Sharpe anything he desired. That alone had assured his participation in the case. But now, after spending hours with Leigh, he was drawn in even further. She was smart and sexy as hell, but it was her drive to find justice for a nameless victim that really hooked him. It spoke to him on a visceral level and matched his own desire to identify the dead.

Ten minutes later, he heard the shout. He was on his knees examining the soil in a small clearing when he heard Paul's voice calling his name. "Over here!" he called back.

"Trooper Abbott needs you. She's found something," said Paul's disembodied voice.

Climbing up a small incline, Matt found Kiko and Paul waiting for him.

"Do you know where she is?" Matt asked them.

Kiko shook her head. "I just heard Juka shout that they needed you."

"Then we'll do this the old-fashioned way." Matt cupped his hands over his mouth. "Leigh!"

"Matt! Over here."

Angling further south, Matt picked up his pace, his students falling into step behind him. They broke through the foliage together, all three jerking to a stop at the sight in front of them.

Leigh and Juka knelt in a small cleared area, only a few feet away from the edge of the marsh. Yet there was no mistaking the shapes rising from the earth.

Right clavicle, sternal manubrium, ribs, anterior surface of the left scapula.

Then he realized what he didn't see.

No skull. Upper left extremities and ribs missing.

"Damn it. No skull." It wasn't until Leigh glanced up that he realized he'd said it aloud. He circled the remains to stand beside her, then slid his pack off before kneeling in the dirt.

The body was partially covered with a layer of soil, leaving the top left side exposed to the elements. The surrounding area was swept smooth of leaves and loose soil.

Matt glanced over his shoulder, out into the marsh beyond. He could hear the rush of the Essex River, perhaps a hundred yards away. "You can see how it happened. The storm surge came through here, roaring across the open marsh, scouring everything in its path. Anything this exposed would be stripped clean by the wind and the water." He focused on the pale bones. "It uncovered the victim." He glanced at Leigh. "This was no hiking accident."

"I agree." She rolled easily to her feet. "I've got to call this in to my sergeant, Crime Scene Services, and the Essex Police. We can't do much until the techs get here and we're quickly losing the light." Pulling out her cell phone, she stepped to the edge of the marsh to place the first of several calls.

A few minutes later, Leigh came back to stand beside Matt. "They're on their way. They understand that we're in a hurry, so they'll get here as fast as possible. I also called the M.E.'s office to keep Rowe in the loop."

"Does he want to check out the site before we start?"

"Rowe?" She started to turn away. "He and his staff don't come out to sites."

Matt reached out, catching her arm to stop her. "What do

you mean 'they don't come out to sites'? Then who does liver temp, lividity, and rigor to determine time of death in a fresh victim?"

"No one."

"What?"

Leigh shook off his hand. "Jurisdictions that can afford it send the M.E. or an assistant to a crime scene to do an on-site examination of the body to help establish time of death. Unfortunately, the Commonwealth of Massachusetts doesn't have that in the budget."

"Then who comes out to get the body?"

"The M.E.'s office will send a couple of techs to properly bag the body and transport it to the morgue. Once there, they do as-is photos, take fingerprints, and then toe-tag the body before storing it in the cooler. And that's all they do until the autopsy, which can be days later. But that's not all."

"I can't believe it. There's more?"

"They base time of death on L.S.A.—the time the victim was last seen alive."

Matt gaped at her in disbelief. "That's incredibly inaccurate."

"I know. So does Rowe. He's well aware that they're losing convictions because they can't nail down time of death more precisely. He's argued for additional funding to cover this for years, but no one is listening. This is just the reality of what the budget will allow and the constraints we have to work with. Anyway, when it comes to this particular case, Rowe will fully review all photos, evidence reports, and your written report as soon as it hits his desk, and will consult with you personally at that time."

"I'm . . . appalled. I haven't worked with the police a lot but I know colleagues back in Tennessee who do. That's not how they do it there."

"It shouldn't be how we do it here. That's why Rowe's trying to change it." Leigh turned back to study the burial site. "So, what's next?"

"Kiko's taking full photos of the area while we're waiting. Then she'll do the in-progress shots as well as the sketch work since she's the one with the artistic eye. Paul, Juka, and I will do the actual excavation."

"How far will you get tonight?"

"That's going to depend on when the techs get here, but even if they arrive soon, we won't get very far. We can't work in the dark; we'd run the risk of damaging the remains. It will likely take us most of tomorrow to excavate and pack the remains for transfer to the lab. The remains will be safe once they're back in the lab, but what about tonight?"

"You're going to cover the site tonight?"

"Yes. But surely that won't be good enough security for you now that you know that the remains are here?"

"I've arranged for the Essex Police to send an officer out here. From this point on, we need to maintain the chain of evidence."

"Just as long as they don't touch anything." At Leigh's withering look, Matt held up both hands defensively. "All right, all right. They're cops and they know better."

"I'd feel better knowing the site is being watched all the time. I know these remains have been exposed like this for at least two weeks, but . . ."

"Now they're yours," Matt finished for her.

"Yes," she said. "Now they're mine. And I protect what's mine."

"I'm with you on that." Seeing that Paul and Juka had already put on their Tyvek suits, Matt tugged his own suit out of his pack and started to pull it on. "Identification is going to be a lot harder because we're missing the skull. It may have been pushed further inland, but I'd bet that it was probably swept out to sea by the storm surge. Luckily, the remains look to be in good shape. We'll be able to pull a reliable DNA sample from the femur. But we'll still need something to compare it to." He studied the expression on her face and the twisted set of her mouth. "What?"

"DNA has to go to the state lab. You guys are not an accredited DNA lab. We need that for it to stand up in court." Her tone clearly conveyed her weariness with this argument. "You have to understand that my hands are tied. It's not that I don't want a faster answer, it's just that I need the right people to give it to me."

Matt frowned. "But didn't you say earlier that DNA results from the state lab could take anywhere from six months to two years?"

Embarrassed color flushed her cheeks. "Yes," she muttered. "But evidence gets bumped up the line if a case is due in court so it's not like we go into court without a complete case."

"How about this then? We'll take duplicate DNA samples. One of the samples goes to the state lab, the other goes to B.U. We'll give you your answer first so you can use it in the course of the investigation. Then the state lab will confirm and you'll have that evidence to go to court. Would that work?"

"It just might," she said cautiously. "Are you always this sneaky?"

"I prefer 'devious,' personally. It's more a matter of knowing how to work the system. I understand that you have a legal case to build and that you'll have your evidence in time for a trial, but how do you investigate when you can't even identify your victim because of a backlog at the lab? It's simply not practical."

"You're right, of course." Leigh stepped closer, lowering her voice. "Your students . . . they'll be okay? They won't . . ." She trailed off, as if suddenly unsure how to continue without offending him.

"Screw up?" he finished for her. "You have my word. They're good kids, and they've got good skills and instincts. This will only help to hone them. I know we don't know each other that well yet, Leigh, but you need to trust me on this."

"You certainly haven't given me cause to doubt your word so far. And you've brought me farther today than I ever dreamed possible. I think that deserves some leeway."

"We just followed the trail that the evidence showed us. But don't worry," Matt added, "you'll be standing alongside the whole time. If you're like me, you're not willing to put all of your faith in someone until they've proven themselves."

Twenty-five minutes later, the sound of raised voices drifted through the trees. Leigh called out to them, directing them to the site. Shortly thereafter, three men broke into the clearing. They all carried heavy cases and were wearing navy windbreakers with "Crime Scene Services" printed on the back in blocky white letters. After a brief conversation with Matt, they immediately started to take photos of the area and initial samples of the topmost layers of soil. Then Matt and his team moved in.

The work of recovering the dead and missing had begun.

CHAPTER SIX:
SALT PANNE

Salt Panne: a calm, shallow pool of standing water after high tide; it usually has an extremely high salt content due to evaporation.

Tuesday, 9:23 P.M.
Abbott residence
Salem, Massachusetts

With a quiet sigh, Leigh settled back into the softness of her overstuffed couch, swinging her feet up onto the seat and slipping her cold toes into the crevice between the cushions. She cradled a steaming mug of jasmine tea between her palms and took a small sip, relaxing into the comforting warmth. Her head fell back against the cushions as the quiet strains of Bach's *Brandenburg Concertos* washed over her.

It had been a long day and it was good to be home.

Tension slowly seeped from her body. Closing her eyes, she let her mind sift through the day's events.

The team had started early and had barely paused during the day. By tacit arrangement, Leigh ran interference with the Essex force and the crime techs, allowing Matt and his students to concentrate on their work. It was well past six P.M. when they were ready to head back to Boston with the remains. Leigh was more than ready to go home—she was hot and sweaty and covered with a layer of fine grit from sieving soil for small artifacts. But she followed Matt back to Boston and assisted with carrying the bones and equipment up to the lab. Once everything was secure, she'd left, promising him she'd be back the next morning to observe his examination.

She took another sip of tea and let herself drift. As tired as she was, the satisfied feeling of a job well done layered over the exhaustion. From a single bone, they had found and recovered their victim. She tried to dampen the triumph that rose in her. Colleagues like Morrison fully expected her to fail at this task, and she was more than happy to prove them wrong. They would certainly never expect her to get so far in such a short period of time. She gave up fighting the feeling and let a satisfied smile curve her lips. She could be triumphant here in the privacy of her own home. Tomorrow, in the bullpen, she'd be all business. And those who had hoped for her failure could simply go straight to hell.

At peace, her gaze roamed the small room. After the death of her father four years before, Leigh sold the larger family house where she had lived all of her life, moving just around the corner to this small fisherman's house built in 1800. Many would find the tiny abode too cramped; yet, for her, the diminutive rooms with waist-high wainscoting and wide plank floors were perfect. The tiny living room, filled with overstuffed furniture and small tables scattered with decorative knickknacks, showed off her eclectic style—a flat-screen TV shared space with hand-thrown pottery, hand-blown glass, seashells, and interesting pieces of driftwood she found washed up on the beach.

Her eyes were naturally drawn to the painting over the mantel. It was a watercolor of a small blond girl dressed in a bright sundress running through the ocean surf. A black Labrador puppy, nearly as big as the girl, gamboled at her feet in the spray from the waves. The familiar wave of longing for the mother she didn't remember washed over Leigh. She had to rely on rendered memories like this one—she was the girl in the picture; this was one of her mother's final paintings before she succumbed to the cancer that finally took her life.

The shrill peal of her cell phone shattered the peaceful quiet.

Leigh gave an audible groan and reluctantly picked up her phone from the coffee table. She glanced at the Caller ID— "Matthew Lowell." She frowned. Had they missed something at the site? "Leigh Abbott."

"Leigh, we've got a problem."

Matt's urgent voice sent a bolt of electricity arcing through her exhausted body, shooting it from relaxed languor to anxious tension. She jerked upright on the couch, her tea sloshing dangerously close to the rim of her mug. "What's wrong?"

"The bones don't match."

Leigh sat in stunned silence as she tried to make sense of Matt's words. She leaned over and set her mug down on the coffee table. "What do you mean 'the bones don't match'? I watched you pull those remains from the ground and the site was guarded last night. No one could have tampered with them."

"I know that," he said brusquely. "But these remains don't match the radius you brought me yesterday."

"*What?*" Leigh swung her feet off to sit on the edge of the couch. "How can that be?"

"It just is. The radius that you brought me is from a much younger person than these remains indicate."

Leigh stood and started to pace the wide hardwood planks in front of her fireplace—the tension in his voice had her pulse rate spiking. "Wait. Back up. How do you know this already?" She heard him heave a sigh on the other end of the line. "Do you need me to come to the lab?"

"No," he said shortly. "There's nothing for you to do here."

Behind his voice, the lab seemed overly quiet. "Are your students still there?"

64

"No, I sent them home." Exhaustion slightly slurred his words. "After you left, we got all the equipment washed and set out to dry. Then I told them to go home. They'd put in enough time for today. But I thought I'd get a jump on tomorrow morning by setting out the remains on the exam table, so we could start right away. As I removed each bone, I examined it to determine position and side. That's when I started to notice something was off. So, I kept going until I had all the recovered remains laid out. Leigh, we assumed that we had the correct remains because we had a skeleton that was missing the entire left arm, so the fact that we already had a left radius made sense. But they simply don't match. These remains came from a woman, likely in her early to mid-forties. The original radius came from someone decades younger."

"You're saying that after all that searching, we've found a set of remains, but not the *right* set of remains? And that the original body is still out there?"

Two beats of silence passed before Matt spoke. "Yes."

Leigh was speechless with disbelief. *A second body found where they expected the remains of a single victim? It simply couldn't be a coincidence.*

"You want the truth and my expert opinion?" Matt's terse voice broke into her thoughts. "Well, this is it—we have the wrong set of remains. We have to go back."

"Of course I want the truth and your expert opinion," she snapped. "That's why I came to you in the first place." She returned to the couch to drop limply onto it, all sense of triumph wiped away, leaving her feeling wrung out and hollow. "But what you're really saying is that we have two potential murders, not just one since we now have two sets of remains." She hesitated, but needed to be sure. "You're sure about this?"

"*Yes.*" His voice sounded strained, as if speaking through gritted teeth.

She closed her eyes and counted to ten much too quickly to be effective in calming her rapidly unraveling nerves. "Look, Matt, you're tired. I'm tired. I'm sorry if it sounds like I doubt you, but I need to be sure."

She heard the rattle of a wheeled office chair being pulled out and his harsh exhalation as he dropped into it. When he spoke, his voice was much quieter, much calmer. "I'm sorry too. I'm snapping at you, but this isn't your fault. I'm just tired and I'd kill for a shower right now."

Leigh gave a small laugh. "I know that feeling. I didn't even eat until after I'd taken a shower. I just felt . . . grimy."

"Food is up there on my list too," he said tiredly. "Lunch was the last time I ate. And, truthfully, I'm more than a little surprised by this. I knew the remains didn't match twenty minutes ago, but I kept looking for where I'd gone wrong, pulling out more bones, checking each one, looking for where I'd made the mistake in my initial evaluation—"

"Except that you didn't make a mistake."

A deep sigh. "No. There's no doubt in my mind."

Leigh tried to massage away the sudden tightness in the back of her neck. But no amount of rubbing would lift the weight that suddenly lay across her slim shoulders.

"You there?" Matt's voice was quiet.

"Yes," she said softly. "I guess I'm a little stunned myself. This isn't Boston, where you can easily see seventy homicides a year. This is Essex County. Over the whole district, we'll see maybe twenty or twenty-five homicides in the whole year and many of them are drug-related because of the heroin problem in this area. But suddenly we've got two deaths, neither of which appears drug-related—no one takes the time to bury those murder victims; they just drop them and walk away. So, yes, we need to go back. We should start early tomorrow, even earlier than today."

"I was thinking that too. Leigh, we only covered about a third of the island. We stopped when we found the remains."

"Because we thought we had our answer," she muttered quietly.

"I think we should finish that first, then the smaller area north of it."

"Then Cross Island," Leigh proposed.

Matt blew out a long breath. "It's like starting all over again."

"Kind of discouraging, isn't it?"

"Yeah." Several beats of silence passed before Matt spoke. "Are you thinking what I'm thinking?"

"I guess that depends on what you're thinking."

"Doesn't it seem a little coincidental to you that we'd find a second victim where we were expecting the first?"

"It does, doesn't it?"

"What if we've got a serial killer on our hands? And we've stumbled into his dumping ground?"

It was out there now, no taking it back. Leigh's mind was suddenly crowded with thoughts of news conferences, screaming newspaper headlines, task forces, and public panic. "Just what we need, another Boston Strangler. We have to consider that as a possibility, but we need to find the second set of remains before we make any leaps like that."

"Yeah," Matt agreed. "I'd better call my students. They're expecting to be here tomorrow at eight but instead they'd better be here before six, maybe earlier. We can be there by six-thirty or six-forty-five. We not only need to find the remains; we need to complete as much of the excavation tomorrow as possible."

"Works for me. Meet you at the same place?"

"Yeah."

"Then you need to go home and get to bed as soon as you've contacted your students. Thanks for putting in the extra time, even if it did make you the bearer of bad news."

"Well, on the good news front, we've found someone else

who needs a name and to be returned to the arms of her family. Someone else to bring home. So it's not all bad."

"That's true." Leigh tipped her head back on the couch to stare dully at the ceiling. "This case is turning out to be a little more than you bargained for, isn't it?" she asked quietly.

"Not your fault. It's just how the chips are falling." Silence rang over the line for a moment, then—"We'll find your missing victim."

"Yes, we will. You'd better go make your phone calls and ruin a few more evenings."

He chuckled, but she could hear how drained he was. "I'll do that. Grad students are infamous for not wanting to get out of bed a moment before they have to. Have a good night, Leigh."

"You too. I'll see you in the morning." She ended the call.

For just one moment, Leigh let herself feel both disappointment and dread at the turn of events. But then she remembered Matt's words. *We've found someone else who needs a name and to be returned to the arms of her family. Someone else to bring home. It's not all bad.*

Her gaze fell to the framed photograph on her side table—her most treasured picture of herself and her father. It had been taken the day of her graduation from the Academy. In it, they stood together, both in full dress uniform, his arm around her shoulders. Her father stood a full head taller than she, but from his wide smile, it almost looked as if pride gave him extra height. She stared at his face, feeling the familiar wave of longing. What she wouldn't give to be able to discuss this case with him, drawing from his knowledge and years of experience.

She rose and picked up her mug to take it back into the kitchen.

She had several phone calls to make and then she needed to get to bed.

It was going to be another early morning and another long day.

CHAPTER SEVEN:
INTERTIDAL ZONE

Intertidal Zone: any area of shoreline subject to cyclical flooding and drying—i.e., covered with water at high tide and exposed to the air at low tide.

Wednesday, 4:52 A.M.
Lowell residence
Brookline, Massachusetts

Bone tired, Matt leaned back against the granite countertop and closed his eyes.

After a late and restless night, he had dragged his sorry ass out of bed at 4:20 A.M. and stumbled blindly into the shower. He lingered there for long minutes, hands braced on the smooth tiles and head bowed under the pounding hot spray, trying to jolt his body into wakefulness.

He now stood in his dim kitchen, the small light over the stove casting long shadows around the darkened room. He wore a charcoal T-shirt tucked into a pair of black jeans. His hiking boots stood by the kitchen door and a long-sleeved black and gray plaid shirt was draped over a kitchen chair to ward off the chill of the early fall morning. His still-damp hair stuck out in tufts from running his fingers through it.

He poured himself a cup of freshly brewed coffee and added a healthy dollop of cream before carrying it to the kitchen table. He took a long sip before setting the cup down with a quiet *click* on the bare wood. He braced his elbows on the cool surface and closed his eyes again as he rested his forehead against his steepled fingers, waiting for the caffeine to hit his bloodstream.

His eyes shot open again when he heard the familiar *tick tick tick* on the hardwood floor followed by the quiet *shush* of rubber wheels coming from the direction of the elevator tucked behind the main staircase. The Belgian Malinois appeared in the open doorway first. His single upright ear perked even higher when he saw Matt.

An affectionate smile tugged at Matt's lips. "Hey, Teak, what are you doing up at this ungodly hour?" The dog trotted across the room, pushing his head against Matt's knee until he reached down and scratched him behind his good ear. The dog laid his muzzle across Matt's thigh and gazed up at him with a single soulful brown eye. Matt scratched carefully around the tattered floppy remains of the dog's left ear. Now his father's faithful companion, the Shepherd was an ex-service dog with the U.S. Army and had lost both his left eye and most of his ear in an explosion in Basra.

"One might ask you the same question."

Matt raised his head to find his father in the doorway, his pajamas covered by a thick, dark burgundy robe. But instead of standing tall, he sat in a wheelchair, his wide, strong upper body a stark contrast to the withered legs strapped into place at the base of the chair. Mike rolled into the kitchen. "You've been up for a while from the smell in here. Pour me a cup, will you?"

"Sure."

Matt joined his father where he had pulled up to the open side of the table as he waited for his coffee. Teak took up his usual spot, stretched out on the floor between the two men as they sat together in easy silence.

"You got in late last night," Mike said.

Matt shrugged. "The excavation went fine. The trouble started after that."

70

"Trouble?"

Matt took another long hit of the coffee, feeling it starting to warm and wake him. "Let's start with this—the remains we excavated yesterday don't match the initial bone that Leigh . . . that Trooper Abbott brought me."

The older man froze with his coffee cup halfway to his mouth before setting it down on the table. "You mean that you went out and found a set of human remains that weren't the ones you were looking for?"

"Kind of hard to believe, isn't it? But yeah, that's exactly what happened. Leigh . . . I mean Trooper—"

"Abbott," Mike finished for him. "You're on a first-name basis now. I've got it. You *are* tired if you're stumbling over something as simple as her name. Have some more coffee."

Matt gratefully took another sip before filling his father in. "So," he finished, "suddenly we have two victims. Maybe more, for all I know."

"So you're going back . . . What's really going on here, Matt?"

Startled, Matt's gaze jerked to his father. "What do you mean?"

"Something's bothering you. You're worried about your safety or the safety of your students."

"I'm always concerned about the safety of my students. They're my responsibility."

"Of course they are, but this is more."

"Why do you say that?"

"Because you don't usually go out to an excavation armed." His father raised his mug in the direction of the counter. "I'll say it again—you really are tired. You left the Glock on the counter."

Matt swiveled around, following his father's gaze. His gun, securely seated in its holster, lay on the dark granite. "Right . . . Something about this case is starting to bother me."

"You think you might be putting yourself in danger?" Mike asked.

Matt let out a self-deprecating laugh. "When you say it like that, it sounds totally over the top. We've found a bone, and then a set of remains, and now I want to weapon up before we go out looking for more."

"No, it doesn't." To Matt's surprise, his father's voice was serious and without a trace of mockery. "We both know from our time in the military that when you have a gut feeling about something, you listen or you run the risk of ending up dead. We've both seen friends ignore that feeling, and we've seen them die as a result."

Matt nodded grimly. "This is as unscientific as it gets, but something about this whole case feels off to me. It just seems too coincidental that there would be two sets of remains in the same area. Something else is going on here. I'm not sure what to expect out there anymore. Leigh can take care of herself, but those students are my responsibility and I watch over what's mine." His mouth tipped up in a half grin. "Although Kiko's trained well enough that she could probably take me down."

Mike boomed out a laugh. "Not a chance. I've met Kiko; she's a live wire but no way does she take down an ex-Marine like you."

"She doesn't even know I served. She probably thinks I'm totally helpless."

The older man's lips went flat behind his neatly trimmed white beard. "You know my opinion about keeping your time in the military a secret. You should share that part of your past with them." He paused. "Or are you ashamed of it?"

"No! Of course not. It's just not something I feel I need to discuss with them. It has no bearing on what I do now." Matt got up to pour himself a little more coffee, using the task as an excuse to put a little space between himself and his father. His reticence to discuss his time in the Marines was a sore point between them, and he was too tired and short of time to rehash it now.

He was relieved when his father let it go, turning back to the situation at hand.

"What time are you meeting your students?" Mike asked.

"Five-thirty." He glanced at his watch. "I'd better get going or I'm going to be late. We have to repack the equipment we left out to dry last night, load up the SUV, and then hit the road." He gulped the last of his coffee before rinsing the mug and leaving it in the sink.

He picked up the Glock and attached the holster to his belt at the small of his back. Then he shrugged into the long-sleeved shirt, letting it fall loosely over the gun, hiding it from view.

"Be careful. I want you back in one piece," Mike said.

"You know I can take care of myself. I'm probably overreacting anyway."

"Possibly, but I respect your feelings on this."

Matt started to move past him, but then stopped, laying his hand on his father's wide shoulder to give it a firm squeeze.

Then he silently left the kitchen.

CHAPTER EIGHT:
SALTMEADOW RUSH

Saltmeadow Rush: Juncus gerardii, also known as Black Grass, is a wetland perennial commonly found in the high marsh zone.

Wednesday, 6:44 A.M.
Essex Bay Coast, Massachusetts

The team members made their way across the salt marsh for the third time in as many days. Feet dragged clumsily and there was an occasional stumble as the sucking mud grasped at their boots. Kiko unsuccessfully attempted to cover a huge yawn behind her cupped hand as she trudged beside Matt.

Leigh adjusted her pack and glanced over at Matt. He wore dark glasses, shielding his eyes from the bright morning glare, but he looked tired and the corners of his mouth were slightly pinched. She angled a bit toward him as they pushed through the salt grasses. "You okay?"

He glanced sideways at her, his eyes unreadable behind his dark glasses. "Just tired. Had trouble getting to sleep last night." Two more slogging steps. "You?"

"I went to bed almost as soon as we got off the phone. It sounds like I'm in better shape than you are. We've probably got another very long day in front of us. If I can help, let me know. I'm not familiar enough with what you do to offer. You need to ask."

He gave a silent nod before fixing his eyes on the higher land rising from the marsh.

Soon they were stepping onto dry forestland under the cool dimness of the trees. Matt stopped to take off his glasses and tuck them into the breast pocket of his plaid shirt.

"What do you think?" Leigh asked. "Same formation as before? Start where we found the remains on Monday and keep moving north?"

"Yeah." Matt started to move into the trees and Leigh fell into step with him. "Is anyone else coming out to help search today?"

"Not yet." Leigh stepped over the trunk of a toppled tree. "I touched base with the Essex force this morning and they're available if we want them. I thought we'd start with just us on the ground search but they can be here in about fifteen minutes if we want to go out to Cross Island." She tapped the phone in a belt holder on her right hip. "I'll call them later, either because we found new remains, or because we haven't." She glanced over her shoulder at the three students behind them. Juka was down on one knee, his shovel laid on the ground beside his boot as he retied his muddy laces. Kiko and Paul flanked him, waiting patiently. "The Essex cops think our remains don't belong to anyone local. They don't have any missing persons listed in this community and they've checked with the Glouces-ter and Ipswich forces as well and they've—"

Matt's hand suddenly shot out and grasped her forearm. She stopped abruptly, her head jerking toward him, all senses sud-denly on alert. "What's wrong?"

Matt's gaze was darting rapidly through the trees. "Do you smell that?"

Alarm spiked through Leigh at both his tone of voice and his expression. "Smell what?"

Releasing her, he took a single step away as if trying to locate the source of the smell. "That slightly sweet, nitrous odor. It's been a long time but I swear it smells like putres—"

A sudden crack split the morning stillness and something hot and furious stirred the air between them with a streaking, high-pitched whine.

"Get *down!*" Matt sprang across the distance separating them, his arms locking around Leigh, the force of his body driving her off her feet. He twisted his body in midair so that when they hit the ground, he landed first with a force that left him gasping as she sprawled on top of him in a small depression.

She lay stunned for only a moment, and then she was rolling off and pulling her gun from its holster. They both flattened to the ground as two more shots rang out. From over their heads came the dull *thump* of a bullet hitting a nearby tree.

Leigh slithered out of her pack and crawled along the ground to crouch behind a fallen tree. Easing her head up a few inches, she peered over the top in the direction the shots seemed to have come from. A movement to her left distracted her momentarily as Matt inched up beside her. Gripped in his right hand was a Glock semi-automatic. *Where did that come from?* She pushed the thought away quickly. If there was more than one of them armed, so much the better.

"Shots were from the north," Matt hissed. "Single shooter. Handgun. Four shots so far. Could be a fifteen-round clip depending on the weapon." He eased slightly higher and immediately dropped flat as a fifth shot broke the silence. "Guys, stay down," he hissed, twisting back toward where his students once stood.

Leigh followed his gaze, but the students were out of sight in the brush. "You stay down too," Leigh snapped. "He's got line of sight on us."

"We can't just lie here, pinned down. There's two of us armed, and one of him. We need to go on the offensive."

Leigh stared at him in amazement—he talked like a man familiar with high-risk situations, and, to her surprise, she found she liked this new trait. "Fine. We can take cover behind the trees and try to outflank him." Surely, their shooter would try to head back to the mainland. "You go left, I'll go right. Keep your eyes open. Do *not* shoot me. Preferably, don't shoot period. But if you pin him down, call for help. We want him taken alive."

"Yes, ma'am," Matt ground out, irritation flashing across his face. He crawled to the left to take cover behind a tree, freezing in place briefly before moving deeper into the woods. Every motion was efficient as he crouched down to stay behind cover, stopping periodically to listen intently, eyes constantly roving.

This wasn't the first time he'd done this. If they made it out of this situation alive, she definitely had some questions for him.

Breaking cover, Leigh darted from tree to tree, pressing close to each, her cheek against the abrasive bark. She quickly peered around each trunk, pausing only long enough to listen for the sound of a branch breaking, or a rock tumbling out of place. Matt had melted into the forest like mist, and he moved so silently she couldn't hear him at all.

Darting behind a scraggly bush, Leigh crouched low, breathing hard. Only silence met her ears—no rustling or running feet. Not even a fluttering of bird's wings or the chirp of a cricket.

Silence.

Matt broke cover, crouching low and sprinting toward a towering oak. He pressed his back against the thick trunk, looking back the way he'd come. *Where were his students? Were they okay?*

It took a moment before his eyes found them, half hidden behind a rock and a scrubby cedar, lying belly-down together on the ground as ordered. Relief surged through him—they were alive and appeared unhurt. But their shock was evident in their upraised eyes. He wasn't sure if it was because they had been shot at or whether it was at the sight of him, gun in hand, as he slid back into the role of soldier. Maybe it was both.

He made a curt hand gesture—*stay down*—and then turned away.

Explanations could wait. For now, there was a shooter out there who had to be stopped before one of them got hurt. Or worse, killed.

Matt melted further into the woods. Every move was unconscious, every action second nature. Even after all these years out of the Marines, the cloak of combat slipped back over him so easily, so naturally, it was like he'd been training only yesterday. There were some things in life that a man simply never forgot.

The quiet snap of a branch breaking far ahead made him freeze in surprise. *He's still on this side of the island.* Matt had expected the shooter to circle east to cross the marsh and head back toward the mainland, so why was he here?

Matt sprinted between the trees, stopping briefly behind each to check for movement, but all he could hear was the sound of his own ragged breathing, the pounding of his heart in his ears, and the dull thump of his boots on the dry, loamy soil. Branches whipped at him and he tried to keep his left arm in front of his face, protecting his eyes.

Then a flash of movement to the left caught his eye. Staring intently through a break in the trees, he thought he could see a smear of dark color moving into the lighter marsh grasses. *Going further* into *the marsh?*

Ignoring safety and cover at that point, Matt sprinted for the edge of the swamp. Forty feet ahead, struggling through the tall grasses was a dark head.

Matt dove into the cover of the tall grasses, shouting, "He's heading into the marsh!" hoping Leigh would hear him and give chase.

Sprinting through the marsh was a challenge—his boots slid in the greasy tangle of rotting plant life covering the slick mud, and the grasses tore at him, unwilling to give way. The shooter spun around, and sunlight glinted off metal. Matt dropped to his knees in the wet muck as a shot sounded and a bullet ripped by, just over his head. The cold ooze of muddy water soaked into his jeans, but he didn't pause as he scrambled to his feet again, running in a jagged zigzag line after his prey. He pulled off two shots, but he didn't have much confidence of hitting his target during this mad chase.

He'd only gone another fifty feet when he heard it—the unmistakable sound of an engine roaring to life.

Son of a bitch! Matt poured on speed, muscles bunching and straining with effort, abandoning evasive maneuvers and simply running full out. At the edge of his consciousness, he recognized the sounds behind him—Leigh was hot on his heels; she must have heard the engine too.

The engine roar increased in volume, followed by the unmistakable sound of water churning. The sound of the motor peaked before dropping in volume as the boat moved away.

Matt ran faster, his breath sawing raggedly, his muscles burning, and his heart racing frantically as he poured every last ounce of energy into the chase. He broke through the grass and slid to a halt at the edge of a wide branch of the Essex River. He overstepped, one foot landing in the murky water at the edge of the wide stream, icy water flowing into his boot.

He was standing near the middle of a short straightaway; twenty feet in either direction the stream curved out of sight, disappearing into the tall marsh grasses.

There was no boat in sight and the sound of the engine was rapidly fading.

They'd lost him.

"Goddamn it!"

Leigh suddenly broke through the grass five feet downstream, breathing hard, her weapon clutched in her fist.

"He had a boat?" she asked between panting breaths.

"Hidden here out of sight in the grass. I didn't see it, I just heard it."

They were silent as they listened to the fading sound of the motor.

"He's gone north," Leigh said. "Into open water." She pulled out her cell phone and Matt listened as she quickly outlined the situation to the Essex police and requested both marine and ground backup. Her words were choppy, short bursts of speech between gasping breaths. Matt bent and braced his hands on his knees, the Glock still in one hand, as he desperately tried to pull some much-needed oxygen into his starved lungs.

"They're never going to find him," Matt stated grimly, his head still bent, when she ended the call. "We didn't even get a look at the boat. He'll vanish into one of dozens of public or private marinas or out into open water long before they can get out there. The only trace of him is going to be the bullets and casings he left behind."

"That's why I requested ground support. I need a team out here for evidence collection." Her eyes trailed down to Matt's gun, still braced on his right knee. "I'm going to assume you have a permit for that. Don't tell me if you don't. Right now, I don't want to know."

"Don't worry, I have a Class A carry permit." He straightened and turned to face the island across the swamp, his mind already back with his students. The tops of the trees were just visible over the tall grass from the stream bank.

He heard her sharply indrawn breath. "Matt! You're hurt."

He spun back to see her staring at his upper arm and the spreading stain of dark blood that marred his sleeve. He remembered the white-hot pain of the bullet ripping along the top of his right biceps as he'd been in midair, his arms locked around Leigh, but he'd forgotten the injury in the hunt and chase that followed. Now, as Leigh brought it back to his attention and his adrenaline level fell after the chase, the wound started to burn and throb viciously. "I've had worse," he said flatly.

Leigh looked at him sharply, her gaze automatically moving to the scar partially hidden under his windblown hair. "Let me see it." Grasping his arm just above the elbow, she gently pulled the material away from the wound.

Matt hissed as she tugged threads of fabric from the wound. "Careful!"

She examined the wound. It wasn't a through and through, but rather a ragged furrow that steadily seeped blood. "This looks bad. We'd better get a paramedic team out here to stitch you up."

Matt stubbornly pulled his arm from her grip. "No paramedics. It's not that bad. The bullet just grazed me. It needs to be cleaned and covered, and I have supplies in the packs for that."

"An open wound like that is going to scar."

"Just one more for the collection," he muttered under his breath.

The expression on Leigh's face clearly conveyed her inner argument. Then she gave a small shrug as if letting it go. "Can you explain something for me then?"

"What?"

"What happened back there? You come armed to a recovery operation and then when all hell breaks loose, you handle yourself like a veteran." She froze as if realizing what she'd just said, then her eyes rose to his slowly. "I'm thinking veteran cop, but that's not it at all, is it? Where did you serve?"

A range of emotions swept through him at her question—

surprise at her intuitive leap, then irritation at her discovery, followed by resignation. "I guess there's no hiding it after this. I was a battlefield medic in Afghanistan with the Marines from two-thousand-and-one to—"

A piercing scream sliced through the air.

Two heads jerked in unison toward the island. *"Kiko,"* Matt said sharply.

They dove back into the grasses, pounding back the way that they had come, adrenaline flooding back in a new, frenzied rush. They ran shoulder-to-shoulder, keeping pace even in full sprint, guns gripped tight in damp palms as they ran. Suddenly Leigh's boot skidded and she started to fall, but Matt managed to reach out with his left hand and grab her right elbow, keeping her upright. She staggered for a pace or two and then found her footing again and fell back into step with him.

They sprinted up onto dry land, both of them frantically trying to identify where the scream had come from.

"Kiko!" Matt called.

"Here!" Paul shouted.

They both veered left, running through the trees and darting around rocks and rotting trunks.

"There!" Matt wheezed between gasping breaths, pointing even further north as he spotted Juka's blue sweat jacket through the trees.

Moments later, they broke into a small clearing and stopped abruptly. Juka, Paul, and Kiko huddled on the far side of the clearing, Paul's arm around Kiko as she hid her face against his shoulder. Paul and Juka's shocked gazes were fixed on the ground.

Suddenly, the nitrous odor he'd smelled earlier hit Matt like a wave and his stomach rolled.

He looked down at the floor of the clearing. Then everything went gray, the forest and its inhabitants disappearing into a dark vortex of misery and pain that dimmed his vision . . .

Falling to his knees beside the soldier, his rifle falling from nerveless fingers.

Ripping open the uniform to reveal tattered, bloody tissue. Warm blood gushing over his hands as he desperately tried to quench the seemingly endless flow. His own blood flowing freely from the gash on his temple, down over his cheek and jaw, soaking his uniform.

The burning heat from an explosion, the shock wave sending him tumbling.

Crawling back to his comrade's body, tossed aside like a rag doll.

Sightless, staring eyes.

Dead eyes.

"Matt. Matt!" Pain from his right arm abruptly brought him back as Leigh grabbed his left shoulder and shook him sharply. "Matt!"

He blinked and forced himself to focus on the woman standing in front of him. Leigh's face was pale, her alarmed eyes fixed on his.

"Are you okay?"

He nodded once, a sharp jerk of his head. Then he forced himself to look back into the clearing, back at the nightmare that had thrust him into the horrific landscape of his own past.

A short-handled shovel lay carelessly discarded on a loose pile of dark dirt, small roots and bits of gravel. Beside the dirt pile was a partially dug oval pit; a pit that was unmistakably long enough and wide enough to hold a human body.

But the true horror lay in the dirt beside the half-dug grave.

The broken, bloodied body of the woman was wrapped in a plastic sheet. She was naked, sprawled as if she had rolled after being carelessly dropped. The upper part of her body was partially exposed, black hair fanned around her bloodless, stark white face. Her lips and tongue had started to swell and dark liquid leaked from her closed eyelids—the tears of the dead.

One ghostly arm had pulled free from the sheet and lay limply in the dirt, palm up and fingers outstretched as if in entreaty, bloody strips of peeled skin falling away from the limb. Her chest was a mass of bloody and lacerated tissue, and blood grotesquely smeared the inside of the clear plastic.

Whoever had killed her had ripped her apart.

CHAPTER NINE:
ENVIRONMENTAL STRESSOR

Environmental Stressor: a physical, chemical, or biological event, either natural or manmade, that adversely impacts the growth and development of the salt marsh.

Wednesday, 7:35 A.M.
Essex Bay Coast, Massachusetts

Matt hung back at the edge of the trees, his eyes fixed on Leigh as she stood at the far side of the clearing. She was far enough away that he couldn't hear what she was saying, but it was her fourth phone call. She ended the call, remaining motionless, her eyes locked on the horror in the clearing and her body rigid. Then she turned, stopping abruptly when she found him silently watching her. "Everything okay?"

"No, everything's not okay. We got shot at, someone's been brutally murdered, my students could have been killed, and we're still missing a body." Matt jammed a hand through his already tousled hair. "What the hell is going on here, Leigh?"

"I wish I knew. But whatever it is, we're damned well going to get to the bottom of it. We're about to have a flood of people arrive—half of the Essex force, a crowd of Crime Scene Services techs, and several state boys as well. And for some reason, Rowe's on his way up here."

"I thought you said he doesn't come out to scenes?"

"He doesn't. I'm not sure why we're so special. If he wanted to tour a crime scene he could find one a whole lot closer to Boston. I guess we'll find out when he arrives." She studied his bloody sleeve. "How's the arm?"

"I told you, it'll be fine." When her expression turned mulish, he said, "Leave it alone, Leigh."

She let the subject drop for the moment. "Where are your students?"

Matt pointed with a thumb back over his shoulder. "When you asked them to clear the area to maintain the integrity of the crime scene, they headed further into the trees. I waited because I wanted to know that help is on the way."

Irritation flashed in her eyes. "Of course help is on the way. Did you think I was going to handle this all on my own? I know what to do, Matt. I'm not a rookie."

She started to push past him, but he caught her arm, his callused palm rough against her skin. "Look, I'm sorry. I'm a little on edge. I brought my students out here and they could have been killed. It's got me a little freaked out. It's one thing to go into battle with trained comrades—"

"Or a cop," Leigh added.

"Or a cop," he conceded. "It's another thing to bring in kids that can't protect themselves and to watch them nearly get killed on your watch. And I—" He broke off suddenly, listening intently. "Is that . . ."

"The sound of someone throwing up? Yes."

Matt spun, pushing through the brush toward the sound, Leigh right on his heels. They found Kiko and Juka huddled together on the trunk of a fallen tree. Paul was nowhere in sight.

"Where's Paul?" Matt asked.

"Here." Paul stepped out from behind a tree, shoving through the scrubby brush. He was sheet white and even from a few feet away Matt could see that the hand he wiped across his mouth was shaking.

Matt stepped forward to lay his open palm over Paul's shoulder, the muscles tight with tension under his grip. "You okay?"

A sharp-edged, strained laugh burst from the younger man. "Except that I just had to toss my cookies like a little girl, everything's great."

"Don't beat yourself up." Leigh had been hanging back, but now stepped toward the group. "I've seen trained officers lose it over less. You guys held up wonderfully when you needed to and you used your heads and didn't contaminate my crime scene. There's no shame in being sick over what you saw in that clearing. I'd worry more if that didn't sicken you."

Matt gave Paul's shoulder a squeeze before releasing him. "Go sit down." *Before you fall down.*

Paul flopped down on the tree trunk on the other side of Kiko, purposely sidling close to her, his long gangly legs sprawled out in front of him while he slumped with his head bent. Juka leaned forward, his worried eyes focused on his friend.

Matt stared at his students, seeing them huddled together for comfort. They were a unit. Hell, together with him they were a team, but maybe it was time to break up that team. It was one thing to ask them to participate in a recovery; it was something else altogether to ask them to put their young lives on the line.

He squatted down in front of them, putting himself on their level. It was then that Kiko noticed the blood that soaked his sleeve.

"Matt! What happened?" She reached out with her free hand to touch his arm.

He swiveled sideways, evading her touch. "It's barely a scratch. It's fine."

Sitting on Matt's right side, Juka leaned in. "You were shot?"

Paul snapped upright, his own misery forgotten. "What?"

"How did we miss that?" Kiko asked.

"It's understandable," Leigh said. "There's only so much that you can take in at a time like that and you were justifiably distracted."

"You need to have that looked at," Kiko insisted before gazing up at Leigh. "You called this in. Are they sending out someone for Matt?"

Leigh opened her mouth to answer, but Matt quickly cut them all off. "Hang on, everyone. It's not serious. I'll take care of it myself."

"It's just a flesh wound." Paul spoke and then his eyes snapped wide as he realized what he'd said.

Relief washed through Matt. Pale and unsteady Paul worried him. Smart-ass Paul was comfortingly familiar. "You're feeling better if you can make Monty Python jokes," he said dryly. "And yes, it's just a flesh wound. It's nothing to worry about."

"Are you sure?" Kiko looked up at Leigh, not even allowing Matt time to answer. "Did you see it?"

"Yes. It looks bad but with a little care, he'll be fine. Don't worry. It'll be taken care of."

"Enough about my arm," Matt insisted. "I'm more worried about you." He scrutinized them, cataloging pale faces, worried eyes, dirt smudged clothes, and the small twig caught in Kiko's ponytail. Otherwise they appeared whole and healthy, even if shaken.

"We're fine. No one got hurt," Kiko said. "Well, no one but you. I really think—"

"We've covered that ground already," Matt growled. He forced himself to inhale deeply and take a moment. "Look guys, I'm sorry if I'm being sharp with you. Truth to be told, this whole situation has me rattled."

Paul snorted. "You too?"

"I never thought when we came out here that something like this would happen. But now that it has, it's clearly time to get you guys out of the field. There's more than enough work for you to do in the lab and that way you can still be involved in the case and—"

"No." Juka's quiet voice snapped out, uncharacteristically backed by steel.

"What?"

"No," Juka repeated. "We're not children needing your protection. We're adults and can make our own decisions."

Matt gaped at him, but was met by Juka's steady unwavering stare. "You hardly ever say anything and *now* you decide to speak up?"

Message delivered, Juka simply continued to stare at Matt silently.

"That's because he's got something important to say," Paul said. "And this time he's speaking for all of us."

"Juka's right," Kiko said. Matt instantly recognized the stubborn set to her mouth and knew he was fighting a losing battle. "We're not kids. You can't make the decision for us to bow out. I for one have no intention of doing that. When the going gets tough, the tough don't head for the hills."

Matt straightened from his crouched position to pace away a few steps before turning on them again. "Do you guys understand that I'm responsible for you? This isn't just a field trip to a dig anymore. *We were shot at.*"

"Do you want us to sign a waiver absolving you of all responsibility?" Kiko asked. "Because we will if that's what it takes."

Matt glanced over at Leigh, who had been quiet through most of the exchange. "Do you see what I have to deal with here?"

"I see," she said. "And I'm with you on this. It was one thing when we were just looking for remains, but now we've got a situation with an active killer. Emergency personnel know the risks and are trained to deal with them. You guys aren't." She met Matt's eyes. "Assuming we find the missing remains, can you do the excavation on your own?"

Matt ignored the objections from all three students. "Yes. It would just take longer."

"This is insane." Kiko shot to her feet. "This has just become the safest spot in all of Massachusetts and you don't want us here?" She turned on Leigh. "You're going to have officers here guarding the site 24/7, right?"

"Yes."

"And they'll be here during the excavation?"

For a moment Leigh looked like she was going to argue, then she sighed. "Yes."

"Then I have a better chance of being mugged in Roxbury than the guy from this morning showing his face here again. We'll have cops on scene at all times." She rounded on Matt. "Hell, we'll have *you*."

"Yeah, that's right," Paul interjected. "Exactly what happened back there? One minute, there you are, the mild-mannered professor. And, in the next, you go all Rambo on us. Where did the gun come from?"

"Look, I don't like to talk about it, but I served with the Marines in Afghanistan after 9/11 and . . ." Matt took in the mixed reactions from his students—shock, surprise, and a little anger. "What?"

"You're a Marine?" Paul blurted.

"Ex-Marine. I've been out of the service since before grad school."

"Hey, once a Marine, always a Marine." Paul gazed at him in astonishment as if Matt had just reached a whole new level of cool in his eyes.

"You don't think you might have mentioned this little fact before?" Kiko asked. "It couldn't have just come up in conversation at some point?"

"Maybe he didn't want it to come up in conversation," Juka interjected, earning the startled gazes of his fellow students. "Sometimes people don't like to discuss their time in combat."

Matt stared in surprise at his unexpected ally.

"I have family members in Bosnia who fought the Serbs during the war," Juka clarified. "They don't talk about it. They *won't* talk about it. We don't know what they experienced, so we have to respect that. If Matt wants to tell us about it, he will."

"I wasn't excluding you guys," Matt explained. "I don't like to talk about it with anyone. Just ask my Dad. For now, let's leave it at the fact that I know my way around guns and a combat situation. And it still doesn't make me any happier that you guys got caught in one."

"Speaking of which," Leigh interrupted, "I want to go walk the crime scene and make some initial notes before the techs get here. Matt, can I talk to you?"

"Sure."

He followed her through the trees back to the edge of the clearing. "What's wrong?"

"Nothing's wrong. I just wanted to give you a heads up as a courtesy."

"About what?" Matt asked suspiciously.

"I want that arm looked after. Properly. Meaning not by you."

"Oh, for God's sake," Matt exploded. "How many times do I need to tell you that I can take care of it myself? I don't like paramedics, and I don't need one."

"And yet a team will be here shortly." Her tone brooked no resistance, and when he started to protest, Leigh pinned him with an icy stare. "I know you don't want them, but I called them anyway."

"You had no right—"

"I had every right," she retorted, the combined weight of exhaustion and stress flashing her temper toward the breaking point. "This is my scene and you were injured during an encounter with an armed suspect," she said. "Add to that you're part of my team and you're my responsibility, just like you feel your students are your responsibility." Before he could reply she stepped forward into his personal space. He stood his ground, staring down at her from just inches away.

"When you came on board, like it or not, you joined a team. And team members look out for each other. I would expect you to do the same for me if our positions were reversed. The current victim aside, you and I still have the responsibility to find the remains we originally set out to look for. And you can't do that if you're distracted by pain." He opened his mouth to speak and she ruthlessly cut him off. "I'm not looking for a discussion. They'll be local, so they'll likely be first on scene. When they arrive, you *will* be treated."

She turned and marched away, leaving Matt seething behind her.

CHAPTER TEN:
TIDAL RANGE

Tidal Range: the difference in height between consecutive high and low tides; it varies as a function of the lunar cycle, with extreme height differences occurring around the full and new moons.

Wednesday, 8:32 A.M.
Essex Bay Coast, Massachusetts

Leigh stood over the body of the dead woman, clipboard and pen in hand. Dr. Edward Rowe, the Medical Examiner for the State of Massachusetts, knelt in the dirt across from her, dressed in Tyvex coveralls.

"Liver temp is 20.5°C," Rowe said, without raising his head.

Rowe was a big man: big in body and big in voice. Many found him gruff and somewhat abrasive, but Leigh genuinely liked him. He was direct to the point of bluntness and never asked for more work from anyone else than he was willing to do himself. He was demanding of his staff but fair and conscientious at the same time. And he was honest to a fault, which Leigh found ideal in a man of his position.

"Ambient air temp is 17.8°C," Rowe continued. Leigh made a note on the Death Investigation form as Rowe handed his thermometers to the morgue tech crouching beside him. "She's been on the ground here for how long?"

"At least two hours," Leigh answered. "We don't know how

much longer. It depends on how long it took to dig this grave."

Rowe bent over the body again, gently lifting one limp, bloody arm to examine the underside.

"You haven't actually said why you're here," Leigh commented. "You just came in, started ordering techs around, and got to work."

Rowe glanced up at her briefly from under a bushy white eyebrow. "Isn't it obvious?" His gaze fell pointedly to the victim before them.

"It would be, except that your office never does on-scene exams."

"Yes, well . . . I'm trying to change that. Let's call this a personal pet project. Best way to change people's minds may be to see the difference it makes when we successfully nail the bastard who did this." Rowe sat back on his heels. "Based upon decomposition, lividity, and lack of rigor, I'd estimate that she's been dead for three to four days. You'll have to give me some time to finish unwrapping her before I can give you a preliminary cause of death." Rowe bent over the body again, carefully folding plastic away from the bloody thorax.

Leigh glanced across the clearing and through a gap in the trees. She'd been surreptitiously keeping an eye on Matt's treatment while she'd attended to Rowe. The paramedic was finally winding gauze around Matt's upper arm. Leigh waited until he'd secured it and packed up his equipment before turning back to Rowe. "Do you need me for the next few minutes?"

Rowe distractedly waved a hand in her direction. "No, no, do what you need to do. I'll call when I need you."

"Thanks. I need to check on Dr. Lowell. The paramedic is done with him now." She excused herself from the scene to cross the clearing and enter the trees where Matt and the team waited.

Matt's students were still perched on the fallen tree trunk

about twenty feet away, talking in hushed tones. Matt sat on the low boulder the paramedic had chosen for him while being treated. His blood-stained plaid shirt lay draped over his left thigh. The paramedic had made short work of his T-shirt, using scissors to cut the right sleeve from the body of the shirt despite Matt's objections. Below the pristine white bandage, Matt's right arm was stained with dark smears of blood. His black jeans were stiff with drying mud from knee to ankle, and mud caked the laces of his left boot.

His eyes stayed fixed on her approach, his mood evident in his tight mouth and furrowed brow.

"Move over," she said softly, indicating the rock, all traces of anger gone. "Please."

He seemed to consider her request, and then wordlessly shifted to his right, making room for her to perch on the boulder beside him.

She settled beside him, laying her clipboard down on the ground. "Rowe doesn't need me hanging over his shoulder while he does his job. I'm giving him some space for a few minutes." They sat in silence, both of them staring at the dirt at their feet before Leigh finally spoke. "How's the arm?"

"It hurt less before your medic started digging around for threads and pouring disinfectant all over it. Now it burns like a bitch."

"I bet." She turned to face his stony profile. "I'm sorry, Matt. I know you wanted it left alone, but I needed to know you were taken care of."

"I don't like being ordered around," he said shortly. "I left the military. I'm done taking orders."

"Okay, maybe I overstepped. But do you understand that it was because I was concerned? You were shot for God's sake."

"Yeah, I noticed," he said sarcastically.

Silence hung heavily between them again.

Leigh frowned. *How were they going to be able to work together if they kept pissing each other off at least once a day?* Then it hit her. *If he can do it, so can I.*

Impulsively, she stuck out her hand.

His gaze skittered sideways and then rose to her face. "What's that?"

"Hi," she said with an almost comical forced cheer. "I'm Leigh."

His eyebrows rose skyward, but a glint of humor lit his eyes for the first time that day. "What's this, a 'do over'?"

"You had one, so now it's my turn."

He gave a rueful chuckle and took her hand. "Hi, I'm Matt."

"We have to figure out how to stop getting under each other's skin."

"We're good at that, aren't we?"

"Too good." They each released their grip, letting their hands fall back into their laps. "New rules," she said. "I think we've proven to each other at this point that we both have the best interests of the case at heart. We just need to avoid irritating each other so we can get the job done. So, how about we both reserve the right to call for a time-out when we start annoying the hell out of each other? The discussion ends right then, at least temporarily. Either of us can call it, and both of us have to respect it, no questions asked. That will let one or both of us cool down before things get out of control."

"That could work. Maybe this way we'll make it out of this case without wanting to kill each other," he said dryly.

Leigh chuckled. "I'd like to think it wouldn't come to that." She slumped forward with a tired sigh. "I need to ask you about what you might have seen earlier. I couldn't see the suspect at all when he was shooting at us. Then when we went after him, he ran into the marsh instead of heading toward the mainland. By the time I caught up to you, he was already gone."

"You didn't expect that, did you? You thought he'd head back across the swamp *toward* the road. I noticed which direction you sent me." He pinned her with a narrowed glare.

"I had to make a fast decision and I didn't know you'd be able to handle yourself. But you know what? You were great out there today. You kept your head and you knew what to do without any explanation or instruction from me. I couldn't have asked for a better partner in that moment."

A smile slowly curved Matt's lips. "Thanks. I thought that I might be a bit rusty—I've been a civilian for years now—but apparently it's just one of those things that you don't forget."

"Can I ask you a question?"

"Sure."

"What happened back there when we first came into the clearing?"

Only because she was watching carefully did Leigh catch Matt's physical reaction as his pupils dilated slightly and some of the color slowly drained from his face.

He cleared his throat roughly. "I don't know what you mean."

"Yes, you do," she insisted. "You were standing there looking at the body, but I don't think you really saw it. In fact, for a brief instant, you weren't 'there' at all."

For the briefest instant, Leigh thought she spotted something akin to panic in his eyes. Reaching out, she laid a gentle hand on his wrist. "Whatever happened back there, it's okay. You're not a cop, and I can't expect you to be accustomed to this kind of thing. But I need to know if there are situations I can't bring you into."

"I'm used to working with bones." He turned his face away to stare into the depths of the forest. "I don't do flesh."

"You were caught off guard because it was a fleshed body?" Leigh tried unsuccessfully to keep the disbelief from her voice. "You told me you worked at two body farms during your training. You must be used to fleshed bodies."

He fussed with the shirt draped over his knee, lifting it to resettle it in the same position. "There's a big difference between a fresh body—or relatively fresh like that woman—and a body that's been buried for a year or left on the surface for insects to colonize for a month or two. Those bodies aren't really fleshed. In many cases, they're hardly recognizable. Or the remains are skeletonized."

Not the whole story. Not by a long shot, Leigh thought. *But now is not the time to push.*

She smoothly changed topics to draw him out again. "Back to the suspect. Did you see anything that might be useful in a description?"

Matt looked mildly relieved to get back to the business at hand. "Not much. Based on what I could see over the top of the marsh grass, he's maybe five ten or eleven. Dark hair. From the way he moved, I'm almost certain it was a man, but I couldn't swear to that in a court of law because he was concealed by the marsh grasses." He shook his head, frowning. "That's about it. I didn't get a good look at him. About the best view I had was when I was on the hill above him but then he shot at me and I dove into the marsh grass for cover." Suddenly his head snapped up. "The gun."

Interest flared in Leigh at the sudden energy in his tone. "What about it?"

"I saw sunlight gleam silver on the barrel when he aimed at me. Only a limited number of guns have that kind of finish. Most handguns and revolvers are matte black."

"You're right. That's a good catch because that will narrow our matches. And your limited description of him is better than I could've done. The techs have bagged the shovel he brought to the scene to dig the grave. Maybe if we're lucky, he's left us some fingerprints or epithelials to use for DNA identification."

"If he was smart, he wore gloves. And even if he didn't, you still need an existing sample to compare that DNA with. If he's not already in the system, we'd have to wait until we've actually caught him to pull a sample for comparison." Matt's gaze returned to the body in the clearing and the man kneeling next to it. "Is there an initial guess on cause of death?"

"So far all I've got is the estimate that she's been dead for three to four days. Which reminds me, I meant to ask you—when you stopped me earlier, before the shooting, you said that you could smell something. What was it?"

"I could smell the decomp gases, putrescine in particular, coming from the body. It's been a while since I've set foot on a body farm, but it's not something you forget easily."

"Abbott!" Across the clearing, Rowe rose to his feet, stripping off a bloody pair of latex gloves.

Leigh immediately stood, picking up her clipboard before glancing down at Matt. "He's done his on-site examination and he'll need to get the body ready for transport. Can you tell your students once I'm done here, I'll need their official statements? Yours too."

"Yeah." He tipped his head in the direction of the scene. "Go. We'll be here when you're ready."

Across the clearing, the naked body lay completely exposed now, and Leigh winced at the sheer brutality of the injuries. The pale flesh was smeared with dark blood, and multiple lacerations and gaping stab wounds were visible, as well as the dark discoloration of large areas from bruising. The hair on one side of her head was tangled and matted with blood, and there were several small circular burns visible on one arm. Narrow strips of skin were peeled from the body to hang in limp, bloody ribbons.

"What can you give me so far?" she asked Rowe, pulling out her notepad.

"Nothing official until I can do the full autopsy, but at this point I'd suggest the cause of death was asphyxiation by manual strangulation, judging from the bruising of the throat and the petechial hemorrhage of the conjunctiva." Rowe's face was set in harsh lines as he considered the broken body at their feet. "But this woman went through significant trauma before she was finally allowed the peace of death. I should be able to give you detailed information about what was done to her when the autopsy is complete. Maybe that will give you a way to track him."

"Good. I want to get this bastard."

"You and me both. I'm not sure if this was a rage killing or just for kicks. Either way, someone brutalized this woman."

"Just get me what you can and we'll take it from there. You're transporting her now?"

"Yes. My tech just went for the body bag."

"Will you have time to do the autopsy today?"

"I'll make time." Rowe's words came out sharply, but Leigh knew that it wasn't directed at her. "Can you be there?"

"I'll make time." Leigh echoed Rowe's own words.

Suddenly one of the crime scene techs broke through the trees on the north side of the clearing. "Abbott!" Leigh whirled to see him frantically motioning her to follow. "You need to come now. And bring your bone guy."

Rowe immediately waved her off. "I've got this."

Leigh turned to locate Matt across the clearing. He had obviously heard the call as he was already on his feet and pulling on his plaid shirt, grimacing in pain as his movements tugged at raw flesh.

Matt skirted the scene, meeting Leigh on the far side. "What's going on?" he asked.

"No idea."

The thin, dark-haired man led them into the trees, talking to them over his shoulder. "You guys need to see this. A couple of us were heading back to the mainland to where we were parked further north on Conomo Point Road. We were going to cut through the marsh from here." His eyes searching the trees, he finally spotted a second technician that he had left to mark the area. They moved through the trees until they approached a woman dressed in a similar windbreaker, her long auburn hair pulled back in a ponytail, the ends dancing in the breeze.

Leigh instantly recognized the technician from previous casework. "Franklin, what did you find?" she called out.

Meg Franklin held out an arm, blocking them from going any further. "This. You were here searching for human remains, right? Well, we found some."

Leigh heard Matt's sharp indrawn breath even as she looked into the clearing beyond where they stood. Shock slammed into her like a physical blow to the gut.

Protruding eerily from the soil were bones from several sets of remains, spaced several feet apart. In one spot, the smooth surface of the brow ridge of a skull disappeared into the dark earth. Nearby, several curving bones of a rib cage arched out of the soil like the ribs of the hull of an ancient schooner, dried bands of desiccated muscle and ligament linking the bones together. Several feet from that, the rounded head of a long bone angled upward and several tiny bones lay scattered on the surface next to an embedded fan of long, narrow bones. *A hand? A foot?*

There must be at least three, or maybe even four more bodies revealed by the storm surge.

For how many years had this small island cradled the dead? And how had so many come to rest here?

One set of excavated remains.

At least three more bodies here.

The murdered woman lying in the clearing.

Leigh glanced at Matt to see the same horror she felt reflected in his eyes as he stared back at her.

At least five dead. Maybe more.

What other horrors could this place possibly hold?

CHAPTER ELEVEN:
SALT MARSH DETRITUS

Salt Marsh Detritus: dead and decomposing plant and animal material that forms the organic mat at the base of the marsh, and constitutes an important part of the local food chain.

Wednesday, 12:19 P.M.
Office of the Chief Medical Examiner
Boston, Massachusetts

Leigh hurried down the hallway, her arms full of Missing Persons files. She glanced at her watch, grimaced at the time, and pushed through the wide single door with her shoulder.

The autopsy suite was all gleaming stainless steel, sterile white tile and bright lighting. A large stainless steel downdraft table was the centerpiece of the room; the female victim lay stretched out on its surface.

Gowned and flanked by a morgue assistant, Rowe bent over the woman's body, scalpel in hand, ready to start the Y-incision. Standing across from Rowe was Meg Franklin, waiting to photograph every step of the procedure.

Rowe raised his head at the sound of the door opening. "Ah . . . I was hoping that you'd get here before I started cutting. Better that you see this in person than just in photographs."

"Sorry," Leigh's voice was breathless. "I had to stop and pick up the Missing Persons files back at the office and then the traffic coming into town on Route 1 was a nightmare."

Rowe set his scalpel down on the draped tray of surgical instruments. "Route 1 is always a nightmare. Don't these damned people have jobs to keep them indoors during the day? No one seems to know when rush hour is, anymore." He shook his head in disgust. "What's going on back at the site? I left the new burials in Lowell's hands, but I haven't heard anything."

"Dr. Lowell and his team are up there right now. Sergeant Kepler stopped by after you left and he gave us the green light to bring in a K-9 team."

Rowe nodded approvingly. "Sensible. At this point, we need to know if we've identified all of the burial sites."

"They'll go over the area this afternoon and mark out any new graves. Dr. Lowell wants to start the excavation this afternoon, even if it's only taking the graves down a few inches to see what they've got. I'll head back up there after we're done here, so I'll call you later to update you on their progress."

"Works for me. Put those down for a minute," he said, indicating the stack of files she held in her arms. "Come and take a closer look."

Leigh set the files on the counter and then, taking a deep breath, turned to face the now clean body of the victim.

The sight hit her like a physical blow and she just managed to hold back a gasp of shock. Even with all the death she'd seen during previous investigations, she'd never seen cruelty like this. "Sweet Jesus. What did he do to her?"

"The question might be more 'what didn't he do to her'? All the years I've been cutting, and this still manages to stretch the boundaries of what I've seen in a single victim."

Leigh forced herself to move closer to the table and examine the victim, taking in each wound. The injuries seemed horrific at the crime scene, but there had been so much blood it had actually camouflaged the true extent of the damage. Over half of the woman's body was marked—bruises, abrasions, slices, jagged tears in the skin, punctures, and even small burns.

With effort, Leigh forced herself to consider each wound. Many appeared to be knife wounds but there were some circular ones that didn't have the typical appearance of a bullet entry. There were stab wounds of various sizes—he must have used a variety of knives or other implements, including a hunting or skinning knife to peel skin from muscle. The burns could have been from a cigarette or maybe a small butane torch.

She leaned in to examine one particular bruise that cut a straight diagonal swath from hip to opposite breast. The bruise undulated as it traversed the deathly white skin.

"I'm not sure what caused that yet. It's an odd configuration." Rowe spoke from behind her.

Leigh couldn't quite put her finger on it, but the pattern seemed familiar. Not a rope, not a wire—those would leave straight, solid lines. It had to be something that would leave intermittent marks. She leaned in to study the mark more closely, then suddenly jerked upright. "Chain links. Someone whipped her with a metal chain."

Rowe's eyes went ice cold. "Bloody hell," he murmured. "What is wrong with this world?" He met Leigh's shadowed eyes. "Don't answer that. We haven't got all day. Let me give you the initial rundown. Chris"—Rowe indicated his assistant—"recovered any trace evidence that we missed at the scene and took fingerprints and x-rays, including a full set of dentals to compare to antemortem x-rays if we can get them. The radiographs show no antemortem healed bone breaks, so we don't have that as a method of identification. Blood and urine were sampled for tox screening. The potassium level of vitreous fluid sampled from the eye will confirm time since death.

"The victim is female, approximately twenty-five to thirty-five years of age, white, five-feet, five inches in height. She currently weighs one hundred and thirty-seven pounds, but keep in mind that ongoing decomposition makes that an approximation of her original weight. There are no surgical scars or piercings other than her ears, but there is a distinctive tattoo of a butterfly on her left shoulder blade that may aid in identification."

"I think I saw something about a butterfly tattoo in my scan through the files while I was sitting in traffic." At Rowe's pointed look, she said defensively, "I was in a rush, so I was making use of the time I had. I'll check the files once we're done here. Go on."

"Each individual defect has been numbered, measured, photographed, and described, and full details will be in the autopsy report. We'll be adding the corresponding internal details now. All injuries are perimortem and show signs of hemorrhage, meaning they all occurred prior to cardiac death. I anticipate additional blunt force trauma will be evident in the internal organs when we move to the internal exam.

"Now, what you can't obviously see here is the extent of bone injury. To begin with, both bones in the victim's forearms are broken. Bruising indicates a single blow with a tool likely less than an inch in diameter. We've taken samples for trace to determine the material."

"Breaking her arms took away any possibility of self defense from that point on." There was ice behind Leigh's words. "What are you thinking of as the weapon? A crowbar or tire iron?" She leaned in to study the right forearm. "The bruising comes from the underside of the arm. Defensive wounds?" She raised both arms over her head, wrists crossed over her forehead as if fending off a blow.

"We'll test for particulate matter but yes, that's a likely theory. Which means that she was awake and aware of what was happening to her." He pointed to several x-rays that hung on the light box on the wall. "Most of her fingers are also broken. From the crush pattern on the x-rays, I'm thinking that something like a hammer was used. Ribs eight through ten are fractured on her left side, consistent with the external bruising you have suggested as being caused by a chain. She also has a crush fracture of the left temporal bone." He patted his fingers against his head, just above his left ear. "Since he's working with us, I'd like your anthropologist to look at that one to confirm, but based on the radiating pattern, my guess is it's from a baseball bat."

Leigh's face flushed with heat as anger started to rise. "Bastard. Was that the cause of death?"

"The internal exam will show for sure, but I don't think so." He pointed to the neck area. "Remember the bruising around the throat we discussed on site and the associated petechiae of the sclera and the conjunctivae of the eye? The head injury would certainly have caused a loss of consciousness but manual strangulation was likely the cause of death. We should find associated breakage of the hyoid bone as well as the thyroid cartilage horns. None of the stab wounds would have been fatal. Whoever did this took his time so that this woman suffered, but she did it quietly. We found fibers in her teeth indicating she was gagged. I've sent them to the lab for identification. I wonder if that means that she was killed in a location where other people might have been able to hear her scream."

"Possibly. Or he was just being very careful and wasn't taking any chances."

"True." Rowe moved around the table, motioning for Leigh to follow him. "Before we make the Y-incision, I want you to see this. I missed it at the scene under all the blood and it's hard to see as it's buried amidst some significant contusions." He pointed to a wound located above the victim's left breast.

Leigh leaned closer as Rowe adjusted the overhead light to shine directly onto the spot in question. A series of interconnected lines were carved into the bruised flesh. "What is that . . . some sort of Chinese symbol?"

"That's my best guess, but that's your department, not mine. We've taken detailed photographs and I'll get them to you as soon as we're done here."

"This could be his signature."

"I know. That's why I wanted to make sure that you saw it."

Leigh was silent as she studied the mark. "How deep does that go?"

"The wound itself?"

"Yes. Would it go right down to the ribs?"

Rowe's eyes lit with understanding. "I see where you're going with this. You want to know if any of the other victims had the same mark, but you only have skeletonized remains." Leigh nodded. "There might be traces left on the bone structure, but the marks could be pretty subtle. Lowell might have to look microscopically for traces of such a wound. On the bright side, if it's a true signature, then at least he'll know where to look. Most serial killers repeat their signatures fairly precisely."

"It's like it's a badge. Look at the placement." With the fingers of her right hand, Leigh tapped the same spot over her own left breast. "Think of a police uniform."

"That's where your shield goes."

"Precisely. It's like he carved it there as some sort of badge or an insignia." Her eyes narrowed on the defect. "But of what?"

"First step is to find out what it means," Rowe said. "Then maybe it will lead you to something. Now, if you're ready, let's get started."

Leigh swallowed and stepped back a few paces to where there was no risk of a splash hazard. "Ready when you are."

Circling the table again to his original position, Rowe picked up his scalpel and bent over the body.

Wednesday, 2:57 P.M.
Office of the Chief Medical Examiner
Boston, Massachusetts

Leaving the autopsy suite, Leigh indulged in a deep breath of fresh air. Bracing one hand against the wall and holding the files to her chest with the other, she let her head drop as she closed her eyes. She just needed to get her balance back—

"Autopsy too rough for you, Abbott?"

The sharp tone scraped along her spine like ice. She raised her head to see the one man she'd like to see taken off the face of the planet even if it meant doing it herself. Len Morrison stalked down the hall toward her, wearing a cheap suit and his typical scornful expression.

Damn it all to hell. Why does he have to be here now?

She schooled her features into a blank mask. "It was just peachy, Morrison. I love a good autopsy. How about you?"

To her surprise, he stepped into her, purposely crowding her against the wall with his bulky frame, his chest bumping the files in her arms, nearly making her drop them. "Bullshit," he sneered.

Leigh scrambled to maintain her white-knuckled grip on the files, but held her ground. She stubbornly wouldn't allow herself to give way to him even as she struggled against the aftereffects of the most brutal autopsy she'd ever attended coupled with the light-headedness that came from not eating in more than nine hours.

Morrison leaned in closer, his eyes narrowing to little slits, his nostrils pinched and his lip curling as if he smelled something putrid. Leigh had to steel herself to not turn her face away from the sour coffee on his breath that made her already unsettled stomach churn in protest. "You look like you're about to crumple. Daddy's little bitch can't handle the tough stuff?"

The venom in his tone shot straight to her heart, but Leigh kept her voice level. "She certainly can. Just as well as the guys."

"I doubt it. You haven't got the nerve. Just one more time when we see you don't have the balls to be a cop. You wouldn't even be with us if it wasn't for your dad. You've been given a free pass from day one and everybody knows it."

His words washed over her like a wave of ice water. The double-edged knife of doubt and uncertainty rose up full force to slice cleanly, its edge as razor sharp as he intended. Morrison took advantage of her moment of shocked silence to twist the blade one more turn.

"I don't know how you live with yourself. You killed a cop, a fellow officer. You might as well have pulled the fucking trigger yourself," he snarled, tiny droplets of spittle flying from his mouth to spray against her cheek. "If you'd been anybody else's kid, you would have been gone after that. But daddy's girl got off with a pat on the head and an early transfer into the Detective Unit like it was some kind of reward for your failure."

Guilt twisted her gut. Tears pricked the backs of her eyes and she furiously blinked them back. *You're done if you let him see that he's getting to you.*

As if sensing weakness, Morrison went in for the kill. "Good thing your father died before the hero could see what his spawn would do. The sight of you would have made him sick."

Hot, energizing anger rushed through Leigh, crushing the guilt and horror that threatened to break free. She raised her head so that she was practically nose-to-nose with Morrison and dropped her voice so no one could overhear. "Fuck you, Morrison," she retorted, her voice low and hard. "You know I was cleared in that investigation. It's over. Stop trying to throw it in my face, because as far as the department is concerned, it's a closed book. And my father would be nothing but proud of my time on the job." She stepped back, squaring her shoulders to stand tall, and allowed a hint of triumph to come into both her expression and voice. "Just because you're jealous of the case I caught when you've got nothing more exciting than a heroin O.D. doesn't mean you need to get nasty."

"Case? What case?" The bafflement in his voice lightened her heart considerably. "You mean that pathetic beaver dam bone? That's hardly a case."

Leigh spun on her heel and started to stride off down the hallway, leaving him standing alone outside the autopsy suite. But she took the time to call back over her shoulder. "Tune into the news tonight, Morrison, so you can catch up with the rest of the world."

CHAPTER TWELVE:
OVERWASH

Overwash: the movement and deposition of sand driven over the top of a barrier beach by storms or strong winds.

Wednesday, 4:11 P.M.
Essex Bay Coast, Massachusetts

Wrapping one hand around the rough bark of an aged elm tree, Leigh pulled herself from the salt marsh onto dry land and walked up the small incline. Flashing a weak smile at the Essex officer stationed at the edge of the marsh, she moved through the trees, heading toward the northern edge of the island.

Exhaustion ran deep in body and soul, and an aching stress headache throbbed rhythmically in her temples. The energizing anger that had come to her rescue during the earlier argument had melted away as she drove north. Now she simply felt unsettled and anxious. Morrison's attack had clearly hit closer to home than she first realized. And after today's incident, it was likely that he would simply redouble his efforts. He wanted to drive her out of the department and she simply couldn't allow that to happen. Police work ran in her blood just like it had in her father's.

She came to the edge of the foliage, stopping just short of breaking through as she peered through the leaves.

Another Essex officer kept watch from the tree line while talking with several Crime Scene Services techs. Inside the clearing, Matt's students each crouched at a different grave. Matt was on his feet, a small trowel in hand as he moved between Juka's excavation and Paul's. He crouched down near Paul and nodded at something the younger man said, his eyes fixed grimly on the burial site.

Leigh took a minute to gather herself. Then, pasting on a pleasant smile, she pushed through the trees.

As soon as she cleared the brush, Matt's head immediately snapped up as if he'd been anxiously awaiting her arrival. Seeing her at the edge of the clearing, he said a quiet word to the group, left his trowel beside the grave, and climbed to his feet to cross the clearing.

Alarm rushed through Leigh at the bleakness in his eyes, wobbling the smile she was desperately trying to maintain. "What's wrong?"

He stopped a few feet away, his brow furrowed. "I was going to ask you the same thing. I can't decide if you're going to laugh or cry."

She let the smile fall away. Clearly it wasn't working anyway. "It's nothing. Everything's fine." Brushing him off, she started past him. "How are we doing here?"

He surprised her by reaching out and loosely clasping her wrist, holding her beside him. Not wanting to make a scene and draw attention, she turned to face him.

"It's not 'nothing.' I can see it in your eyes. What happened?" he insisted.

She gave a small tug, but he held firm. Frustration made her snappish. "This case isn't enough for you?"

Matt's gaze flicked to the floor of the clearing and the exposed bones. "It's more than enough," he said harshly. "But that's not all it is."

She stared at him intently, green eyes fixed on unblinking hazel. "Why won't you let it go?"

"Because something's wrong. I can see it."

Leigh stared at the man planted solidly beside her, not willing to budge and not willing to let her run. Over his shoulder, she noticed that all three students had stopped working as if waiting for something to happen.

"Was the autopsy that bad?" he prompted.

"Yes. No." She blew out a frustrated breath and closed her eyes, trying to center herself. When she opened them again, she realized he'd moved so that he physically blocked her from the students' view, giving her a modicum of privacy. He didn't press; instead, he just waited in silence for her to continue.

"The autopsy was worse than any other autopsy I've seen, and all the other ones were nightmares, so I'm not even sure how to classify this one. But that's not the issue."

"Then what's the issue?"

"I had a run in at the M.E.'s office with another detective."

Matt's expression went sharp at her words. "What do you mean a 'run in'?"

"We had words. Look, Matt, it's nothing. You have to be tough to do this job. You show any sign of weakness, especially as a woman, and your credibility is gone. I can handle it. I have to handle it."

Indecision flickered over his face before he forced himself to step back. "If you're sure you can handle it, I'll back off."

She pulled her arm from his loose grip, but gave him a half-smile of thanks. "It's not the first time. This one just hit a little too close to home. I need to grow a thicker skin. But thank you." Shaking off the upset, she turned back to the crime scene. "So, what have we got here?"

Matt's expression turned grim again. "You're not going to believe what we have here."

"It's bad?"

"Yes, but you need to see for yourself." He started across the clearing, carefully cutting a wide berth around the exposed remains.

They crossed the clearing and joined the rest of the group. Leigh acknowledged Kiko's small smile of welcome, but the men's serious expressions didn't change. Dread started to pool in the pit of her stomach.

Matt crouched down beside Kiko, motioning for Leigh to join him. "What I originally wanted to do was simply determine the outer boundaries of each grave site. The goal was to take each site down just a couple of inches, so we had an idea of the position of the remains. Kiko was the first one to notice that something was off."

"Off?"

Matt pointed down into the grave. "Look here. You see this skull?"

The smooth lines of a skull rose from the dark soil, the eye sockets shaded with packed dirt. "I see it," Leigh said.

"Kiko was trying to orient the scapula and clavicle. But she found something else instead." He picked up a whisk and, with a few quick flicks, brushed the loose dirt from another bone, almost completely buried inches below the skull and slightly off to the side.

Horror blossomed. "Is that what I think it is?"

"It is if you think it's a second skull."

Leigh shot to her feet. "Two bodies in the same grave?"

"It gets worse."

For a second, Leigh thought she could hear buzzing in her ears. "How?"

"Once we realized that Kiko's grave had two sets of remains, I had Paul and Juka concentrate on depth in a small section to see if there was a second skeleton in theirs. All three graves have at least two bodies in them. We need to excavate deeper to know if there are any more than that."

Leigh opened her mouth, closed it, then tried to sync her mouth with her shell-shocked brain again. "At least two? In each grave?"

"Yes."

Leigh had to turn away to pace off a few steps while she tried to process this new information.

The case that had started as a single bone now involved at least eight victims: three double graves here, a single grave on the west side of the island and this morning's victim.

She turned around to find Matt watching her, concern etching his features. "We're looking at a minimum of eight victims."

He nodded.

"Eight?" she repeated, disbelief ringing in the single word.

Matt simply met her eyes in silence.

"But why the change in burials? We have the single grave that we found Monday and the single interment that we interrupted this morning. But there are three supposedly double graves here. Why the change? Are we looking at two different killers sharing the same burial ground?"

"Maybe once we've fully excavated these remains, we'll have some answers for you. Until then . . ." Matt's voice trailed off.

"Tonight's media conference is going to be a circus once this information gets out. The locals are going to panic when they hear about this because they're going to think 'serial killer.' "

"You have to have a press conference now? Tonight?"

"The wheels are already in motion for seven o'clock." When Matt opened his mouth to speak, Leigh cut him off. "It's standard protocol during any homicide investigation. We give out only minimal details, and, if necessary, a warning to the public if there is any perception that they may be in danger."

"How do you warn the public about this?" Matt asked. "In the victims we've examined so far, they all seem to come from different age groups so there doesn't seem to be any pattern.

116

And whatever you do, don't announce the body count yet. I'd like to do the full excavation before making any sort of official announcement," Matt clarified.

"You want to be sure."

"Yes. We'll know in a matter of days, but you have to give us time."

"We'll just say multiple victims then and leave it at that."

"Thanks. Where will the press conference be?"

"We're setting up to do it in front of the Essex police station since they're the local police department. I have to be there, but the D.A.'s press officer will run it." She glanced at her watch. "Damn. I still need to get back home and change into soft clothes." She brushed at a dark stain on her jeans, and self-consciously tucked a loose strand of hair behind her ear. "This is not the image the department wants to project as their finest."

"Looks to me like their finest has simply been hard at work. You don't think the public would understand that? Wouldn't they rather you work hard than just *look* like you work hard?"

"You'd think that, wouldn't you?" Leigh's tone implied that it was anything but.

Matt pointed to his silent students who now stood nearby, clustered around Kiko's grave. "We're going to put in another hour or two today. Now that you've seen what we're up against, we'll pair up on two of the graves and really start the excavation. We'll cover everything overnight and just pick it up again first thing in the morning."

Leigh frowned. "I'm not sure when I'll be able to get here tomorrow."

"Come when you can but don't worry about us here. You've got enough on your plate without worrying about this too."

"And no time to do it in." She suppressed the urge to check the time again. "I have to go. I'll make calls from the car so that everyone is in the loop but I'm still cutting it fine for time." She started for the trees only to stop when Matt called her name.

"Good luck tonight."

"Thanks." She gave him a half-smile that came out more like a grimace, and pushed her way into the foliage, heading back toward the mainland.

CHAPTER THIRTEEN:
TIDAL FLUSHING

Tidal Flushing: the process of seawater washing through an estuary twice daily at high tide, restoring salinity levels and nutrients and removing toxins.

Wednesday, 6:45 P.M.
Lowell residence
Brookline, Massachusetts

Matt accidentally slammed the front door closed with enough force to rattle the flanking leaded-glass sidelights. He quickly toed off his muddy boots, glancing down the hall toward the family room, his father's preferred spot to relax at this time of night. *Deserted.* His shoulders relaxed fractionally. He'd be able to get cleaned up before his father saw him like—

"Matt! What happened?"

Damn. He swiveled to find his father rolling through the kitchen doorway. He held up a hand. "I'm okay."

"You look like you've been through a war." Mike rolled up to stop only feet from his son, his eyes fixed on his blood soaked sleeve. "And you're hurt. What happened?"

Matt's shoulders sagged. He'd wanted to avoid this until he'd had a chance to clean up and get off his feet. "I'll give you the *Reader's Digest* version for now because I'm filthy and would kill for a shower. When we got out to the marsh, we interrupted some guy burying a fresh murder victim." He ignored his father's exclamation and continued. "There was a firefight. I got winged." He pulled up his sleeve to reveal the white bandage. "It's just a graze. Bled like a stuck pig and burns like hell, but it's not serious. Leigh called in paramedics and made me get it treated on site."

"I'm beginning to like this Leigh."

"It wasn't that bad," Matt protested. "I would know. Anyway, I'll explain more fully, but let me get out of these clothes first." He glanced at his watch. "Leigh's got a live press conference in just over ten minutes that I'd really like to see. Then I'll answer all your questions, I promise."

"It's so bad that they need a press conference?" Mike shook his head as Matt started to explain. "You're squeezed for time. Go shower and we'll talk later. What channel will it be on?"

"WKAC should be covering it. Back in a few." Matt took the stairs two at a time, heading for the master bedroom.

Minutes later, he was striding toward the family room in bare feet and faded jeans, pulling a navy T-shirt over his damp hair. His father had the big screen TV on across the room, the volume muted. He circled the wheelchair and dropped in an exhausted heap on the couch. Teak got up from the floor and followed Matt, leaping up after him. The dog immediately started pushing his nose against Matt's left shoulder. Matt gave him a good-natured shove in return. "Sit down, Teak. No one wants your wet nose down the back of their neck."

Teak flopped onto the couch, laying his muzzle on Matt's thigh and staring up at him from under a heavy eyebrow. Matt absently dropped one hand onto the thick, ruddy-brown coat, rhythmically stroking his fingers through it. The dog sighed deeply in pleasure.

"You're just in time," Mike said. "They're starting now." Reaching over for the remote, he turned up the volume.

The words "Special Report" stretched across the bottom of

the screen. A small group of people were standing in front of a jostling crowd of media personnel. Matt searched for Leigh's now familiar face. He found her quickly, standing in the back row beside a tall man with neatly cut gray hair wearing a navy suit. *Detective Lieutenant Harper?*

Leigh was dressed in a mannish suit similar to the one she wore the first time they met, her hair once again neatly knotted at the nape of her neck. *She dresses like a man when she's on the job as a way to fit in,* Matt realized. He'd never considered how hard it was to be a woman in what was likely an overwhelmingly masculine vocation, especially in the homicide division. But today's stresses left him with an inkling of the challenges she faced every day in her chosen career.

His father's voice broke into his musings. "That's your lady cop on the left? In the black suit?"

"Yeah, that's Leigh. And she's not 'my lady cop.' "

"Pretty," Mike commented lightly.

Matt's head slowly swiveled to stare at his father. "Do *not* start in on my love life again."

"How can I?" Mike retorted. "You don't have one."

Matt sent him a mock glare and turned back to the TV.

A woman in a burgundy suit stepped forward to speak. Her tone was calm and straightforward and she clearly was comfortable dealing with the media. "Good evening. I'm Sharon Collins, Press Officer for District Attorney Aaron Saxon. I will be making a statement and then I will take a few questions. Earlier today, several sets of human remains were discovered in a coastal area on the outskirts of the Town of Essex. In addition, the body of a recent homicide victim was also discovered. Detective Lieutenant Harper of the Massachusetts State Police has assigned Trooper First Class Leigh Abbott of the Essex Detective Unit to lead the case. Trooper Abbott is working closely with both the District Attorney's Office and the local

Essex police force in this matter. The most recent victim has been tentatively identified but a name will not be released pending confirmation and notification of the family. We do not perceive any immediate danger to the public at large, but, as always, we encourage you to lock your doors and be aware of your surroundings at all times. Details are limited at this time, but the investigation is ongoing and we will release new details as they become available. I will now take a few questions."

A cacophony of raised voices exploded around her, yet she remained unruffled. As she called for the first questions, Matt's gaze moved to Leigh. He sat up abruptly, leaning forward. "Look at that."

Mike glanced from the TV to Matt and back again. "Look at what?"

"At Leigh. Look at her watching the crowd. Damn, I wish I'd gone to this. I could have been helping her."

Mike leaned forward, squinting at the screen. "Helping her with what?"

"She's looking for the guy who shot at us today. She must have realized there'd be a chance he'd show up at the press conference to bask in his own glory."

Ms. Collins fielded another question from someone off camera. "You said that there were several sets of remains. Is this the work of a serial killer?"

"At this point we can't rule out that possibility. You, in the blue jacket."

"Are there any suspects?"

"The suspect was interrupted on scene and a confrontation occurred between him and Trooper Abbott. All leads from this incident are being examined and the investigation is ongoing." More questions were shouted, but she calmly closed down the press conference. "Thank you very much for your time, ladies and gentlemen. We will let you know as soon as there are any new breaks in the investigation." The feed immediately cut to an anchor sitting behind a desk.

"She said it was only going to be minimal details. She wasn't kidding." Matt reached over and picked up the remote, muting the TV before swiveling to face his father. "Okay, the real story. What they reported is accurate. When we got there this morning, we interrupted the guy digging the grave of his latest victim."

"So you're looking at related deaths then? This new victim and your remains?"

"And then some. I'll get to that. When he heard us coming, he opened fire. But he probably wasn't prepared for return fire."

"I guess it was a good thing that you had the Glock then."

"Yeah."

"And to think that you were questioning your gut. You should know better than that."

"Subtle 'I told you so,' Dad."

"Just making a point. Now, the press officer said that *Trooper Abbott* was involved in a confrontation with him. But if you were there, were the kids there too?"

"Yes, but they're okay. They hit the dirt pretty fast when the bullets started flying. I was the only one who got hit. Anyway, Leigh and I split up and went after him." At his father's upraised eyebrows, he said, "She's damned sharp. She figured out pretty fast that I knew my way around a firefight. And she used it to our advantage." He pushed his damp hair back from his forehead. "It was like stepping back in time. You get into a situation and you just react. You don't have time to think. Anyway, the guy escaped into the marsh where he had a boat moored on a branch of the Essex River. Crime Scene Services arrived later on to collect evidence for this fresh victim and they stumbled across a new burial ground north of where we'd searched, so suddenly we now have a third crime scene. We would have found it this morning ourselves if we'd kept going, but we got a little sidetracked."

"Just a little. Do you have an idea as to how many victims you've got?"

"Our current best estimate is at least eight victims in total." He refrained from smiling at his father's almost comical expression of shock; he empathized with his reaction. "The state police brought in a cadaver dog, confirming the currently identified graves are the only ones in the area. But I suspect they are all double graves. I hope that's the worst they are."

Mike sat back in his chair as he considered the details. "Two bodies buried at once? So he had to carry two bodies through the marsh from the boat and then bury them?" He met his son's eyes. "What if someone comes across the boat with the second body while he's moving the first one to the burial site? And then why only one body at the grave you just excavated and only one body at this newest grave? Why not two?"

"All excellent questions. There's still a lot to figure out, but the first thing to do is to recover those remains, which will take a few days. Considering what's at stake here, we need to be very careful about recovering all of the evidence."

"Because he's still out there and he's still killing."

"Clearly." Pushing off from the couch, Matt rose. "How about some dinner? Did you eat?"

"No, I was waiting for you. Teak's the only one who's eaten."

"He's a bottomless pit. He can always eat again." Matt leaned over and ruffled the dog's ear affectionately. "Give me five minutes. I want to call Leigh and touch base about what they said tonight about a victim ID. How about we grill some burgers after that? I'm starved."

"Sounds great. I'll start pulling things out and get the grill going while you make that call. Will you still have time to take Teak out?"

"Later tonight. A run would do me good too. Burn off some of this excess energy." Matt strode down the hallway and picked up his cell phone from a shallow wooden bowl on the table in the entry hall. Glancing back down the hallway, he changed direction and opened the front door, stepping out into the cooling autumn evening and closing the door softly behind him.

He paused in the slowly fading light of the day, simply absorbing the peace of day's end. He wished he could be out on the Charles; some of his most centered moments came when it was just him and the boat out on the open water, man against nature. The excavations were going to be long and wearing, and he suspected a good hard row would be the best way to work off some of the tension.

He crossed the wooden floor of the porch to sit on the top step. He dialed Leigh's number from memory and then relaxed comfortably against the porch pillar, crossing his ankles.

"Leigh Abbott."

"Leigh, it's Matt."

There was a pause and Matt could hear someone talking in the background. Then, "Hold on a moment, please." Matt heard muffled speaking and then the sound of heels on pavement before Leigh came back on the line. "Sorry, I was trying to get free from the press conference. Thanks for giving me an out."

"My pleasure. I caught the broadcast. You weren't kidding about it being bare bones."

"That's about all we can say. We can't allow any information getting out that might compromise the investigation."

"You didn't mention anything about a victim ID earlier today."

"Sorry, I meant to tell you earlier but you derailed me with your updated body count. The woman we found this morning had a butterfly tattoo on her shoulder blade that matched one of the missing person reports I'd collected. Rowe has requested dental x-rays from her practitioner and we'll be getting them first thing tomorrow morning for confirmation, but we're both pretty certain we have the right woman. If so, her name is Tracy Kingston."

"That fell into place quickly."

"Sometimes you get lucky. Most of the time you don't, so it's nice when it happens. But there was something else we found at the autopsy. It's a mark, potentially a signature, on her chest."

Matt jerked upright on the step. "A signature? What was it?"

"It's some kind of symbol, carved into the flesh just above the left breast. I think it's Asian in nature, but it could be Chinese, Japanese, Korean, or Vietnamese. I'm looking into it."

"I could put you in touch with someone in linguistics at the university. Maybe they could help."

"I'll keep it in mind."

"So . . . did you see him in the crowd?"

She didn't pretend to misunderstand him. "Caught that, did you?"

"I'm a scientist. Observing is what we do. Sometimes the most important details can be buried in the minutia. Was he there?"

"I don't think so. I didn't see anyone who set off alarm bells for me."

"Damn."

"My bet is he's too careful to make a mistake like that. He probably just watched the press conference on TV." There was a brief pause, then, "Matt, I have to go. Detective Lieutenant Harper wanted to have a word with me before he heads back to Salem and it looks like he's getting ready to go now."

"Go. We'll be on site first thing tomorrow morning. We'll see you whenever you can get there."

"If we get ID confirmation then I need to inform next of kin tomorrow, but I'll come up to the site later on. I'll see you then." She ended the call.

Matt set his phone on the step beside him. He gave himself a moment to enjoy the fresh air and the peace of the deepening dusk.

He would need all the fortitude he could muster for the coming days.

Refreshed and somewhat recharged, he rose from the porch and went inside to share a meal with his family.

Chapter Fourteen:
Family

Family: an interrelated group of animals living in a community. Monogamous Sandhill Crane pairs return annually to the same nesting ground in the marsh to raise their young, and migrate as a family unit in the fall.

Thursday, 9:51 A.M.
Kingston residence
Topsfield, Massachusetts

With dragging steps, Leigh forced herself to march up the front walk of Tracy Kingston's parents' home.

She hated this part of the job more than any other. Hated seeing that moment where hope flared in the eyes of loved ones when they thought she arrived with good news. Hated even more seeing that hope wither away to a blank stare of confusion and pain when she delivered the news that someone they loved would never come home again.

Ignoring the knot forming in her stomach, she took a deep breath and knocked sharply on the front door. She heard slow footsteps inside the house and then the door opened to reveal an older woman with short, curling silver hair. Harsh lines of worry formed deep grooves around her eyes and mouth, betraying each of her seven decades.

Leigh extended her badge toward the woman. "Mrs. Kingston? I'm Trooper Leigh Abbott of the Massachusetts State Police. May I come in?"

Mrs. Kingston lost what little color she had. "Kevin?" Her voice rose stridently. "Kevin, the police are here."

A slightly balding older man instantly appeared at the door to the living room. He was dressed casually in a navy cardigan and leather slippers, and had a comfortably worn air about him.

Leigh stepped through the open doorway. "Mr. Kingston, I'm Trooper Leigh Abbott . . ." For just the briefest of instants, she hesitated as knowledge and understanding shone in the old man's eyes, eclipsed by bone-deep sorrow. *He knows she's gone.*

"Do you have news about Tracy? Have you found Tracy?" Mrs. Kingston's hands twisted together, unconsciously wringing in agitation. "We've called the police several times. They're very nice, but they haven't been able to tell us anything."

"Could we sit down for a moment, ma'am?"

But it was as if the woman hadn't heard Leigh speak. "Something must be terribly wrong. It's not like Tracy to go away like this and not tell us. She calls us every night, but we haven't heard from her since last Thursday. If she had a sick friend and had to go away she would have told us. And they haven't heard from her at the college either—"

"Dorothy." Mr. Kingston cut in gently. "You're not letting the officer talk." He put an arm around his wife, deftly steering her into the living room. "Let's sit down."

Leigh followed the couple into a comfortably furnished living room. A well-padded couch and two comfortable chairs were grouped in front of a large fireplace, hardwood piled high beside the grate in a brass log rack.

The heart of the house was proudly displayed in the framed photos of Tracy on nearly every surface in the room. But they weren't just pictures of Tracy alone; there were easily as many photos of the three of them together through the years. Leigh's gaze fell on a graduation picture on the mantel—Tracy, clad in cap and gown and grinning exuberantly, stood with her arms thrown around her proud parents. It was a picture of family unity and mutual affection. Leigh studied the young woman in the photo—all bright eyes and overflowing laughter. So vivacious and full of life. A life cut short.

Leigh's heart squeezed in sympathy as the knot pulled tighter.

She followed the older couple, taking one of the armchairs after they chose the sofa. Mr. Kingston clasped his wife's hand before taking a deep breath and raising his eyes to meet hers. Leigh read resignation there and felt a wave of sympathy for him—the truth was already clear to him. But Mrs. Kingston's shock was yet to come, and it would shatter her world forever.

She folded her hands in her lap, hardening herself to deliver the blow with all possible speed. "Mr. and Mrs. Kingston, I regret to inform you that your daughter's body was recovered near the coast outside the Town of Essex."

Stunned silence filled the room. Mr. Kingston's head dropped even as his hand clutched his wife's, but Mrs. Kingston simply stared at Leigh. "Her body . . . you mean . . . she's gone? Tracy's gone?" Stricken, she turned to her husband. "Kevin, this can't be right." She whirled back to Leigh. "You can't be sure. You said a body was found, but you haven't had us identify that body to make sure it's Tracy."

"Dorothy." The word came out as a harsh whisper as Mr. Kingston raised his head, tears welling unashamedly in his eyes.

"No!" She tried to pull her hand from her husband's, but he held on tightly. "It can't be her. There's been a mistake."

"I'm sorry, Mrs. Kingston, but there's been no mistake. I was able to identify her from the Missing Persons report you filed. The Massachusetts Medical Examiner confirmed the identification through dental records. Please accept my condolences on your loss."

"No, I won't believe it." Her husband pulled her into his arms and she collapsed against his chest, weeping openly as he whispered to her, his voice thick with tears.

Motionless, Leigh sat across from them, her back ramrod straight and her hands clasped in her lap, her fingers clenched so tightly that her nails left deep imprints in the backs of her hands. She felt like the worst of intruders, an eyewitness to the most raw and brutal kind of grief; the kind of grief that shouldn't be seen by any stranger. Yet here she was.

Their pain was palpable and she steeled herself against the depth of their sorrow. She still had a job to do, and she couldn't do it unless she kept her emotions wrapped tight. She remembered Matt's words to his students—*Put emotion aside for a few minutes. This is how we can do the most good.* Matt was right—she served the victim best when she put her emotions aside.

For now, anyway. But this kind of anguish always left a mark on those who witnessed it. She swallowed thickly, pushing down sympathetic grief, and simply waited.

After several minutes, Mr. Kingston raised his head to meet Leigh's eyes. The devastation in his eyes was almost a physical ache. "How did she die? Was it an accident? You said her . . ." His eyes closed briefly and then he forced himself to continue. "You said her body was found on the Essex coast. Did she drown?"

"No, sir. Current evidence indicates that she was murdered."

"Murdered?" Mrs. Kingston's head finally came up. Her eyes were red-rimmed and her face was blotchy. "Someone murdered our girl? But why? Everyone loved her."

"We're investigating that now. There's a possibility that her death might be related to other remains that were found in the same area."

Mr. Kingston stiffened. "Other remains?"

"Your daughter's body was found close to several sets of

older remains. We suspect they are connected, but it's too early to be sure. We have a forensic anthropology team currently working with the medical examiner to investigate this possibility."

"But I don't understand," Mrs. Kingston whispered. "Are you saying that she was the victim of a serial killer?" Tears started streaming down her cheeks again. "Someone just randomly decided that she should die?"

"We're pursuing all available leads at this time. It would be helpful if I could ask you a few questions now if you feel up to it."

Anger flushed Mr. Kingston's face with color. "Can't it wait?"

"Sir, I could ask these questions later, but every minute we delay is a minute that we could be out tracking down the person responsible."

The older man seemed to crumple into himself slightly, but he gave a small nod.

Leigh pulled out her notebook and pen. "Was Tracy personally involved with anyone? Did she have a boyfriend or a partner?"

"Tracy was dating someone last year but they had a messy breakup and Tracy decided to stay out of the dating pool for a while."

"A messy breakup? Was it violent? Did he ever threaten her?"

Mr. Kingston shook his head. "Not that Tracy ever mentioned."

"She would have told us. She told us everything." Mrs. Kingston pushed away from her husband to sit straighter, but gratefully accepted the handkerchief he handed her to wipe her eyes and cheeks. "He hurt her emotionally, but never laid a finger on her. We can give you his contact information, but the last I heard from Tracy, he'd transferred to the West Coast to take another position in his company."

"I'd still like to follow up on him. Was there anyone at work that she was having problems with?"

"No, Tracy got along with everyone." The older woman's voice started to wobble. "Everyone loved her. Kevin?"

"I'm right here, love." Putting his arm around his wife, Mr. Kingston pulled her against his side as she dropped her face into her hands and her body shook with sobs.

Leigh laid her notebook and pen in her lap, patiently waiting out the storm.

Finally, Mrs. Kingston quieted, her head rising slowly. "How did she die?" When Leigh paused, the older woman pushed. "I need to know."

"She was severely beaten, but the cause of death was manual strangulation."

Mrs. Kingston jerked, a low moan of pain breaking from her.

Leigh tried to cushion the truth as much as possible. "We believe that she was unconscious at the time of death. She didn't know what was happening."

Mrs. Kingston abruptly surged to her feet, crossing the room to the nearest bookshelf. She picked up a crystal frame, gazing at the family in the picture. She returned to hand the photo to Leigh.

It was taken in a hospital room almost thirty years ago, based on Mr. Kingston's clothing and glasses. Mrs. Kingston lay in the hospital bed, exhausted, but her face was lit with an inner joy. Mr. Kingston perched on the bed beside his wife, his chest puffed out with pride. In Mrs. Kingston arms, wrapped in a pink blanket, lay a tiny baby. *Tracy.*

"They told us we couldn't have children," Mrs. Kingston said tearfully. "We'd given up hope. And then, a miracle happened. I got pregnant at forty-five. Tracy was that baby. She was our life." Her voice broke. "She was our whole life."

The older woman covered her mouth with a shaking hand

and sank down onto the sofa, leaning against her husband. Closing her eyes, she took several deep breaths. Then she looked up at Leigh. "Can I tell you about her?"

Leigh smiled gently. "I'd like to hear about Tracy. She's mine now, so I want to know her."

She settled back in the chair and let Mrs. Kingston talk herself out.

CHAPTER FIFTEEN:
SALTMARSH CORDGRASS

Saltmarsh Cordgrass: Spartina alterniflora; a wetland perennial grass that typically grows at the border of tidal creeks in the marsh; the dominant plant species in the low marsh, it enables the rest of the marsh to form around it.

Thursday, 2:47 p.m.
Essex Bay Coast, Massachusetts

Raising his head from the remains, Matt called over one of the Crime Scene Services photographers to document the next stage in the excavation. Sitting back on his haunches, he rolled his head from side to side, trying to release some of the tightness that was building in his neck and shoulders from so many hours hunched over the grave.

The team had advanced well over the day and the contents of both excavations were exposed to view, although Matt's was progressing faster than Kiko's. Wearing Tyvek and latex gloves, Juka sat opposite Matt, taking advantage of the brief break to quench his thirst from the water bottle he kept nearby. Kiko and Paul crouched over the second set of remains, brushes in hand, as they meticulously worked to sweep away the soil surrounding the bones. Two other Crime Scene Services techs moved around the burial site, recording the scene in both video and still photos. Several Essex police officers were stationed at the periphery, talking quietly to one of the techs and watching intently as the scene was slowly revealed.

Leigh suddenly broke through the brush to stand at the edge of the clearing. Standing all alone, she looked worn and tired, as if the investigation was wearing her down. But she gamely smiled at Matt and he returned the gesture.

Leigh crossed the clearing as Matt rose to his feet, pulling off his gloves to ball them in his fist before stuffing them into the pocket of his coveralls. "Hey."

"Hey, yourself. You guys have really made progress today."

Juka, still kneeling beside the grave, smiled and offered a silent nod of greeting.

"We have," Matt agreed. "Granted we've been at work since seven and we only took a twenty minute break around eleven."

Leigh glanced at her watch. "Maybe you should let them take another break and grab some food if they brought any. It's almost three o'clock and you don't want them dropping from exhaustion. We've all had a busy few days. They must be worn out."

"Is it that late already? You work on an excavation like this and you sort of get into the zone and you lose track of time." Matt critically surveyed the excavations before nodding. "I think we can afford to take a break now. Guys! Take twenty. Get something to eat. Then we're back at it until we lose the light and have to shut it down for the night."

The three young people stood, giving small groans of relief at the change in position. The photographers wandered off to talk to the cops.

Leigh circled the grave to study the tangled remains that lay below the surface of the surrounding earth. There were clearly two sets of remains inside the grave, excavated laterally so that only the lower legs were still encased in soil. The first victim lay stretched on its back as if placed there with some care. In contrast, the second body lay partially covering the first, its head pillowed sideways on the chest below, its limbs bent at awkward angles. The cause of death was startlingly clear in the topmost skull—the front of the skull was brutally fractured, with pieces of the smooth forehead section shattered into large shards and collapsed into the partially dirt-filled cranium.

"I was really concerned after yesterday that there might have been more than two sets of remains," Matt said. "But we're sure now it's only two. It's the same in Kiko's grave."

"As bad as it is, it feels like a small blessing it's not more." Ignoring her neat charcoal slacks, Leigh knelt in the dirt at the edge of the excavation, bracing her hands at the edge of the grave so she could lean over. She bent close to the shattered skull, her eyes narrowed in concentration as she studied it. "Any idea what happened here? Blunt or sharp force trauma?"

"Single gunshot round to the head, likely at a moderately close range, execution-style. Fairly high velocity, but not from a rifle. Probably a small caliber handgun."

"Can you clearly see the back of the skull? Did the bullet pass right through?"

Matt shook his head. "I don't think so. Not from what we've uncovered so far or from the estimated trajectory. You might get lucky—if the bullet didn't go through, it might have bounced around inside the skull a few times, but it'll still be there. If so, we'll recover it for you, and ballistics can run it."

"We'll be able to do a direct match because Crime Scene Services pulled several spent bullets out of tree trunks after our run-in with him. If there's a positive match, then we've got a direct tie between him and these victims. Not that he would necessarily be using the same gun, but if he was, then that would go a long way toward starting to tie up some of our loose ends."

"Loose end number one being 'is it the same killer?' " Matt proposed.

"Definitely."

"What are we looking at, bullet-wise?"

"Twenty-two caliber. More specifically, between the bullets themselves and the casings that the techs collected yesterday, we know that he's using a Remington .22 LR, 36 grain, high-velocity hollow point."

He glanced back at the damaged skull again. "Small caliber bullet, as I thought. But it's also pretty common. Lots of those around."

"All we need is one to compare it to." She turned back to the grave. "Any sign of bullet trauma in the second body?"

"Not so far. There isn't a bullet wound in the front of the skull. However, there could be something in the back we can't see yet. But, we've found signs of significant trauma."

Her gaze shot to his. "What kind of trauma?"

"On a first quick examination, it's similar to what we saw in yesterday's victim. There are multiple kerf marks on the bone."

"Then we have more to tie into the serial killer theory if the injuries match the newest victim. Can you tell what caused these marks?"

"Not yet. But once the remains are back at the lab and all traces of the soil are removed, I'll be able to magnify the defects and start matching them with potential tools. Different tools and weapons leave characteristic marks just like a bullet does."

Raising her head, Leigh indicated the second grave. "Anything different there?"

"Not too much. A slightly different body positioning—those two bodies went in side-by-side. Between the two graves, cause of death looks identical at this point with one victim shot in the head and the other having multiple tool marks. It's also a more recent burial—we've found desiccated tissue, the hair cap, and more significant clothing remnants. We may have something interesting there. Kiko noted early on that the remnants only seem to be associated with one set of remains, so she thinks that one body went into the grave clothed, but the other was naked."

Leigh's gaze jerked from the grave on the other side of the clearing to Matt's face. "That has to be significant."

"You would think so. We can't tell that from this grave yet due to degradation, but when we unearth the feet, that may tell the tale. Cottons and natural fabrics can degrade quite quickly in the grave, but the synthetics used in shoes don't. That may tell us if one of the bodies was naked."

"Why the difference? Was there evidence he was trying to hide so he didn't bury the clothing with the victim? Or were they a keepsake from the victim, something to treasure so he could relive the experience? Why from only one victim and not both? And why the difference in killing methods? There has to be a reason for that if it's in his MO." Leigh climbed to her feet, bending momentarily to brush the loose soil off the knees of her pants. "Maybe he's taking the two victims as couples. What if he grabs a couple, and the fun is to torture one of them while making the other watch while he slowly kills? He's physically torturing one victim, but mentally torturing the second. Then when the first victim is finally dead, the fun is over."

"So he finishes off the second victim quickly. Half of the killer's fun is to terrify the second victim and the first is potentially only a means to an end in that respect? Then once the first victim is dead, the game is over and he just caps the second? It might go down that way."

Leigh picked up a small stone from beside the grave, worrying it absently in her hand. "It might, but something about this isn't playing for me. If the point of the double murder is to torture the second victim, why stop then? That ends the game too quickly. Why not stretch it out and torture the second victim too if that's how you get your enjoyment out of the act? They'd already be terrified out of their minds before you even started in on them. Also, if we had couples disappearing together, even over a large area, that would be noticed. These disappearances have been completely under the radar." She shook her head, her lips pursing. "We might have an idea of what's going on here, but something's still not right. Which reminds me . . ." Reaching into the breast pocket of her lightweight jacket, she pulled out a color print of one of the digital photos taken by the photographer during the autopsy. She held it out for him. "This is the signature I told you about last night."

Matt examined the mark closely. "Very careful and precise markings. I don't recognize the symbol. Where was it on the body?"

"Here." She patted the spot over her left breast. "But because of the positioning in the grave, I can't see that area."

Matt squatted down to examine the remains. "You're right, with the one set of remains overlaying the other, we can't see that part of the rib cage yet." He straightened. "You're hoping that we'll be able to find a trace of that kind of carving on the bones to prove that it's a true signature and to tie all the victims together?"

"Yes. If it's a true signature it should be in approximately the same place."

Matt studied the picture again. "I wonder if Kiko might recognize the symbol. She's American but with her Japanese background . . ."

"It might make no more sense to her than to us, but it's worth a shot," Leigh agreed. "She may be able to tell us what kind of symbol it is, even if she doesn't know exactly what it means."

"Let's ask her." Matt cocked his head in the direction of his students.

Together they crossed to where the students lounged on the

ground just inside the tree line. Their packs were open and water bottles and pre-packaged food lay scattered around them.

"Kiko, would you mind looking at this?" Matt held out the photo.

"Sure." Reaching up, she took the photo. "What am I—" Her lip curled and she winced when she saw the carved flesh. "Matt, next time warn me you're handing me autopsy photos."

Paul and Juka exchanged glances.

"Sorry, should have given you a heads up. We were wondering if you know what that symbol is. It's Asian, right?"

Kiko stared at the symbol before shaking her head. "It looks like a Kanji symbol to me, but I don't know them. I can speak Japanese better than I can write it. I could have my mother look at it. She might recognize it."

"We can't show your mother this photo, but we could copy out the symbol for her," Leigh said.

Juka held out his hand and Kiko passed him the print. "I've never seen it before. Sorry."

"Hold on. Let me see that." All eyes shot to Paul, who was staring at the photo in Juka's hand. Reaching out, he snatched the print to examine it more closely. "That's 'Death.' "

"It's what?"

Paul raised his head to find everyone staring at him. "It's the Chinese character for 'Death.' "

Leigh's hands fell to her hips as she stared down at Paul incredulously. "How do you know that? I mean, you don't look . . ."

"Like I'd know Chinese?" Paul laughed. "No, not really." His gaze slid back to the symbol. "And I pretty much don't know any of it, except for this particular symbol."

"So how do you know what that is then?"

"I had this horrible pain-in-the-ass roommate while I was an undergrad at Fordham. You know the type—total slob, a jerk with the women, spent most his time playing video games, never studied . . . and blessedly dropped out after Christmas when his parents no longer wanted to pay seventeen-thousand dollars per semester for him to drink and screw around." He realized everyone was staring at him and he cleared his throat, suddenly awkward. "Anyway, he was into this multiplayer online video game called 'Death Orgy.' It was brutal, an absolute bloodfest. I used to call it torture porn." He turned the photo outwards to face them. "This symbol was the icon for the game. Whatever character or team won was awarded a badge with that symbol on it in the game."

"Where?" Leigh's question came out more sharply than she intended. "Where did they wear the badge?"

Paul looked at her curiously. "Here," he said slowly, patting his upper left chest.

Leigh whirled to meet Matt's eyes. "That's it."

Matt stared at her incredulously. "This has something to do with a video game?"

"Maybe not directly, but there must be something related to it. If I've learned anything as a cop it's that there are no co-incidences in a murder investigation."

"Wait, what's going on?" Kiko asked. "That mark came from yesterday's victim, right?"

"Yes. We think it's the killer's signature. It was carved into her chest, just above her left breast."

"Holy shit," Paul breathed, before flushing in embarrassment. "Um . . . sorry."

"That mark was on the newest victim. You're thinking that it might have been carved into those victims as well?" Kiko interjected, ignoring Paul's outburst.

"We're going to be looking specifically for it," Matt said. "But we're going to be looking at everything. Every kerf mark, every fracture, all of it. Take another ten minutes and then we're back at it." He turned to Leigh. "Come on, I need to grab some water and an energy bar."

They crossed the clearing toward the bag he left near his excavation. Sitting down with his back against a tree, Matt tugged his pack toward him and retrieved a water bottle, indulging in several long swallows before pulling out an energy bar and a bag of trail mix. Opening the bag, he offered it first to Leigh, who sat down beside him on a smooth, wide rock. With a small smile, she reached in and pulled out a small handful of mixed nuts and dried fruit.

"How did you do with the ID?" Matt asked.

"Of Tracy Kingston? Dental x-rays confirmed her ID. I drove out to Topsfield this morning to break the news to her parents."

He noted the way her eyes stayed fixed on the trees on the far side of the clearing. He suspected she wasn't seeing the trees; she was likely still seeing the couple whose hopes she had crushed that morning. "Hey." He reached out to brush his fingers lightly over the back of her clenched fist, then waited patiently until she looked at him, pain and regret clearly etched on her face. "I'm sorry you had to do that."

She sighed. "Yeah, me too. Worst part of the job, hands down. Not even watching the autopsy is that hard. But for a homicide cop, it's a necessary part of the job. Giving the victim an identity and giving closure to the family is what we do. Informing them of the fate of their loved one is simply the first step." She let her head drop and massaged her forehead with the fingers of her left hand. "If I seem a little obsessed today about finding out who's doing this and why, it's probably because of having to break the news to the Kingstons this morning. It was pretty bad. She was their only child and the mother completely broke down. The father was expecting it though. You could see it in his eyes. *He knew.* Even before I said a single word, he knew."

Matt stiffened. "Do you think he had knowledge of her death?"

"No, not at all. I've seen this kind of thing before. Some people cling to hope right up until the point that you bring them in to see the body at the morgue. Some know the moment that you knock on their door or even before that. He was one of those. He knew his daughter wouldn't just stop calling them. They were elderly, and she was the miracle baby they never expected to have. They were totally devoted to her, and she to them. You could tell by the house. Pictures of not just her, but of all of them together. They were a real family."

"Did the father tell you all of this?"

"No, Mrs. Kingston did in between bouts of weeping. I don't know . . . maybe one of the guys would have just done the 'I'm very sorry for your loss' routine, and asked a few questions and left, but I can't do that. As a mother, she needed to tell someone about her child. It was part of her grieving process." She slumped forward, bracing her elbows on her knees. "But it also allowed me to get to know Tracy, and that kind of knowledge about a victim is always good."

"It makes her real," Matt said. "And it probably lights a fire under you to give her justice. Not that the fire wasn't there before."

"It was. But I admit the flames were fanned a little higher." She took the time to chew a small handful of trail mix and Matt stayed silent beside her, giving her a moment to regroup. "Her parents reported her missing. She would call them every night but she didn't call last Friday. By Saturday morning, there was still no word and they couldn't get a hold of her on her cell phone or landline. They were concerned so they drove down to Beverly. They have a key to her apartment so they let themselves in, but it was deserted and her car was gone. They tried to report her missing but standard protocol on an adult is a minimum of twenty-four hours before a report can be filed. The official report was filed with the Beverly P.D. on Saturday night. The mother never gave up hope, but the father knew that she was gone. He was shattered by the loss, but he knew."

"No matter how old that child is, it's always wrong for a parent to see their child die." Suddenly Matt stilled. "Hold on, did you say she was gone on Friday?"

"I thought you'd catch that. Yes, she taught a class on British literature late Friday afternoon at Endicott College. She disappeared sometime after that."

"But that means . . ." He closed his eyes as the details crystallized in his mind with bone-chilling clarity. "That means that he held her for a least a day, by Rowe's time of death estimate. That means that he killed her slowly over that time."

"We knew from her injuries that it wasn't quick."

"Yeah, but I guess I didn't really think about how 'not quick' it must have been. Bastard." Matt blew out a breath, trying to diffuse the slow burn of anger because he knew it would distract him from the task at hand. "So what's next for you?" Opening his energy bar, he took a bite.

"I need to go to the college and retrace Tracy's footsteps from last Friday. What courses she taught, what students she interacted with, if she was having trouble with any of the students or anyone else in the department. Her parents at least were not aware of any men in her life currently."

"You really think this will come down to her having issues with a student or a coworker?" Matt asked. "Because I really can't see that, considering the rest of the victims. If she was the only one, sure, but not as victim number eight."

"I agree, but every lead has to be followed. So that's where we need to start. She was last seen on campus, so that's where I need to pick up the trail." She checked her watch. "It's too late today. By the time I got there, many of the departments would be shutting down for the day. I'll go first thing tomorrow and spend the day trying to get to know Tracy Kingston. If you need me for anything, you can reach me on my cell."

"I think we'll be okay. We'll be here excavating all day tomorrow, so we'll be busy too. We should be in the lab on Saturday though. Why don't you stop by and we can compare notes?"

"Sure."

They fell into a comfortable silence, their gazes fixed on the graves in the clearing but their minds fixed on the trail that could lead them to a killer.

CHAPTER SIXTEEN:
BREACH

Breach: a manmade gap in a seawall or dike to allow flooding. Demolishing the barrier allows saltwater intrusion and normal tidal exchange to restore the salt marsh.

Thursday, 7:10 P.M.
Abbott residence
Salem, Massachusetts

Leigh pushed the refrigerator door shut with her foot, fumbling the vegetables cradled in her arms. She watched a red pepper roll across the floor as she leaned back against the stainless steel door, frowning at her own clumsiness.

She was definitely ready to put this day behind her.

She crossed over to the sink, putting the carrots, mushrooms, and broccoli into the strainer before picking up the pepper. As she rinsed the vegetables, she tried to relax into the soothing strains of a cello solo playing in the living room, but instead she found herself almost twitching with agitation, her movements abrupt and unfocused.

The day hadn't been all bad. They were making progress— Matt's excavation was coming along well, they had an ID for the latest victim and she had interviews scheduled for tomorrow morning. But the task of telling the Kingstons of their daughter's death had affected her more than she first thought. Leigh still felt echoes of their sorrow hours later.

She placed the strainer beside the heavy oak chopping block on the granite countertop. Selecting a large knife, she started to thinly slice the vegetables, her mind turning to what she'd learned that day—

The sharp knife sliced into her index finger, blood welling to trickle onto the chopping block. Leigh froze, not seeing her own injury, but instead seeing Tracy's cold body, laid bare on the forest floor, a multitude of slices oozing blood—

"Stop it!" She gave her head a sharp shake, dropping the knife with a clatter and reaching for a tissue from the box on top of the fridge, pressing it to the small wound. Small dots of blood instantly seeped through the tissue staining it deep red. She tossed the carrot into the sink before wiping down the board, and reaching for the knife again—

With a violent crack, the window shattered behind her head in an explosion of razor sharp shards. Instinctively ducking down below the countertop, Leigh reached for the gun that wasn't on her hip. She stayed low, her arm raised protectively over her head as jagged pieces of glass rained down and scattered across the granite counter and floor. Something solid smashed into the dishwasher door and there was a sound like marbles falling to the tile.

Then silence, broken only by the wind whistling through the gaping hole in her window.

Her mind immediately leaped to the worst-case scenario— somehow the killer had found her and was shooting at her. But when she raised her head, she saw the small, craggy rock on her kitchen floor.

Not a bullet. But definitely an assault.

"Goddamn it!"

She snapped upright, whirling to look out her kitchen window into the tiny yard that ran alongside her long, narrow house. *Empty.* But someone *had* been there.

She sprinted out of the kitchen, glass crunching under her shoes, heading for the front door at a run, ignoring the fact she was unarmed. She wrenched it open to run down the front walk and out onto the cobbled sidewalk. She stopped dead, her heart pounding and breath sawing as she scanned the street.

The last fading rays of sun reflected off the windshield of her own car parked in front of the house. She scanned up and down the narrow, crowded street, but there was no movement around the clapboard houses or under the huge ash trees that lined the curb. Unless . . . *was that something moving in the shadows down the street?*

Again, she reflexively reached for the non-existent gun.

"Leigh! Is everything all right?"

Leigh spun around to see the young blond woman who lived next door running down the front steps, her face pale and one hand pressed against her chest. When Leigh looked back down the street, the shadows were still.

"Are you all right? You ran out your front door like the house was on fire."

Leigh cast one more glance down the empty street before turning back to her neighbor. "Some jackass just hurled a rock through my kitchen window. Did you see anyone in my yard just now?"

"No. I was just coming out to sit on the porch with my coffee when you ran out the front door." The young woman looked sheepish. "I'm sorry, I didn't see anyone else."

"Don't apologize. Thanks for coming to lend a hand."

"Are you going to call the police?"

"Sue, I *am* the police."

"But this isn't the kind of crime you deal with. Shouldn't you call Salem P.D.?"

"For this? This is just some pain in the ass kid playing a prank for kicks. He probably doesn't even know he hit a cop's house. I'll just clean up the mess and board up the hole for tonight." No way in hell was she going to report this to Salem P.D. The Essex Detective Unit cops worked with Salem P.D. often enough that she didn't want any chance of word spreading to her own unit.

Leigh took the time to walk her yard looking for any trace of her intruder, but the ground was too dry for shoe imprints. She was certain of one thing—because the kitchen was at the back of the house, whoever had thrown the rock would have to have been standing in her yard looking in her window. *Watching her.*

Back inside, she surveyed the mess, taking in the blood-spattered tissue on the floor in front of the chopping block, glass shards on the counter, the small dent in her dishwasher door and sea glass scattered into nearly every corner.

Her temper spiked when she saw the sea glass. Two Mason jars of different heights still sat on the windowsill, filled with multicolored bits of glass, washed smooth by the ocean's hand. The third jar was in pieces on the charcoal granite below the windowsill, the softly rounded jewel-toned treasures pouring onto the floor, mixing with razor sharp shards of window glass. Leigh picked her way gingerly across the floor, carefully collecting the tiny bits of memories until they formed a small, bright pile on a clear section of counter.

As she bent down to start sweeping up the broken glass, the sound of a motorcycle engine roaring to life drifted in through the shattered window . . .

Friday, 9:04 A.M.
Salem, Massachusetts

Leigh glanced at the clock in her dash as she pulled into traffic behind the Detective Unit. She had arranged to meet with the Dean of the Arts and Science program at Endicott College at 9:30 A.M., but Beverly was just across the Essex Bridge, so she would arrive in plenty of time.

Leigh had been pleased to find headquarters blessedly quiet that morning. After last night's incident, the last person Leigh wanted to see was Morrison, but, to her relief, she found he was off-shift today, so she wouldn't have to deal with his insufferable attitude all day. That alone put a spring in her step.

She turned onto Bridge Street. Traffic was busy at this time of morning, but compared to the summer season, it was quite reasonable. This late in the season, the majority of the fair weather tourists who came to Salem to explore the culture of witchcraft were now gone and the town was enjoying a brief period of normalcy. Leigh knew the tourists would return in droves in time to celebrate Halloween, but she pushed that thought away. She had enough on her plate right now. She didn't need to worry about 100,000 tourists flocking to her city to create mayhem in a few weeks.

Traffic flowed onto the Essex Bridge and Leigh glanced out her window at comfortingly familiar surroundings. To her left, bright sunlight glinted off wind-swept waves in Beverly Harbor. To her right, a large cluster of boats hugged the shoreline, safely moored at the marina away from the open sea.

A motion in the rearview mirror momentarily distracted Leigh as a dark motorcycle swung into the outside lane. The rider was dressed to match his bike in black leathers and gloves. His helmet carried the only splash of color—twined behind the mirrored visor was a fierce red dragon, its mouth open in a silent scream. The motorcycle briefly pulled up beside her, but then dropped back to veer in behind her car. He continued to ride her bumper as they topped the apex of the bridge before falling back to a respectable distance.

With one last glance at the cyclist, Leigh fixed her eyes back on the road just as the bridge ended and they were back on dry land. A block further, she took the turn to Route 127, driving east, turning directly into the blinding morning sun. Pushing her visor down to block the glare, she concentrated on the road in front of her.

Five minutes later, she left Beverly proper and drove into the outskirts of town. Traffic was lighter here, but a steady stream of cars in front and behind her carrying students and teachers made their way to the college for morning classes. Following both the posted signs and Dean Campbell's instructions, Leigh pulled left to turn at Witch Lane. Suddenly, with a roar, the black motorcycle abruptly swerved out from behind her, nearly grazing her back bumper. As it came even with her passenger window, the driver slowed to look directly into the car.

Directly *at her.*

Leigh's palms went suddenly damp against the steering wheel as an icy chill ran down her spine, her nerves jangling as she experienced the sensation of being watched for the second time in less than twenty-four hours.

Horror dawned. *The sound of the motorcycle from last night.*

The cyclist revved his engine and kicked the bike into high gear, speeding off down the street. Leigh contemplated following her gut and going after him, but she was blocked by the cars around her in the turn lane as well as those streaming after the motorcycle. Craning her neck, Leigh straightened in her seat trying to see the rear license plate of the bike, but the car in front of her blocked her view.

Helplessly trapped in place, Leigh's gaze followed him as he disappeared from view.

When the car behind her honked for her to move forward on the green light, she told herself her pounding heart was from being startled by the car horn, not by the surge of alarm caused by the cyclist.

CHAPTER SEVENTEEN:
ICE RAFTING

Ice Rafting: the transport of materials by moving ice; pieces of ice in the low marsh are broken off by high tides and deposited in other areas of the marsh.

Saturday, 1:47 A.M.
Lowell residence
Brookline, Massachusetts

Matt gave a low moan as his body jerked in sleep. He tossed restlessly in the darkness, his legs tangling in the sheets as his breathing became ragged.

The hot sand burning his skin as he fell to his knees beside his comrade. The brutal wind whipping grit into his eyes and scoring his face, a multitude of tiny knives.

Ripping apart ragged fatigues to find torn flesh beneath. Blood welling thick and dark, pouring out onto dirt and rock.

The warm flow of his own blood down his cheek, trickling to drip from his jaw and trail down his neck.

His body flying through the air. Searing heat. Agony.

His body sliding uncontrollably across the grit, razor sharp gravel scraping off skin like coarse sandpaper.

Crawling through a trail of his own blood, back to the soldier.

The stab of shock as he found himself looking down into the sightless, staring eyes of the woman in the clearing, found himself kneeling in those same woods. His blood-soaked desert fatigues, heavy boots, and combat helmet so jarringly out of place in what should have been a peaceful glade. But instead was rife with death.

Ice-cold blood leaking from dozens of gaping wounds. Harsh bruising even darker under drying blood. Tangled hair matted with blood and gore. Tears of dark decomp fluid leaking sluggishly from the corners of her eyes.

Turning away so he didn't have to look. There was nothing for him to do here. She was long gone.

"You didn't save me."

The staggering shock of her rasping voice, the almost dizzying motion of his head whipping back to stare at her. The air rushing from his lungs, never to return.

The sightless eyes fixed on his, the blood-red petechiae vibrant against the ghostly paleness of her skin. "You didn't save me."

"I wasn't there when you died. I couldn't save you."

"You could have saved us."

Looking up with a jerk to see the corpse of his fallen comrade feet away from her ruined body.

"You let us die." Black fluid starting to trickle from the corner of her bloodless lips.

"I couldn't stop it." Desperate words, tumbling from his mouth. Who was he trying to convince? "I couldn't save him. He was too badly injured." He held up his bloody hands for her to see, vibrant trails running down his forearms. "I tried. I couldn't stop the bleeding."

"You could have saved us." Her voice was growing weaker and weaker. "You let us die."

"No . . ."

"You let us die. Our deaths, all our deaths, are on your hands . . ."

"No!" With a ragged gasp, Matt sat bolt upright in bed, his heart pounding frantically and the heavy sweat on his bare skin chilling instantly as the blankets pooled around his hips. He instinctively groped for the lamp on the bedside table, fumbling for the switch, almost frantic for the light to drive away the dark images in his mind.

Bright light suddenly flooded the room and he turned his face away, closing his eyes against the glare even as his breath rasped raggedly from his lungs. "Not my fault, not my fault," he chanted in a broken whisper as he dropped his face into his hands. He pulled his knees up, curling into a ball for warmth and comfort.

For long moments, the only sound in the room was his own harsh breathing. Finally he fell back against the headboard, his legs sprawling out limply as his head tipped back and his eyes closed. His heart rate slowed toward normal.

He hadn't dreamed like that in years. He thought he'd moved past it. He'd worked for years to move past it.

Now the flashbacks were back, dragging the nightmares with them.

He opened his eyes to fix on the ceiling above his wide bed. The single lamp threw a circle of light on the white plaster. He concentrated on the brightness of that circle.

Not real. Just a dream.

But it had felt real. Terrifying and real, and it left him shaken. Empty.

He raised a trembling hand to run a single finger along the scar at his temple.

You let us die.

He swore softly.

It was a long time before sleep returned that night.

Saturday, 8:22 A.M.
The DeWolfe Boathouse, Boston University
Boston, Massachusetts

Matt slid on his sunglasses before stepping from the dimness of the boathouse into blinding morning sunlight. His gaze instantly found his father, seated in his wheelchair on the dock, swapping stories with one of the rowing coaches as he waited while Matt and one of the riggers stored the scull after their early morning row.

Matt's gaze drifted out over the choppy blue water of the Charles.

He'd needed the time out on the water. Time to throw off the dream. Time to push himself hard, letting physical exertion drive away some of the darkness. He rolled his shoulders, feeling some of the tension loosen.

His father laughed, drawing his attention back to the dock.

The morning's exercise had been good for the older man as well. Since they'd moved to Boston, they regularly used rowing as part of Mike's physical therapy and it was one of the reasons his father remained strong despite being trapped in his wheelchair. Mike might not be able to use his legs, but Matt suspected his father could easily overpower him in an arm wrestling match, despite their age difference.

A shrill ring cut through the still morning air. He fished his phone out of his sweatshirt pocket, glancing at the display. *Leigh.* "Good morning."

"Morning. I know I told you I'd be into the lab later today, but I'm afraid there's been a change of plans."

Instantly, dread swept through Matt. "What happened?" He couldn't keep the edge out of his tone. "Did we find another one?"

"No, no, nothing like that," Leigh quickly reassured him. "I just have work to do here. We found Tracy Kingston's car."

"Where?"

"In the parking lot at the Cummings Center. There's no overnight parking at the mall but management is pretty lax about it. However, after several nights in the lot, the car was called in to be towed away. Beverly P.D. ran the license plate number and when they saw the name on the registration they called the state police. We impounded it right away."

"You're going over the car for evidence?"

"Crime Scene Services is. But what I have is even better. The mall's had problems in the past with car thefts, so they have security cameras covering the parking lot."

Matt found her excitement contagious. "And her car was in view of those cameras?"

There was a smile in her voice, and anticipation. "It was. So I have hours of security camera footage to go through. It's a pretty wide window to cover when she might have disappeared but if we can see anything in the camera footage, we might get our first real lead in this case. There's no guarantee I'll find anything, of course. They may not have taken her from anywhere near her car, so if this doesn't pan out I'll try the footage from other security cameras in the vicinity." She sighed, and he could hear an echo of exhaustion behind the excitement. "I'm supposed to be off today, but no one's getting time off when there's a case like this."

"Why don't you bring it down to the lab?"

There was a pause at the end of the line. "Bring the footage to the lab?"

"Sure. We're all meeting there at nine-thirty to start examining the remains. But I could lend you at least one of the students to help. Two sets of eyes will be able to scan the footage faster than one. Bring a few copies down; all the students have laptops. We can do it right in the lab so security isn't an issue. Better than hanging out alone in the office on your day off, right? Besides, I need to bring you up to date on the excavations. The third grave has given us some valuable insight."

"That would work. And it would be nicer than working alone at the office. Thanks, Matt."

"You're welcome. See you in an hour." He hung up and hurried across the dock. "Dad, we've got to get going. Leigh needs the team."

CHAPTER EIGHTEEN:
DECOMP CYCLE

Decomp Cycle: the recycling of organic and inorganic materials within the marsh from dead and decomposing material into living plants and animals.

Saturday, 9:29 A.M.
Boston University, School of Medicine
Boston, Massachusetts

Matt and Kiko both looked up at the knock on the closed laboratory door. The small window framed Leigh's face as she peered into the lab through the glass.

Circling the gurneys, Matt crossed the lab to open the door. "We really need to get you your own key card so that you can have full access to the lab and the case evidence."

Leigh stepped into the room and Matt closed the door behind her. "It would certainly make it easier on you every time I stop by to see how you're doing." She patted the messenger bag tucked under her arm. "Thanks for the offer to help me review all this material. I admit it was a welcome invitation."

Matt sent her a quick flash of a smile. "No problem. There's enough of us that we can share the work load."

"How are the examinations coming?"

"We got the remains laid out last night, but we're just getting started on that now."

"Good. I'll start to collect Missing Persons reports for

potential victim matching once you can give me some kind of time estimate as to when they died."

"That's all part of the examination—sex, race, age, postmortem interval. The remains will tell me all that."

Leigh studied the remains, a slightly puzzled expression on her face. "I understand Rowe's methodology of time since death—it's all based on soft tissue biology—but how do you do it? You've got nothing left but bone."

"Well, in this case, that's not quite true. I didn't talk to you yesterday after we excavated the last two sets of remains. They were so fleshed we opted to put them in cold storage at the M.E.'s office because we just don't have the ventilation system needed for bodies still undergoing decomposition."

"They're *that* recent?"

"Well, not as recent as it sounds. Bodies decompose about eight times slower when they're buried than if they're left on the surface. These remains aren't undergoing putrefaction, but they are still in the advanced decomp phase. I called Rowe directly and he agreed that we should examine those bodies together. We're hoping that will be Monday, but I'm kind of at the mercy of his schedule. It's high on his list though."

"You said those remains gave you some insight?"

"Yeah, they're pretty straightforward. We have a male who died of a single gunshot wound to the forehead and we have a female who died of traumatic injuries similar to Tracy Kingston. The male went into the grave dressed; the female, naked." He caught Leigh's eye. "The female victim is marked over her left breast. The marks aren't clear due to decomposition and shrinkage of the skin, but there was clearly a pattern of lines carved there. We can macerate the flesh to remove it from the bones to look for matching kerf marks once a full examination has been done, but I think we're looking at an identical signature to the one on Tracy Kingston."

"Another link between the victims," Leigh said. "Good work. You're building a solid case."

"We're trying. The soft tissue degradation on the third set of remains gives me something to work with to estimate time since death. It's clear these were the last bodies buried. The internal organs are completely liquefied, but there's skin present, as well as muscle and connective tissue. It's only the extremities that have progressed to skeletonization."

"This extra tissue will help pinpoint how long the remains have been out there?"

"Yes. The biggest question forensically is to determine when the remains were buried. Decomposition takes place much faster during the warmer months. We also know how deeply the bodies were buried and can correct for how much soil was lost in the storm surge. The deeper the burial, the slower the rate of decomposition because of lower ground temperature and protection of the remains from insects."

"I know you need to do a more extensive examination, but can you give me a rough initial time frame? I know you haven't likely had a chance to examine the remains nearly enough for an official opinion for your report. This is just for me and my interest."

Matt was silent for a moment as he weighed how comfortable he was with a rough estimate. "I don't normally do this, but for you and your interest, I would place the most recent burial interval at fourteen to sixteen months. In other words, June to August of last year."

"What about these skeletonized remains?"

He shook his head. "It's too soon. I haven't had a chance to examine them because we've been focused on the excavations. With only minimal tissue remains at best, I need to look for erosion of the cortical bone due to acidic burial conditions or cracking and warping because of weathering. We can look at the degree of DNA degradation through PCR and there's soil chemistry that can be run on the soil from beneath the remains. Or there's microscopic examination or UV fluorescence or—"

Leigh held up a hand, cutting him off. "Bottom line, what's your guesstimate on the skeletonized remains?"

Irritation rose. *Scientists don't guess.* "I told you it's too soon. I gave you an estimate on the other remains. You'll have to be satisfied with that for now."

"I need an estimate on these remains too. I told you I won't hold you to it."

"I can't just guess, Leigh, and that's exactly what I'd be doing here. I need to be sure of our results and that takes time."

"I'm not asking you to testify to it in court. I just need some sort of window so I can narrow my search."

"Unless you want a time frame that will simply waste your time, you need to be patient. This isn't like working with flesh. There are multiple markers that need to be considered and we have multiple victims to work with."

"I know that. Even just a few to start with would—"

Matt's temper started to unravel. "Time-out." The word came out clipped short and edged with anger.

"You don't need to call for a 'time-out' here," Leigh argued, her cheeks flushing with anger. "I'm not asking you to open a vein and write it in blood. But I need this information to start the Missing Persons search. Even if you make the range too wide, it at least gives me a starting point."

"With skeletonized remains, sometimes a large range is the best I can do," Matt grated.

Leigh closed the distance between them to only inches, standing so close he could see the tiny flecks of forest green that shot through the jade of her eyes. "That's fine," she insisted stubbornly. "Give me a range then."

His jaw locked and his eyes narrowed. "You're pushing." He

started to turn away from her.

Her hand shot out, grabbing a fistful of shirt at his shoulder. She yanked him back toward her. "Don't turn away from me. I need something to go on. Give me *something*."

Fury flared and before he could stop himself, his hand grasped her wrist where she clutched his shirt. *"Time. Out."*

Leigh opened her mouth to argue, but the words seemed to die on her tongue. She stood stock still, held in his grasp, her eyes searching his face. Then she eased away slightly. "Okay, time-out."

"Time . . . *what?*" He didn't shift back, but simply waited her out, allowing her the next move. His grip around her wrist loosened slightly.

She released his shirt and his fingers immediately dropped from her wrist. "We made a deal," Leigh stated, all animosity gone from her voice. "You and I can be pissy with each other all we want but that doesn't help the victims and they're the only ones that really matter. It's just that this case is sitting so heavily on me right now and I feel like we don't have any idea who we're fighting for yet and—"

He reached out a hand and then hesitated, not knowing if she'd welcome his touch. His hand hovered in mid-air before finally dropping limply to his side. "I know the pressure you're under. I'm not oblivious. I can make time since death my first priority and then go back to cataloging injuries if that's what you need. I can be flexible but I just can't stick my neck out and give you incorrect information because I'm making a guess rather than an educated assessment."

Leigh tried not to look discouraged. "Can you look at that first then, please?"

"Absolutely. Now, are you ready to review that footage?"

"Yes." She started to turn away, but then glanced back at him, concern in her eyes. "Are you okay? You look really tired."

Matt drew back at the slight and she rushed to cover any insult. "It's not that obvious. I mean, I can see it but—"

"It's okay." Matt cut in before Leigh could dig herself in even deeper. "I just had a rough night. This case . . ."

She gave him a small, twisted smile. She reached out to run her palm over his shoulder, smoothing out the twist in his shirt, but he suspected she was also trying to soothe him. "I know exactly how you feel. I've had murder cases that have left me sleepless too. You know it doesn't help the situation, it only makes it worse, but you can't turn it off."

"Hopefully tonight will be better because it's wearing me down. Come on. We'll grab Juka to help you."

As one, they turned toward the grad students, only to stop dead when they found the three young people standing across the room, staring at them, various expressions of intrigue, alarm, and surprise on their faces.

"Busted," Paul murmured.

"Don't you guys have anything to do?" Matt snapped.

"No, no . . . we've got lots to do," Paul said lightly with a grin, clearly unperturbed by Matt's icy gaze.

"Then go do it," Matt said flatly. "Juka, you come and set up here with Leigh. Paul, you can help me with the examination unless Leigh needs you." He turned to Leigh. "You can set up at my desk over here." He indicated the desk in one corner of the room, its surface cluttered with numerous piles of papers and journals, and a skull perched atop a stand on one corner.

The students watched Matt and Leigh cross the room. Kiko glanced sideways at the men. "Did you just see what I just saw?"

"Oh yeah," Paul said, grinning. "The temperature in this room jumped about ten degrees during that argument. And did you see Matt? He actually looked flustered, like we'd caught

him in the act. This is going to be very interesting to watch. I'll
bet they don't really even realize it themselves yet."

Kiko nodded. "Maybe not, but if those fireworks are any
indication, it's going to be damned hot when it happens. Two
years with Matt and I've never even seen him give a woman
even a passing glance, let alone that kind of intensity." She gave
Juka a push toward Matt's desk. "Enough about Matt's sex life.
Let's get to work."

The group broke apart, each heading to their own task.

Chapter Nineteen:
Human Disturbance

Human Disturbance: the disruption of an ecosystem by human activity.

Saturday, 11:52 A.M.
Boston University, School of Medicine
Boston, Massachusetts

Leigh set up on Matt's desk, while Juka settled at his own writing station a few feet away. She'd brought several DVDs of security camera footage, so she and Juka each selected a disc and started to scan the footage. On one DVD, Tracy's car was not visible at the beginning of the footage. On the next, her car was visible but it was impossible to say if she had already been taken since the car was still there days later.

There was very little noise as everyone got down to work, with only quiet murmurs between Matt, Paul, and Kiko as they examined remains and cataloged kerf marks.

An hour and a half later, Leigh shifted stiffly in Matt's desk chair and rolled her shoulders, trying to ease the kink in her neck before leaning back over the desk and propping her chin on her hand. Carefully scanning the footage to ensure nothing was missed was time consuming. Finally seeing Tracy pull into her parking spot had given her a jolt of adrenaline. But after watching Tracy get out of her car, the footage continued with no sign of her return. Cars came and went. People entered and

165

exited the mall. But no sign of Tracy.

Leigh realized that her knee was bouncing restlessly, and forced herself to stop. *Settle down. You knew this was going to take time. You can't afford to miss anything.*

Pausing the footage, she glanced up briefly to see how the rest of the team was faring. Kiko was seated at a workstation, meticulously fitting and gluing fragments back into place to reconstruct one of the skulls. Matt and Paul were bent over one of the older sets of remains, discussing some aspect of the examination, the low murmur of Matt's voice interspersed with Paul's slightly higher tone. As if sensing her eyes on him, Matt glanced up, their gazes locking over the span of the lab before Paul pulled his attention back to examine a section of bone.

Leigh considered the frozen scene on her laptop screen, but then abruptly surged to her feet. She just needed a quick break—a drink of water, a walk down the hallway, some air. Anything to soothe her suddenly jittery nerves.

Without a word, she slipped from the lab, silently making her way down the deserted corridor. Some of the other labs had lights on, but the offices were all dark. *It's Saturday. Not everyone works seven days a week—*

"Leigh? Everything okay?"

She turned to find Matt standing in the hallway, pulling the door of the lab closed behind him. She didn't want to make a big deal out of this. "Yes. I'm just . . . restless. I just wanted a quick break."

He started down the corridor toward her. "That's understandable. You've been sitting for a while and probably need to stretch your legs."

"It hasn't been that long." Her shoulders slumped. "Maybe the pressure's starting to get to me."

"We've been running for almost a week straight and no one's had a break," Matt said. "It's wearing us all down." He took her arm, pulling her down the corridor.

"Where are we going?"

"The lounge. I'll make some coffee. Nothing fancy but it's faster than running out for one and I think you could use the pick-me-up."

"It's got to be better than what I'm used to. Cop coffee is like liquid tar. But are you sure you have time for this? I'm taking you away from the lab."

"Paul and Kiko will be fine without me for five minutes." He steered her into a small room at the end of the corridor.

One side of the lounge comprised a simple seating area with several couches and chairs gathered under a large window, bathed in the afternoon sunlight. A small kitchen with a sink, fridge, and microwave filled the other side of the room.

Matt indicated the seating area. "Have a seat. I'll put on a pot. The students will want some too."

Leigh flopped into one of the overstuffed armchairs, tipping her head back and closing her eyes, trying to let the tension seep from her tight muscles. She could hear Matt moving around the small room and, eventually, the gurgling of the coffee maker. A minute later, the couch creaked as he sat beside her.

"You're tired." It wasn't a question.

Leigh opened her eyes, peering at him sideways through her lashes. "You could say that. It's been an interesting few days."

"What do you mean?"

"You know . . . everything that's going on with the case and the ID."

"And that jackass at the department who's been giving you a hard time?"

She laughed, but there was no joy in the sound. "Oh yeah, him too. And . . ."

When she hesitated, Matt leaned forward. "And . . . ? What else?"

"It's nothing."

"I'm learning that when it's 'nothing' with you, it's always something. What else happened?" When she remained silent too long, Matt pressed again. "Maybe there's something I can do to help."

"Do you know a good window guy?" At his baffled look, she explained. "Two nights ago, after work, I was in my kitchen making dinner when someone hurled a rock through the window."

"What?" Alarm spiked into his tone. "Were you hurt?"

"I was fine, except for being seriously pissed off. It made a huge mess and I've still got a piece of board nailed over the broken glass because I haven't had time to call anyone yet."

"Did you report it?"

She fixed him with a deadpan expression. "I didn't need to report it. I'm a *cop*. If I'd called Salem P.D., they'd have wanted a description of the perp, but I didn't get a look at one. Besides, it's probably just some kid showing off for his buddies." She shifted uncomfortably in her chair. "The stupid thing is it's making me jumpy. Yesterday I was driving to Endicott College and I thought I picked up a tail."

"What do you mean you 'thought' you picked up a tail?" Matt's voice was pure suspicion.

"It was just a feeling I had. Some guy on a bike in full black leathers following too closely. It set off alarm bells for me, but I probably just overreacted after the rock escapade the night before." She dropped her face into her hands. "I'm just tired. It's making me see things that aren't there and I'm second-guessing my own instincts."

She felt Matt gently pull her hands away from her face. She opened her eyes to find him leaning in close. "You're running non-stop and under a huge amount of pressure," he said. "And you're exhausted because you're not sleeping well."

"And you are?" Leigh countered, a defensive edge creeping into her tone.

"Not as well as I'd like, especially considering how exhausted I am when I fall into bed. But that's not the point. All I'm saying is give yourself a break. No one is pushing you harder than you, yourself." The coffee maker beeped three times. "Coffee's ready. How do you take it?"

"Sweet and light."

"You've got it."

He was halfway across the room when Kiko dashed in the door. "There you are!"

Leigh sat bolt upright in her chair, instantly on alert. "What's wrong?"

"Nothing's wrong." Kiko grinned. "Juka's got it. He found Tracy."

The coffee was forgotten in an instant as all three raced down the hallway and back into the lab.

"What have you got?" Leigh crossed over to Juka, bracing her hand on the desk beside his laptop as she peered over his shoulder. The picture on the screen was frozen, and Leigh's eyes instantly found Tracy's car, a sporty little hatchback. It occupied a parking space two rows above the bottom of the screen, the frozen figure of a woman beside it, her arms loaded with bags. There was only one other car in the picture, an older model four-door sedan, parked one row farther away from the camera. The timestamp read 9:08 P.M.

"Roll it back, please, Juka. Back to when she appears."

Juka placed his cursor over the time bar and dragged it back a minute before starting the footage rolling forward again. Leigh met Matt's gaze over the top of Juka's head. The hope she felt lit his eyes as well. *This is it; our first real clue as to the identity of the killer.*

"Right here." Juka's words broke into the silence and they turned back to the screen. Paul and Kiko crowded in behind Juka's chair.

The black and white footage showed a nearly empty parking lot.

"That's no coincidence," Leigh said. "He waited until the end of the night to grab her. The parking lot is almost empty, so there are no witnesses." Her body tensed as the recognizable face of the victim entered the picture. Tracy's arms were laden with shopping bags and she walked with a quick step. Moving quickly to her car, she unlocked her doors. Opening the passenger side, she laid the packages and her purse on the front seat. She closed the door and hurried around the hood of the car toward the driver's door.

Leigh found herself chanting *keep going, keep going,* in her head, even though she knew how the scene would play out.

Tracy reached the front of her car when she suddenly stopped and turned around.

"She nearly made it," Matt said softly, "but someone called for her attention."

A person climbed out of the only other car on screen. The details were grainy, but the tall, slender man wore a jacket with the collar turned up and a baseball cap pulled down over his eyes. His hands were deep in his pockets. He and Tracy talked briefly and then Tracy circled her car to open the hatchback, the man meeting her at the back of the car. She rummaged in the back of the car and then pulled out a tangled jumble of cables.

Leigh leaned in, squinting at the screen. "Jumper cables?"

"Yeah," Matt agreed. "He probably faked having a dead battery and asked for help. Then when he had her closer he likely—" He cut off abruptly just as Leigh's sharply indrawn breath sounded beside him.

A second man entered the picture, wearing a flat cap pulled low. He silently slipped behind Tracy as she turned to the man in the baseball cap, both hands full with the tangle of cables.

"Goddamn it, there's *two* of them," Matt breathed.

They watched in helpless horror as Tracy gave a sudden jerk, whirling to face the second man, the jumper cables tumbling from her hands. He quickly grasped her upper arms as the first man put a hand over her mouth. She struggled, but her efforts were short-lived as she quickly weakened and sagged to the ground. The first man caught her, supporting her weight as the second man picked up the cables, tossing them carelessly in the car before closing the hatch.

Leigh's hand came down firmly on Juka's shoulder. "Stop!" She turned to Matt. "What just happened there? We couldn't see clearly, but could he have had a cloth in his hand with some kind of inhaled anesthetic? Something to knock her out?"

"I doubt it. Most inhaled anesthetics have longer induction times and they reverse as soon as the patient breathes oxygen again. It's more likely an injected anesthetic, but his body blocked our view of what his hands were doing." Matt's tone was harsh with barely banked anger. "Whatever it was, it was fast-acting. It only took ten or fifteen seconds and she was starting to lose consciousness."

"Start it again, Juka, please," Leigh requested.

The video continued. Both men glanced around before the man in the flat cap moved to take part of her weight and together they walked her to the car at the edge of the picture. They opened one of the back doors and proceeded to lay her on the back seat. Then the man in the baseball cap got into the driver's door, but the other returned to Tracy's car.

"What's he doing?" Kiko asked.

"He's grabbing her purse and her purchases," Paul answered. "An abandoned car with a visible purse and bags might attract attention. They wanted this car to stay under the radar for as long as possible so they took her belongings with them."

On screen, the man carelessly tossed the bags into the back seat with their victim before getting into the front passenger seat. Then they drove away, leaving Tracy's car alone in the picture.

Leigh straightened and started to pace the floor in front of the workstation. "Two men. Not just one killer but two working together." She whirled suddenly on Matt. "Why did we only see one man last Wednesday? Did we miss one?"

His answer was immediate, his voice sure. "Not a chance. I suppose there could have been someone in the boat. But . . . no, that doesn't make sense. Why have only one man dig the grave if there are two available? It would take much longer that way and you'd run a higher risk of getting caught in the act. No, there was only one man out on the marsh that day. I'm sure of it."

Leigh started to pace again. "Me too. So then why two men working together here? We never anticipated that." She stopped again. "Do you know how rare it is to have serial killers working together?"

"I bet it's very rare. Lucky us." His sarcasm was unmistakable.

Leigh wanted to put her hands into her hair and yank hard in frustration. One bone had become eight victims. One killer had become two. She made herself focus on what she had just seen. "This just shows how organized and staged this whole scene was. I don't know where the second man was waiting but he was never on screen before that moment. Juka, roll it back a bit please. Yes, about there . . . stop! Hold it there. Perfect."

On screen, in grainy black and white, the two men supported

Tracy between them as they stood beside the car.

"What are we looking for?" Paul asked.

"Anything that we can use to identify these men. They're both wearing gloves so fingerprints are out. They're both wearing hats that hide their faces from this angle. But standing beside the car like this, we can estimate height and weight."

"Why do you think they left it there?" Kiko asked suddenly. When everyone turned to her in question, she clarified. "Her car. Why did they leave her car? Wouldn't they have been wiser to take the car at the same time they took her? They could have dumped it somewhere so it looked like a carjacking or something."

"It's a valid question," Leigh said. "There could be a couple of reasons. For starters, they simply might not have thought about it. Some criminals don't think things through that well."

Matt made a sound of derision. "You can't believe that in this case."

"No. Not with what we just saw. This required advanced planning. Whether Tracy was chosen and they followed her to this location or whether she was a random victim, they had their trap planned out. 'Miss, can you help me? My car won't start and I don't have AAA. Do you have any jumper cables?' Most people will willingly help someone they see as being in need, often not considering their own safety because they never think they might be in danger. They just think they're doing a good deed. I agree though. This wasn't a case of not thinking it through."

"I'll bet they *did* think it through," Matt interjected. "They hardly had any contact with that vehicle. The less contact, the less chance of leaving anything in the way of incriminating evidence—epithelials on the steering wheel, hair on the headrest . . . anything that could lead the police back to them and link them definitively through DNA analysis to the crime scene."

"You also have to wonder if they were hoping someone else might steal the car if it was just left there," Paul suggested. "There's not enough detail to see if they left the keys, maybe in hope of inviting some poor sucker to steal it. Then whoever had the bad luck to pick that vehicle would suddenly be linked to a potential kidnapping case if he got caught."

"That would nicely throw the scent off the real culprits wouldn't it?" Leigh leaned in again, studying the frozen image. "But now we've finally got a concrete lead. The first one to the killer—" She stopped abruptly, and corrected herself. "—*killers* instead of the victims. We've not only got a picture of the killers, but of the car they used in the abduction."

Matt pointed at the image with an index finger. "The footage is pretty grainy, but it looks like a Chevy. Maybe an older model? The license plate is visible, but you can't see the plate number on it. The print quality is too poor."

"*We* can't see the plate number on it, but the computer forensics guys back at the office can work miracles. Juka, let's mark it. What's the timestamp on the footage?"

"It starts at nine-oh-eight P.M. and is finished at nine-twelve P.M.," he answered.

"This is a copy. The original is back in the office." She pulled out her cell phone. "I'll call it in and see how fast we can get someone on this."

Matt reached out to briefly touch her shoulder, bringing her eyes up to his. "We need to get on this right away. All these other killings seem to be spread out over time but that was before we interrupted one of them at the burial site. There's nothing to suggest they won't strike again, and quickly. What if they take someone else?"

"I agree. We need to move on this as fast as possible."

She speed dialed a number on her phone. "Richards, it's Abbott. I need computer forensics to contact me ASAP." She caught Matt's gaze and held it. "We've got a break in the case."

CHAPTER TWENTY:
GREENHEAD FLY

Greenhead Fly: Tabanus nigrovittatus; a species of horse fly that is an important pollinator and lives its entire life cycle within the salt marsh. Females require a blood meal for egg production and development, and have a sharp bite that often causes a skin reaction.

Saturday, 3:20 P.M.
Boston University, School of Medicine
Boston, Massachusetts

Matt set the T-6 vertebra back into place on the table just as his cell phone rang. He hurriedly stripped off his gloves to dig into his lab coat pocket. "Matt."

"It's me." Leigh's words were hurried. "I'm at headquarters. The computer forensics boys managed to tweak that security video enough that we could get a license plate number from the footage. We've compared the owner's Massachusetts driver's license photo against the security footage. Even as grainy as that footage is, we're sure it's the same man—a Mr. John Hershey. My warrant just came through, so I'm organizing backup and heading there now."

Matt froze. "Heading where?"

"The registered address on his driver's license is in Middleton. I've checked the tax records—it's owned by Hershey's father, who is currently a guest at one of the Commonwealth of

Massachusetts' correctional facilities following the beating death of his wife. There are no other children, so our guy should be the only occupant."

"I want to come with you."

There was dead silence on the line for a moment. "Matt, I didn't call to invite you along. I was just keeping you in the loop. This is a police investigation. It's a job for cops, not scientists."

"What if that's where Tracy was killed? If you find weapons there, I might be able to identify them. We've gotten a lot further with the investigation in just the last few hours and we're compiling a list of bone trauma. I can tell you if there are implements there that might have been used on the victims."

"I don't know . . ." But her words dragged, and Matt knew she was at least considering it.

"I was helpful to you out on the Essex coast," he reminded her.

"I can't deny that. Okay, if you can get up there fast enough to meet us, you can come along. But you have to stay back until we've cleared the residence, and Matt . . . no gun. Your word on that. We'll have more than enough firepower as it is."

"Yes, ma'am," he said obediently and with only a touch of sarcasm. "I'm on my way right now. What's the address?" He quickly scribbled down the street address she recited to him. "See you there in forty minutes."

Saturday, 4:03 P.M.
Hershey residence
Middleton, Massachusetts

After pulling his SUV to the curb behind Leigh's Crown Vic, Matt met her on the grassy side of the road in front of a fenced yard.

He quickly scanned the area. It was a quiet neighborhood

with large, leafy trees and single-family clapboard dwellings on large lots, well separated from their neighbors. At the far end of the street, several uniformed field troopers were climbing out of their patrol cars. "Which house?"

Leigh pointed down the street. "The brown bungalow a half block down on the right."

Matt fell into step beside her, noting she now wore a light blazer covering her holster and had tucked her shield into the waistband of her jeans.

The brown bungalow seemed starkly out of place. The other houses on the street were neat and bright while the bungalow shouldered an overall air of shabbiness. Overgrown shrubs surrounded the screened-in front porch, weeds grew in between the concrete paving stones in the front walk, and paint peeled from worn siding. Instead of the paved driveways next to the other houses, this house had a simple gravel off-street parking area.

"Check out that car," Matt said quietly, pointing to the older model navy Chevrolet sedan parked near the house. "It's the same one."

"They know the body's been found, yet the car they used for the kidnapping is still sitting in the driveway? I don't buy it. They should be a hundred miles from here." She quickened her pace. "I'll go in with the backup. You wait out front. I'll let you know when it's safe to come in and check the place out."

Leigh smelled it the moment she peered in through the dingy screen at the scattered mess of discarded shoes, old newspapers, and rotting garbage inside the porch.

Blood.

Human excrement.

Death.

She opened the screen door and stepped into the porch. The

smell was even stronger inside the enclosed space. She signaled the backup team to stay behind her, then moved forward.

Leigh quickly scanned the interior of the porch, focusing on one of the front windows. It was unscreened and open several inches.

Then she heard it. A low moan of pain.

Alarm shot through Leigh's system. Someone was alive in there.

She pulled her gun from its holster, before pounding sharply on the door. "Mr. Hershey, it's the Massachusetts State Police. Open the door." Silence. She knocked again. "Mr. Hershey!"

She tried the door handle—locked. Moving quickly to the open window, she pushed her hands under the window sash and pulled upwards. With a screech, the window reluctantly gave way. Putting her back into it, Leigh opened the window further until the gap was wide enough for her to scramble though. Throwing her leg over the sill, she squeezed her body through the gap.

She threw the deadbolt to open the door for her backup team, then scanned the gloomy interior. There were no lights on; only late afternoon sun filtered through filthy glass. The front room was full of worn furniture and strewn with old pizza boxes and dirty glassware. A cluster of beer cans sat around a high-tech computer in the corner.

There was no sign of anyone injured or dead.

Gun held ready, Leigh moved through the room and down the dim hallway. She moved cautiously, with her back to the wall, every sense on alert. The acrid, metallic smell that permeated the house was all too familiar.

Another low moan. Down the hall and to the right. Her pulse kicked in response.

She came to a doorway and peered in cautiously, thankful for the armed men behind her.

The kitchen seemed deserted until her gaze tracked downwards to see the toe of a shoe. She slid around the doorway, gun extended, about to call out her designation when the words died in horror in her mouth at the sight before her.

A young man, maybe still in his teens, lay on the floor inside a spreading pool of blood.

Or what was left of him . . .

There was blood everywhere—on the linoleum in puddles and smears, soaked into what was left of his clothing, dripping off deathly white skin. There was even a bloody handprint on the wall.

Her eyes dropped down to the man and her stomach rioted in protest. She tamped down brutally on the need to vomit.

She'd been a detective with the Essex unit for years and this surpassed anything she'd seen before. But the similarities to Tracy Kingston were starkly obvious.

Someone had viciously attacked this man and then left him to die. His shirt was in bloody tatters beneath him and his jeans were pulled down below his hips. His groin was a mass of shredded tissue. He was covered with stab wounds, ragged slashes, and tears. A deep bloody furrow ran from his jaw across his cheekbone toward the opposite eye, nearly amputating his nose. A straight diagonal slash from rib to hip opened the abdominal cavity and loops of pink intestine burst through the layers of fat and skin. A plethora of small stab wounds, each oozing blood, were scattered over the torso, and flaps of skin had been peeled back leaving long, weeping wounds that dripped blood onto the floor. A knife was buried to the hilt in the man's inner thigh, blood flowing freely around the blade. A bloody serrated knife lay on the floor beside the body next to what Leigh was sure were the man's testicles.

Her gaze moved up his body, back to his face. To find his eyes fixed on her. Eyes that were filled with fear and pain.

Holy mother of God, he was still conscious.

Leigh bolted from the kitchen and through the living room to the front door. "Matt! I need you *now!*"

When Leigh frantically called his name, Matt didn't pause. He sprinted up the walk and burst through the open front door, only half-aware of the cautious looks the backup team shot his way. "Leigh!"

Her voice came from down the hallway. "Here! Matt, hurry!"

He raced down the hallway and skittered around the corner into the kitchen.

Straight into hell.

Torn flesh. Exposed organs. Bone and cartilage gleaming through bloody tissue. Dully imploring eyes with dilated pupils.

He wasn't prepared for the memories that crashed over him, and couldn't fight them off as they rose to swamp him, hurling him back into the heat and blood and pain.

Then Leigh was in front of him, grabbing his arms, giving him a harsh jerk. "Matt! I need you to stay with me." He blinked, focusing on her frantic expression. "Help is coming, but they're minutes out. You were a battlefield medic. You must know how to keep him alive until the paramedics get here."

He pushed away nightmare and memory as instinct and training took over. He fell to his knees beside the wounded man, cataloging the damage and trying to decide what to deal with first. "He's bleeding out. He needs a surgical team, but I'll do what I can to slow the bleeding until we can move him."

Leigh took up a position in the doorway of the kitchen. "We interrupted whoever did this. We need to check the house in case he's still here."

Matt nodded distractedly, his attention on the man in front of him. "Throw me your jacket." Leigh stripped out of it quickly, tossing it to him before disappearing down the hallway toward the back of the house.

Matt pressed two fingers against the right side of man's throat, searching for the carotid to feel just the faintest of flutters under his fingertips. The man was fading fast. Matt's gaze flicked up to see terrified eyes focused on him. "Stay with me. Just hold on. Help is coming." Quickly undoing his belt, Matt wrapped it around the man's thigh, several inches above the knife, tightening it until he detected a slowing in the stream of blood seeping around the blade.

With his bare hands, he started to tuck intestine back into the abdominal cavity so he could close the lips of the gaping wound. But the more he pushed in, the more slippery, bloody loops slid out. Cursing quietly, Matt tried again. Finally, he took Leigh's jacket in his bloody hands and rolled it up to lay it over the wound, applying pressure as he quickly scanned the other wounds, deciding what to do next.

He jerked as the ear-splitting shriek of furniture sliding across the floor came from down the hall.

Leigh had just cleared the first bedroom when the screech split the air. Sprinting after the sound to the end of the corridor, she tried the closed door, but it only opened an inch before jamming against something solid. One of the men joined her and they each pressed a shoulder against the wood, pushing hard, hearing the satisfying squeal of furniture legs skidding over wood from the other side. When the gap created by the open door was about eight inches wide, Leigh carefully peered in, leading with her gun, two members of the backup team right behind her.

The small bedroom was completely deserted. But the window on the far side of the room was open, the dingy drapes that hung on either side blowing in the light breeze.

Leigh squeezed her body through the tight space before bolting to the window just in time to see a slender dark-haired man, dressed all in black, sprinting through the back yard.

"Stop! Police!" she yelled as she scrambled through the window, landing lightly on the ground four feet below and tearing after him. He was easily forty feet ahead of her as she wove through the trees, and she lost sight of him as he shoved through a row of cedars that separated this yard from the next. She desperately poured on all her speed.

She crashed through the same bushes herself, woody branches scraping her face and arms as she determinedly pushed through. She could hear the footfalls of the other officers behind her as they spread out, widening the search. She scanned the yard and disappointment rose in a wave as nothing moved. Then she caught sight of a movement to her right, toward the back of the lot, and the chase was on again.

Ahead of her, the man scrambled over a six-foot wooden fence at the end of the yard. For just one instant they made eye contact as he hung at the top of the fence. There was victory and a manic joy in his eyes, an almost unholy light.

She fired, aiming for his hip, trying to wound him, to slow him. But she was still running and the bullet harmlessly struck the fence post inches below him. Then he was gone, rolling out of sight.

But the sound of his laughter carried clearly over the top of the fence.

"Goddamn it!" Leigh ran harder, holstering her gun to take the fence at a running leap, scrambling ungracefully over the top and landing in a heap on the other side. She rolled quickly to her feet, to find herself in a parking lot behind a small strip mall.

From around the corner came the unmistakable sound of a motorcycle engine starting up with a roar.

The mental image of the black garbed cyclist with the dragon helmet crashed over Leigh. She'd been feet from him yesterday and hadn't sensed the danger until it was too late.

Leigh sprinted across the parking lot, rounding the corner just in time to see him crouched over the same dark motorcycle, rounding the corner into traffic, the now familiar image of the screaming dragon emblazoned on his helmet. He swiveled his head to see her standing in the parking lot.

He raised two fingers to his brow in mock salute. And then he was gone.

She pulled out her phone, panting raggedly between sentences as she put out a bulletin for all units in the area, local and state, with a description of the motorcycle and the best description she could give of the suspect.

She wasn't hopeful that anyone would catch him. On a motorcycle, he could easily vanish among back roads and fields until the heat died down.

Leigh simply stood there, beaten, her heart pounding wildly and her breath heaving. Forcing herself to push the frustration, anger, and disappointment aside, she whirled and ran back toward the house.

Leigh came in through the front door at a run and skidded to a halt inside the kitchen.

Matt sat back on his heels, his bloodied hands lying limply in his lap. Her jacket still lay across the victim's abdomen, one sleeve sliding off to sag into the puddle of blood and gore that surrounded him. There was a belt around one thigh, a tourniquet to stem the flow of blood from the femoral artery. He had used pieces of the man's shirt as field bandages to try to stem the unending streams of blood.

But it was no use. The man's open eyes were dead and lifeless.

Leigh spared only a small glance at the man they had tried to save as her focus shifted to Matt. He was abnormally pale and his eyes were glassy and fixed sightlessly on the body. She knelt beside him in the blood, noticing for the first time the discarded syringe in the puddle beside his knee. She took his cold, sticky hands in hers where they lay unresponsive in her grasp. "Matt?" No response. She squeezed his fingers and tried again. "Matt!"

His eyes slowly rose to hers, horror and memory locked in their depths.

A shout from the front of the house made her break eye contact. Heavy, thudding footsteps came toward them and then paramedics followed two troopers through the doorway of the kitchen. They, too, recognized that they were too late.

Letting go of Matt's hands, Leigh rose to call for Dr. Edward Rowe and Crime Scene Services.

Their killer had struck again. They had a ninth victim on their hands.

CHAPTER TWENTY-ONE:
TIDAL FLATS

Tidal Flats: Nearly flat intertidal surfaces that are sheltered from direct wave action by a barrier beach.

Saturday, 7:12 P.M.
Lowell residence
Brookline, Massachusetts

Leigh pushed open the door, letting Matt enter the foyer before stepping in after him.

"You're home late." A disembodied voice came from around the corner, before an older man in a wheelchair rolled into the hallway. "Did you get through everything you—" He froze, his face going slack with shock when he saw his son.

Leigh followed his gaze, seeing Matt with fresh eyes. He was covered in blood: It soaked into his jeans and splashed in obscene arcs over his shirt, his hands and forearms were stained dark red, and a smear covered one cheekbone.

Matt's father reached out a hand. "Matt! What—?" His tone was sharp with alarm.

"It's not his blood," Leigh quickly interrupted.

After sparing her only the quickest of glances, the older man rolled forward into the hall to stare more closely at his son's blank expression and dull eyes. "Matt?"

Matt never even looked at his father. He simply walked past him in silence and climbed the stairs.

The older man pushed his chair toward the bottom of the staircase, but Leigh stepped forward, laying a hand on his arm before he could call out. "Mr. Lowell, please, let him go," she said quietly. "He needs a minute."

His gaze stayed fixed on the now empty staircase. "What happened?"

Leigh circled the wheelchair to sink down onto the third step so she was eye-to-eye with him. "I was following a lead on a potential suspect and was going to go check out his residence. Matt asked to come along in case we found any of the weapons used on the victims. He thought he might be able to recognize if something at the scene produced the bone trauma that he'd already identified. I agreed as long as he stayed out of the way until we'd cleared the residence." She sighed heavily. "But when I went in, I found our suspect in a pool of blood on the kitchen floor. He'd been attacked and was bleeding out fast."

From upstairs came the sound of a shower turning on.

"I called for Matt then," Leigh continued. "He'd told me he was a combat medic, so I knew he'd know field triage. I thought he might be able to save the suspect's life."

"That explains the blood then."

"Yes." Leigh rubbed her hands roughly over her face, unmindful of the dark crescents of blood that still stained the cuticles around her nails and the creases of her knuckles. "Matt did everything he could, but the wounds were too severe. Multiple stab wounds and he'd been eviscerated and—" The older man winced and she cut off abruptly. "Sorry." Giving into exhaustion, she hung her head, letting her eyes fall shut. "We're both a little rattled." She pulled in a deep breath, trying to compose herself. "I had to go after the attacker. While I was gone, Matt did what he could, but the suspect died anyway. Matt was just kneeling beside him, covered in blood and completely still. He had that same blankness you just saw in his eyes. I had to call his name twice before he even heard me. I knew we were contaminating the crime scene, kneeling there together, but I needed to reach him. I did get through, to some extent, but he's been shut down ever since. He answers questions if asked directly, but other than that, he hasn't said a word. I drove him back, but he was silent the whole time, like he was lost in his own personal hell." She met the older man's gaze. "Was his time in Afghanistan that bad?"

Mike gave a curt nod. "When William Tecumseh Sherman said 'War is hell,' he was giving us the straight goods. Matt experienced some horrible things. As a medic, he saw the worst of what humanity can do to its own. He saved many lives, but he lost too many—in firefights, explosions, and roadside bombs. War is ugly and raw and brutal, and it affected Matt deeply. He has physical scars from his time in the Marines, but it's the invisible scars I worry about. He doesn't like to talk about it, but it's got him twisted so tight that sometimes I wonder how he can breathe. It certainly changed his long-term career goals. He wanted to be a doctor once, but by the time he came home, he wouldn't even consider it. The memories associated with being a medic just hurt too much. I suspect today threw him back into those memories."

"I hate to think that I've done this to him."

"You haven't done this to him. He's a grown man, and he could have turned this case down." His gaze flicked over her blood-smeared clothes. "But let's not make this worse for him than it has to be." He backed up his chair a few inches before deftly turning toward the kitchen. "Follow me. I've got some fresh laundry and I think one of Matt's old T-shirts might do. It'll be too big, but it's better than what you're wearing now. And I can probably find a pair of drawstring shorts."

Leigh followed him into the brightly lit kitchen. He wheeled out of the room but returned a minute later with a soft, faded blue T-shirt, a pair of black shorts, and a plastic bag lying across his knees. He held them out to her. "The bathroom is just down that hallway," he said. "Why don't you wash off the rest of the blood and get yourself changed. There are towels under the sink. Help yourself."

"Thank you, Mr. Lowell."

" 'Mike' will do just fine. No need to stand on ceremony with me. Go on."

The water turned off above them and deep concern shadowed Mike's face briefly before he composed his expression. Leigh turned away to give him some privacy, and left the kitchen in search of the guest bathroom.

She returned a few minutes later, her face and hands scrubbed and her hair neatly pulled back into a ponytail. She glanced around the kitchen, but Mike was alone. "Matt's not down yet?"

Mike cast worried eyes toward the ceiling. "No. He's taking too long. I need to go up there and make sure he's okay."

He started to roll toward the hallway but Leigh reached out to grasp his shoulder. "No, I'll go. I know he's your son and no one knows him better than you, but I was there with him. I know what he saw and how it affected him." Her voice dropped. "Please, Mike. I brought him into this situation. If I've done damage, I need to fix it."

Mike opened his mouth to reply, but then closed it again before nodding. "If you need me, I'll be here."

She pushed back her chair to stand. "Thank you," she said quietly.

She left the kitchen, feeling Mike's worried gaze on her back until she rounded the corner.

Hand on the railing, Leigh stopped at the top of the stairs.

Silence.

Of the three doors in this hallway, only one was closed. She stared at it, sure that Matt was on the other side. She crossed over to knock lightly on the door. "Matt?" she called. "Are you okay?"

When he didn't respond, she repeated the knock, a little louder this time, before laying her palm flat against the cool wood. "Matt? I need to talk to you." More silence. Concern spiraled higher. "I'm coming in."

She pushed open the door, stepping into the room and closing the door behind her.

Matt stood at the far end of the room, in front of the windows. His feet were bare and his hair was a damp tangle, but he wore a fresh pair of jeans and a gray T-shirt.

Crossing the room, Leigh circled the double-wide chaise that angled toward the windows for nighttime star gazing or daytime dozing in the warm sun. As she passed the open door to the master bath, a bloody pile of clothes on the tile caught her eye. He had taken them off, dropping them where he stood, and then walked away, not yet ready to deal with them or what they represented.

"Matt." The single, softly spoken word finally seemed to penetrate and suddenly he looked startled to see her standing in his bedroom.

"I knocked several times, but you didn't answer." Coming to stand beside him, she laid a hand on his shoulder. "Are you okay?"

He nodded once, jerkily.

She looked into his shadowed eyes. "No, you're not. Talk to me. What did I do to you?"

That snapped him out of his silence. "You didn't do anything," he said, his voice rough and uneven.

"I took you into that situation." He opened his mouth to speak, but she interrupted him. "You're not the cop, I am. To be honest, I was being selfish. I knew you'd be helpful."

"Some help I turned out to be."

He angled his body away from her, but she caught his arm to pull him back. "I would have been lost in there without you. I have basic first aid, but I wouldn't have known what to do in that situation. You didn't even question what was going on, you just did what needed to be done."

"Fat lot of good it did." Disgust coated his words. "He died. Just like she did in the dream." He squeezed his eyes shut as if to block out the visions in his mind.

They flew open again in surprise when Leigh's fingers came to rest softly against his jaw. "What dream?"

"It doesn't matter. Look you probably need to get going. I'm sure you've got—"

"There's nothing I have to do right now that's more important than this. Don't tell me you're okay. It's as clear to me as this scar that you're not." She reached up with gentle fingers to touch the scar at his temple, only partially visible under his damp hair.

His eyes went wide and he jerked his head back out of her reach. "Don't!"

She froze, her fingers suspended only an inch from his temple. "Don't what? Don't touch you? Don't touch *it?*"

"It's ugly." His words were harsh, a bitter whisper.

"It's a badge of honor," she contradicted softly. "It's a wound you received while fighting for your country. There's no shame in that. You nearly *died*. Another inch to the left and they would have sent you home in a body bag." She reached out again. He flinched slightly as her fingers nearly touched him and she hesitated, but then resolutely closed the distance between them, slipping her fingers under his tousled hair, her fingertips feathering along the hard, twisted furrow of scar tissue. He winced once as she made contact, but then held still beneath her touch.

"You take such pains to hide your scar. You shouldn't."

"Most people think scars are ugly. They stare, or worse, ask questions. And I don't want to talk about it."

"Then they're insensitive idiots. It's a battle scar. *It means something.* It's like a cop being injured in the line of duty. You're there for a greater purpose. You should wear that mark proudly." Understanding suddenly dawned. "But you don't just mean 'people,' do you? You mean 'women.' Well, if some woman told you it was ugly, or wouldn't touch you because of it, then you're better off without her."

Matt laughed roughly and shook his head in consternation. "You're one of a kind."

"I doubt that." Her tone softened and she let her hand drop from his face. "Are you okay? You shut down on me for a while there." Embarrassed color suffused his cheeks, but she was past allowing him to shut her out. "Tell me what's going on."

He turned away from her to cross the room toward the wide king-sized bed. He sat down on the edge of the bed and she followed to sit beside him.

"Tell me what happened back there. It's the same thing that happened back on the Essex coast when we found Tracy's body, isn't it? When you walked into the kitchen I knew you were in trouble from the way you lost all color just before your eyes went blank."

"Yes."

Leigh's eyes searched his face. "Can I ask you a personal question?"

He nodded.

"Do you suffer from PTSD?" She asked the question flat out, as if she was asking him if he liked sugar in his coffee. No disgust, no blame, no derision of a diagnosis of Post-Traumatic Stress Disorder. Just a simple, straightforward question.

But one that packed a hell of a punch. Matt's whole body jerked and he pulled away from her grasp as he abruptly shot to his feet to pace the room. "Why would you ask that?"

She didn't answer immediately as she simply gauged his reaction. "Because it would be entirely reasonable seeing what you've gone through. Your dad told me a little about it. No, don't blame him," she said, when she saw him stiffen. "I asked him about your time in the Marines. I'm an investigator. If I can't put your past together along with two significant reactions to horrific attacks and your own words—*I don't do flesh*—then I'm not very good at my job." She patted the bed beside her. "Matt, sit down. Please."

He hesitated for the space of several heartbeats before complying.

Leigh simply waited in silence beside him, thigh to thigh, giving him the time he needed to collect himself.

"I joined the Navy after dropping out of medical school. I'd always wanted to be a doctor, but in the end, med school itself took that away from me when my best friend, another med student, committed suicide. The impossible work hours, the debt, and the stress all combined to bring on clinical depression. We all saw the signs. Hell, we all displayed them ourselves, but we never thought Dave was that bad. *I* never thought he was that bad. It was all right in front of me, but I just couldn't see it."

"Probably because you were busy and struggling yourself," Leigh said quietly. "You took on too much if you blamed yourself for his death."

"I was too wrapped up in myself to see that he needed my help," he said bitterly. "In the end, it made me question what I was doing there. Would I be the next one to snap under the pressure? Was it worth all the mental and financial anguish? Finally, I decided it wasn't, and I dropped out. After that, Mom and Dad and I spent a lot of time talking through where I could go next. They helped me see that medicine was right for me, but not necessarily the traditional route that included med school. In the end, it was Dad's idea to join the Navy that felt right. He suggested that I join as a Hospital Corpsman, that way I could still have the medical angle that I was interested in and I might see a little of the world at the same time."

"When was that?"

"I enlisted in July of nineteen-ninety-nine. I went to boot camp, then did the fourteen week Hospital Corpsman training. Then I spent a year with the Fleet Marine Forces, training to move to the Marines." He could see her doing the math in her head and beat her to it. "I had just been officially transferred over to the Marines at the beginning of September, two-thousand-and-one."

"9/11," Leigh breathed.

He nodded. "9/11. It changed everything."

"You deployed overseas?"

"As part of Operation Enduring Freedom. I was part of one of the frontline Marine battalions. We deployed in November of two-thousand-and-one and I was with the Marines until January of two-thousand-and-three when I was granted a hardship discharge following my parents' car accident. There was a blizzard and they were just trying to get home . . ." He cleared his throat roughly. "My mother was killed and my father ended up in that wheelchair."

Leigh reached out to touch his knee. "Oh, Matt. I'm sorry."

He swallowed harshly but pushed on. "There was no one else. I'm an only child. My father needed care, so I applied for a hardship discharge. I left the service, and never went back." He paused, weighing his words. "The first few years . . . they were hard. I'd have flashbacks to some of the worst battle scenes, and I'd get the sweats or I'd have spells where my heart would race, kind of like a really bad anxiety attack. That went on for months. Later, there were nightmares." He rubbed his hand over his forehead. "Those were worse and lasted for years."

"Can I ask you a question?"

"At this point? Sure."

"How did you manage working at the body farms?" He frowned, but she pushed on. "Most of the bodies donated to those facilities are pretty fresh. That must have taken you back, must have brought on some PTSD reactions."

"It did." He took a moment to choose his words carefully. "I knew that I wanted to go into osteology, but you can't just study that. You have to learn decomposition from death onwards. So I took it as a challenge, sort of as my own psychological therapy. If I could force myself to deal with bodies like this on a regular basis, then maybe I could desensitize myself."

"Did it work?"

"Sort of. I still had nightmares." His shoulders rose on an uneven breath. "But then I graduated and came to Boston, and specialized strictly in osteology. And eventually the nightmares went away."

"Until now."

Matt's head shot up. "What?"

"You said earlier today that you had a rough night last night. At the time, I thought you meant you didn't sleep, but there's more to it. Am I right?"

His eyes stayed locked on hers. "Yes."

"The murders, the attacks, they're bringing it all back for you, aren't they?" Guilt layered over the regret she already felt. "I'm sorry, Matt. I had no idea that this case would turn into the nightmare it's become." She reached out to comfort him, lifting her hand to clasp his jaw. "How could one bone spiral into such chaos and so many deaths?"

She was only inches from him. His gaze flicked from her eyes to her lips and back again. Her eyes went wide as she realized his intent just a moment before he moved in, covering her mouth with his.

There was a moment suspended in time and then heat exploded between them.

She gasped in shock and he took advantage, sliding his tongue over the tender skin of her lower lip before sinking in deeper. His hands delved into her hair, his fingers unerringly finding her ponytail to tug the elastic free. It fell unnoticed to the bed behind them as his fingers entwined in the loose strands, angling her head up for his kiss.

She framed his jaw, the stubble of his late afternoon beard rough against her fingertips. She backed off to change the angle of the kiss, tangling her tongue with his and hearing his low groan of satisfaction when she slid her arms around his neck and pulled him in.

Gripping her shoulders, he tipped her backward, pressing her into the duvet as he rolled his weight partially over her. Her fingers speared into his hair as she sucked his lower lip into her mouth before nipping at it and then soothing the small sting with a swirl of her tongue. His weight felt heavy and satisfying, his body solid and muscular. Pulling her hands from his hair, she ran them over the wide breadth of his shoulders and down the solid planes of his back.

His hands slipped from her shoulders to run down her ribs, his fingers only inches away from the sides of her breasts. Reaching out with one thumb, he stroked it over soft flesh, smiling against her lips at her soft intake of breath.

He rose up on his forearms to look down at her, his gaze suddenly fixing on her jaw. He reached out with gentle fingers to trace the length of an angry red scratch that followed her jaw line before bending to feather his lips over it. "Is that from chasing—"

"No more talking." Leigh's hand curled over his shoulder as she pulled him down for more, arching up off the bed to meet him, mouth to mouth and breast to chest.

They sank into each other again, falling back onto the softness of the duvet. She brought one knee up to flank his hip as he settled against her, his weight pressing her further into the bed. His warm palm cupped the back of her knee, drawing her leg even higher before sliding down her bare thigh to skim his fingertips teasingly under the edge of the shorts.

With a quiet murmur, she ran her palms over his back to find the waistband of his jeans, gliding her hands under the hem of his T-shirt to find warm, smooth skin below. She traced her fingertips over the strength of his back, over muscles made strong by rowing, sliding her left hand over his side toward his chest—

Her eyes flew open in surprise as her fingers contacted hard, twisted tissue. Her hand froze in shock and then her fingers spread wide. *More scar tissue. More than her hand could cover.*

His eyes jerked open, his body stiffening as her body stilled and her fingers froze over his ruined skin. He abruptly pulled back, rolling off her to sit at the side of the bed. He yanked his T-shirt down to cover the waistband of his jeans, hiding himself from view as he stared at the floor, his body hunched tight.

Still lying on her back on the bed, her breath heaving, Leigh stared at him in shock. She had thought that the scar on his temple was bad enough but it was nothing compared to the mass of scar tissue hidden under his shirt. She pushed herself up on one elbow and reached over with her other hand to touch his back. "Matt?"

He sprang to his feet as if burned by her touch. He looked down at her, but Leigh noticed he wouldn't meet her eyes. "We'd better get downstairs. My father must be concerned and I'd like to put his mind at ease."

She held out a hand for him to help her up off the bed. When he averted his eyes and half-turned away, she rolled off the bed to stand beside him.

He glanced over just as she was shaking her hair out over her shoulders. For one brief moment, temptation warmed his expression as his gaze flicked from her toward the bed and back again. But then his face went blank and his eyes turned cold as he turned toward the door.

She stepped closer, reaching out to purposely lay her hand against his scarred side. "Matt, I—"

But he pulled away so her fingertips only brushed fleetingly across him as he turned away from her to open the door and disappear into the hallway without a backwards glance.

Following him, Leigh paused at the threshold of the bedroom, watching him stride down the hallway away from her. Clearly, there was a lot more than met the eye when it came to Matt, including his discomfort with the damage done to his body. She'd been surprised at the extent of the scarring, but surprise was all it had been. He had clearly read something else into her hesitation and she needed to make it right with him.

But, for now, she put it aside.

They had a case to solve and if Matt's head was now back in the game, they had work to do.

Chapter Twenty-Two:
Erosion

Erosion: the wearing away of the Earth's surface by the action of water or weathering; the salt marsh efficiently protects coastal areas from erosion.

Sunday, 1:08 P.M.
Hershey residence
Middleton, Massachusetts

Hands planted on her hips, Leigh surveyed the damage to John Hershey's kitchen. The body was long gone, but vestiges of the attack remained.

Blood stained the dirty peel-and-stick vinyl flooring in an obscenely wide puddle. It spread over the floor and oozed into the cracks between the tiles in grotesque tendrils. Dark arcs of blood splashed over the walls and nearby cupboards, and the acrid odors of blood and urine still hung heavily in the air.

Signs of the forensics investigation were also clearly evident. Every light-colored surface was coated with fine black fingerprint powder and hundreds of prints were visible. Small, bright yellow numbered evidence markers littered the floor. But one thing was clear from the search of the house—the only victim to die here had been John Hershey, who had lost his life, slowly and in agonizing pain, on his own kitchen floor.

The room was still horrific, but to Leigh it wasn't nearly as bad as it had been the day before, when she stood in that same spot with a murdered man at her feet, and Matt kneeling shattered and blood-drenched beside him.

She needed to call him today to see how he was doing. He should be at the lab by now, continuing his work on the remains.

Work was good. Work was something to concentrate on when other aspects of your life fell apart in pieces around your feet.

Yesterday's experience had rattled him. She had no doubt about that. However, as she came to know Matt better and better, she sensed a strength in him that wouldn't yield. It had knocked him back a pace or two, but he'd been willing to open up about some of his experiences with her the night before. He may have closed down for a while, but it had only been temporary.

He wasn't the kind of man to give in to weakness. He was the kind of man to fight the challenges life threw at him and to come out of the experience stronger. But a call to check on him might not be amiss. She just hoped he wouldn't mention their shared moment in his bedroom. She didn't think either of them was ready to examine that yet.

Leigh checked her watch. She had at least twenty minutes before anyone would be here.

She pulled out her phone, and speed dialed Matt's cell.

As soon as he answered, she could hear uneasiness in his voice and an awkwardness that wasn't there earlier yesterday. So she concentrated on the case. "How are the remains coming?"

"Good. You beat me to calling you." Relief filled his tone at keeping things on a strictly professional level.

"You've got something for me?"

"The examination is going well. I have some basic information for you now that will help with your Missing Persons search—age, sex, and race approximations. We're still working on time since death. But we're getting close."

Leigh wedged the phone between her shoulder and her ear as

she reached into her pocket and pulled out her notepad and pen. "Great. Give me the details."

"I think it would be easier if we walked you through it here. Can you drop by later today?"

"You can't give me anything now?"

She heard the smile in his voice at her wheedling tone. "I could, but it will make more sense if you see the remains. Trust me."

"I do." The words were out before she even stopped to consider the significance of them. "Okay, if I can, I'll stop by later. But I'm at the Hershey house now and I'm waiting for someone from the computer forensics team."

"The computer forensics team? Why?"

She briefly considered how much she should share with him, quickly deciding that after his experience yesterday he deserved to know something about the life he had tried so hard to save. "Are you sure you want to talk about this?"

There was a pause, and then his voice was muffled. "Guys, I'll be back in a minute." She heard footfalls and then the sound of a door closing before his voice came back clearly. "Sorry, I wanted to go somewhere private. Look, Leigh, about yesterday . . ."

She broke in before he could say any more. "Matt, no explanation is required. It's water under the bridge as far as I'm concerned." *Well, part of it is . . .* "Are you okay to hear about our suspect?"

"Yes." His voice was hard and sure.

It was good to hear the confidence in his voice again. "I spent the morning running background checks on John Hershey," Leigh reported. "It turns out he's got a record."

"Why am I not surprised?"

"I wasn't either. He started with small stuff, petty theft, that kind of thing. Then he graduated to breaking and entering when he was seventeen. As part of his sentencing for the B&E, he was required to attend behavioral modification treatment at a Beverly health clinic."

"Behavior modification? For theft?" Matt sounded confused. "Was that simply because of his age?"

"No. It was apparent to the judge that Hershey was a disturbed young man with a history of abuse and mental health issues. I tracked down Hershey's therapist this morning. She was quite accommodating once she saw I had a warrant for his records."

"She remembers him?"

"Yes. And that says something considering it was over a year ago and she sees hundreds of teens a year in her position at the clinic. She described him as a very troubled young man, one who was raised in an abusive household and who she identified as having anger management issues. He lived in a group home for some time while undergoing therapy, but returned to his family home after his father was jailed for the murder of his mother."

"That kind of home life has to produce a pretty screwed-up kid." Matt paused. "Not that I'm making excuses for him."

"I know," Leigh said. "But it starts to paint a picture of his personality. His therapist also said he was extremely resistant to any sort of therapy."

"So he did his time and got out as soon as he could. Which likely means he didn't get much out of therapy."

"That's exactly what I thought. But I did get one other very interesting piece of information from the therapist."

"What's that?"

"He was obsessed with video games, both the console and online kinds. This was a real concern for her since he tended to prefer the ultra-violent variety. First-person shooter, gang violence games, that kind of thing."

"The online game that Paul suggested." There was excitement in Matt's voice. "The symbol found on Tracy Kingston."

"That's right," Leigh agreed. "We needed a connection and now we have it. That's why I'm waiting for the computer forensics expert. You probably didn't notice it yesterday, but Hershey has a shiny new computer system sitting in the middle of all the trash in his living room."

"Leigh, this could be our link between the two men." The intensity in Matt's tone was unmistakable. "If we can trace from one man to the other . . ."

"We might be able to nail the son of a bitch who did this. Yes, I know." She heard a voice call out from the front door. "Matt, he's here now. I have to go. I'll try to stop by the lab later this afternoon."

"Go," Matt insisted. "If you can't make it, make sure you let me know what you found out."

"I will." Leigh ended the call and left the kitchen, moving through the dingy, shabby living room.

A young man stood at the front door, holding a leather bag. He had shaggy red hair and was wearing black jeans, high top sneakers, and a red-collared navy sweatshirt emblazoned with "Patriots." He also wore a disgruntled expression.

Rob Tucker was the best and the brightest of the computer forensics boys. Leigh had asked for him specifically.

"You made good time. I thought it might take you longer to get here."

Her smile of welcome was met with a level stare. "Sunday is a sacred day, Abbott. It's a day for chicken wings, pork rinds, and football. But you had to haul my ass out here today because it couldn't wait for tomorrow."

"Gee, Tucker, I don't know how you manage to keep your girlish figure when you eat crap like that. And here I thought all you computer geeks did at home was watch *Star Trek* reruns."

"Not when the Pats are playing. Which they started to do—" He glanced at his watch. "—about five minutes ago."

"Welcome to working for the cops. Today is my day off too, you know. Nobody gets a day off during a case like this."

"But someone else was on call today. It's not my day to—"

"I wanted you." Leigh's flat statement broke through his protests. "I know Delancy's on call, but I wanted you because you're the best. We have suspicions of an online gaming connection in this case, so I need the best hacker I can get. At this point in the investigation, Harper will give me whatever I need as long as it goes toward solving this case, preferably before there's public panic, or, worse, another death."

Tucker simply stared at her in silence, but she caught it—a barely perceptible softening of his expression.

"So that's why your Sunday afternoon got hijacked. I'm sure you set your DVR, and I promise not to tell you how it ends." She pointed at the chair in front of the computer in the corner. "Now, sit. We've got a serial killer to catch."

Mollified, he raised a single eyebrow at her in a mock glare. "You're a hard-ass, Abbott." But his tone lacked its previous razor-sharp edge.

She glared right back. "Don't I know it. Now, get us into that system."

They picked their way across the refuse strewn over the living room floor.

Tucker stopped half way across the room, nearly causing Leigh to walk right into him. "Whoa . . ." He whispered the word almost reverently.

Leigh leaned sideways, trying to see what he was staring at so intently. "What? What's wrong?"

Tucker whistled before continuing across the room. "This is one sweet system." He pulled out the chair in front of the monitor and sat. "This guy really wanted his computer to kick ass."

Leigh contemplated the strange looking computer. It was mostly black, but a neon stripe glowed ghostly red down one edge while oddly spaced rectangles sprouted from one side. "This may be the strangest computer I've ever seen," she said. "Where's the case?"

"Where's the case?" Tucker looked up at her, clearly dismayed by her ignorance. "That *is* the case. And it's one of the most expensive ones out there. Only the most serious gamers shell out for something like this. I bet the components he used are just as extreme." He swiveled in the chair to critically study the room. "Does the rest of the house look like this?"

"You mean a run-down, disgusting mess?" Leigh's lip curled as she took in dirty dishes, moldy food wrappers, and discarded clothing. "Yeah, pretty much."

"I've seen it before." Tucker swiveled back to the system. "Some guy who lives in a pathetic hole in the wall, but his electronics are totally state of the art. This is a perfect example. Unless he made a lot of money at work, he likely skipped a few meals to pay for this baby. And was happy to do so."

"So we're not just talking about someone who likes to game, then. We're talking about someone with a serious addiction."

"Oh, yeah." He unconsciously reached out to run a hand lovingly down the chassis. "You can kind of understand it though. She's a thing of beauty."

"Stop being a fanboy, Tucker. Just get me in."

"Yes, ma'am," he said, in a tone slightly edged with sarcasm. He wiggled the mouse. "Oh look, it's password protected," he sneered.

"Is that a problem for you?"

Tucker's expression bordered on arrogant. "Unless this guy was really smart, I bet I can crack his password in under sixty seconds."

"Sixty seconds?" Disbelief rang in Leigh's tone. "It can't be that easy."

"Lucky for us, it usually is. And if it isn't, then I have a host of other tricks up my sleeve." Bending, he rummaged through his bag, flipping through several DVDs until he found the one that he was looking for. Putting it in the drive, he restarted the system.

"What are you doing?"

"Running a password cracker I wrote. So, is there something in particular we're looking for? You said something about an on-line gaming connection."

"There's a potential connection between the victims and a multiplayer online game called 'Death Orgy.' " At Tucker's perplexed look, Leigh reached into her blazer pocket and pulled out the picture of the Chinese symbol, handing it to him. "It was suggested, and I've now had it confirmed, that this is the Chinese symbol for 'Death.' We found it carved above the breast of the most recent victim and we are investigating whether any of the skeletal remains have any trace of the same injury."

Eyes fixed on the picture, Tucker's expression was solemn. "Nasty, for sure. But what's the connection to this game?"

"I've been working with a scientist, and one of his students identified it as the symbol for this game, so I want to explore the possibility that he was a player. Our now deceased suspect had a record with the local police—mostly small stuff like petty theft, but the last charge was a B&E so that shows a potential escalation. As part of his sentencing, Hershey had to attend behavior modification with a therapist. That therapist has confirmed that Hershey had a proclivity for violent video games. I need to know if he used this computer to participate in this particular game and, if so, who he gamed with. Because one of those people just might be his killer." Her eyes locked on the window now open on the screen. "It's done? *Already?*"

Tucker tapped the lower right corner of the screen where a small box read "Time elapsed: 0hr, 0m, 37s." "It only took thirty-seven seconds. And check out the password: 'mankiller.' "

Fury swept through Leigh at Hershey's casual reference to his life of crime. "Bastard."

"Kind of flaunting his secret life, which is seriously not cool. But it didn't take long to crack because it's a weak password." He rebooted the computer and then took in the filth that surrounded them as well as the flashy electronics. "My guess is he was no computer genius. He may have been addicted to gaming and was willing to throw serious money at that addiction, but he likely only knew the basics, just enough to do what he wanted and needed to do. This is likely the only security we'll encounter." He logged onto Hershey's account. "Here we go." A curvaceous blond woman sporting only the tiniest of G-strings splashed across the screen in a provocative pose. "Well, hello."

"Put your hormones in neutral and focus, Tucker. Although . . . I do want to know if he was into porn, and if so, what kinds. An acceptance or an approval of degrading women may play into how he acted out his fantasies and how these women were killed. But first, gaming . . ."

"Gotcha." Tucker opened Hershey's default browser and started searching through his bookmarks and history, keeping up a running monologue as he did. "Here we go . . . Okay, we're into the gaming right from his homepage. This is one of those social network sites that compiles lists of games for easy searching. Your game is listed here near the top. It rates very high in popularity in the online gaming community, but it carries the top age appropriateness rating—AO or Adults Only. AO games contain extremely graphic depictions of sex, violence, or worse, sexual violence."

Leigh stomach clenched at the thought. "They portray rape in these games?"

"Nothing is sacred. If it sells, someone will code it. There's some pretty horrible stuff out there, some even based on real life. Programmers will take their inspiration for new ideas where they can find it." He reorganized the history in order of sites visited, scrolled down the list for several seconds, and then stopped, sitting back in the chair. "And there's your proof. He not only played that game, he played it *a lot*. I'll bet he felt secure enough that he wasn't going to be caught to have the browser save his log-in information. Care to log in and see what the game's all about?"

Leigh's eyes went cold. "Show me."

"You're sure? This is probably going to be pretty nasty stuff."

"I need to know what interested the man who would do this to these women. There may be some relation between what's portrayed in these games and what was done in real life. Maybe this was how he honed his skills. Maybe this was where he got his ideas. Maybe this was where his aggression was stoked to the extent that he had to take it out on living, breathing women. Maybe it was none of those things, but I have to know what he knew, and see what he saw." She squared her shoulders, preparing to face the worst. "Show me," she repeated.

Then, bracing her hand on the desk, she leaned over his shoulder and let him take her into hell.

Sunday, 3:24 P.M.
Hershey residence
Middleton, Massachusetts

Stepping out into bright afternoon sunlight, Leigh took a deep breath of fresh air. After the darkness and the rancid odors in the house, the outside air was fresh and crisp with the scent of the last of summer's flowers and the earthy smell of oncoming fall.

Two children rode by on bicycles, shouting to each other.

One of them rang the bell on her handlebar as she coasted past, smiling and laughing. It was a picture of life proceeding as it should, innocence and youth distanced from the horrific world of murder and cruelty just feet from where they played.

She and Tucker had entered into the hellish world of multi-player gaming, ill-prepared for the brutality of what they would see. "Torture porn" was certainly a good name for it. Violent torture, brutal death, and an overt and careless disdain for women, children, animals, and the sacredness of life. Nothing but blood, pain, despair, and the glorying joy of those who enjoyed death.

They had only been in the game for a few minutes, when other players started to talk to them, using Hershey's screen name.

Thanatos, where you been? It's been days since you were here.

We've been challenged to a match by Team Scourge next Wednesday. We need to grind them into the ground. They don't stand a chance against us.

Where is Orcus? Has he contacted you? He missed the last game too.

They stayed in the realm of the game for just over half an hour, but in that time they had seen more than enough. Finally, blessedly, Tucker had exited the game and shut down the computer.

He said he would be able to trace the IP addresses of the other players, both those online today and the missing Orcus. There were no more complaints about missed football games. Leigh knew she had his attention now, and he would get the information to her as fast as humanly possible. Even if that meant dragging in the staff of Internet service providers on a Sunday and serving them with warrants to gain access to their records.

Tucker had left with the computer only minutes before, mut-

tering under his breath about the depths sick minds could sink
to.

Leigh understood what he was feeling. The concept that human beings could derive enjoyment and pleasure from such a pastime was beyond her understanding.

She wanted to talk to Matt and his students, to move forward with all the possibilities their investigation could produce. To close this case.

She re-engaged the secondary police lock on the porch door and walked quickly toward her car. Away from death and toward hope. Toward the answers that might identify those who existed now only as skeletons, ravaged by wind, weather, and scavengers. Toward the men and the woman who had taken on her cause as their own.

Toward Boston.

Chapter Twenty-Three:
Productive Natural
Systems

Productive Natural Systems: the salt marsh is one of the most productive ecosystems on Earth; it produces more food per acre than the average Midwestern farmland.

Sunday, 4:16 P.M.
Boston University, School of Medicine
Boston, Massachusetts

"How did it go?" Matt asked.

"We found all the connections we could want to Hershey's life inside 'Death Orgy,' " Leigh answered as she strode into the lab. "Tucker took us into the game and it was . . ." Her mouth tightened as she searched for the correct word. ". . . enlightening."

Matt caught her arm when she would have kept walking. "It upset you."

"It certainly disturbed and disgusted me. The thought that other human beings play realistic games like this for sport makes me lose a little faith in the purity of the human spirit."

"It was that bad?"

"It was an absolute horror. Chainsaw beheadings, crushed skulls, disembowelments, burning victims alive, complete with screams of agony in full surround sound . . ." She shook her head as if to clear it. "I just can't wrap my mind around it. This wasn't going after 'Dawn of the Dead' zombies or alien creatures—something that's clearly not based in reality. This was killing innocent human beings in the most realistic and violent ways possible for fun."

"Can you ever wrap your head around violent death like that?"

"Actually, some of it I can. Some of it I have to. It's all part of understanding who I'm looking for. I understand some murders, even if I can't condone them for any reason. As a person, you understand the concept of killing for money or love or out of revenge even if you don't agree with it. But this . . ."

Matt's lips formed a grim line. "This is simply causing pain for the joy of seeing someone else suffer."

"Maybe I'm blowing this way out of proportion." Leigh pushed her hands into the pockets of her blazer, hunching her shoulders defensively. "I know no one actually dies in the game. It's a virtual world, and yet what kind of person could take pleasure in that? I came out of it feeling . . . dirty."

"I'm no psychologist, but to me it says something about the kind of people who'd get involved in that kind of gaming"

"I'm no expert either, but I agree." She glanced over at the remains, spread over the tables in the lab. "It really makes me want to kick some serious ass in this case. Tucker felt the same way. He hauled away all the equipment with promises of finding out the IP addresses of the other players in the game."

"Can he do that?"

"He says he can. An interesting thing though—when we were in the game, other players from the team started talking to us. Hershey was apparently someone called 'Thanatos' and the other players were asking where 'Orcus' was, because they had both been missing in action for some unknown period of time. Orcus might be our missing suspect."

"Thanatos and Orcus?"

"Yes. Those names aren't familiar to me." The expression on

Matt's face made her pause. "Are they to you?"

"Sure. Thanatos is from Greek mythology. He was the supernatural personification of Death. He was a daemon, a being somewhere between the frailty of man and the omnipotence of the gods. Orcus is from Roman mythology. He's the god of the Roman underworld and was known to torment souls in the afterlife. He's also the punisher of broken oaths."

Leigh stared at him incredulously. "How could you possibly know all that?"

"My mother loved literature and cultural mythology and shared that with me. See—I told you'd I'd come in handy."

She shrugged. "I'm not going to look that gift horse in the mouth. So, they both had names that personified those who ruled over death or represented it in the game. Lovely."

"Not so much." He gave her arm a tug, leading her toward the gurneys and the remains they held. "Let me give you an overview. Want to take notes?"

Leigh pulled her notepad and pen from her blazer pocket and waved them at him. "Yes. I know the formal report is coming, but this helps me keep it in my head."

"Good enough for me. Guys, just leave that for now so Leigh can see everything."

They waited patiently as the students laid down the bones they were examining and stepped back from the table.

"We have the remains laid out in pairs as found in two of the three double graves." Matt moved over to his desk and picked up a photo and his notebook before returning to hand the photo to Leigh. It showed the clearing on the island in the salt marsh on the Essex coast, just as Leigh remembered it, but this photo had grave markers written on it in black ink. Matt pointed to the furthest table to the left, sitting slightly apart from the others. "We set up a labeling system to keep things straightforward in court. We're calling the burial sites 'A' and 'B.' 'A' was the first site we found, the one we excavated last Tuesday." He walked to the foot of the gurney. "This is 'A1-1,' the single set of remains that was found there, the bones that didn't match the beaver dam radius."

"Site 'B' then is the mass grave site?"

"Yes." Matt moved to the next pair of gurneys. "The photo you're holding shows the grave designations: 'B1,' 'B2,' and 'B3.' The remains closest to the surface are labeled as '-1'; the lower remains are designated '-2.' "

"Sounds straightforward."

"I know you wanted time since death, but we took the time to run the basics on these remains because this information is also crucial for victim identification. As you recall, I told you the 'A1' remains were that of a woman between forty and forty-five years of age. Now, we have some consistencies within the 'B' graves, but we also have some inconsistencies."

"Such as?"

"Do you want the long explanation or the short and to the point explanation?"

"You know I'm going to want the long explanation, but I have a feeling there's so much information I might get lost. Maybe we can circle back?"

"Sure. Okay, short and to the point. Ask questions as they come to you." He opened his notebook for reference. "In each of the 'B' graves were two sets of remains. In each of those graves, one set of remains is female and one set is male. With the exception of 'B2-2' who was African American, all the victims were North American white."

"What about sex?"

" 'A1-1,' 'B1-2,' 'B2-1,' and 'B3-2' were female. 'B1-1,' 'B2-2,' and 'B3-1' were male." He caught her eye. "By the way, we know now that the radius found in the beaver dam that started this whole case matches the 'B1-1' remains." He glanced back at his notes. "The approximate ages of the female victims in the graves were quite varied, even with the estimate range figured in: 'B1-2' was twenty to twenty-seven years of age and 'B2-1' was forty-five to fifty years of age. 'B3-2' is still unknown, but we'll hopefully be looking at her tomorrow. But from a rough estimate of the bone structure that I could see—the visible cranial sutures, for example—I'd place her at older than thirty-five years of age."

"Damn," Leigh murmured under her breath. "That makes MO kind of hard to work out. No consistent pattern."

"We do have one consistency within the females from both the 'A' and 'B' graves and Tracy Kingston."

"The signature," Leigh breathed.

"Yes. We were very careful to examine the ribs of all of the victims, especially the first to fourth ribs on the left side. Of special note is the fact that only the female victims bore this mark. To confirm the pattern we were looking for, Kiko took pictures of the anterior surface of the ribs and arranged them in anatomical order, compensating for physiological spacing."

Leigh's gaze shot to Kiko. "And?"

"All four of the women carried the 'Death' mark in the same approximate location. Some of the kerf marks were clearer than others, indicating the force used in carving them, but each defect was carved using the same smooth, single-edged blade."

"Excellent. That speaks to an organized and consistent method of death, even if victim selection was inconsistent."

"Victim selection for the male remains was a more consistent process," Matt said. "We noted at the site that one victim in each grave had a gunshot wound to the head; each of those victims was male."

Leigh's eyes narrowed speculatively at that information.

"By the way, we found a hollow point bullet in each of those two skulls. You can take those back with you for ballistics."

"Thanks. Any other consistencies with the males?"

"Yeah. Each of the victims was between fifteen and twenty-five years of age, although, honestly, I'd put them toward the lower end of that range."

Surprise lit Leigh's eyes. "That young?"

"Yes. Juka and Paul did a lot of this work, but I double checked their results and I'm one hundred percent in agreement with their analysis."

"That's going to narrow down the search parameters nicely." She met Matt's gaze, and his eyebrow cocked, almost in challenge. "Where are we on time since death?"

Matt smirked. "I knew that would be your next question."

"Then apparently I'm getting too predictable and need to start changing things up."

A strangled laugh escaped him. "No, that's okay. This whole case has us on our toes enough. I have some timeline estimates for you."

"You do? I didn't actually think you'd have anything this fast."

"I do." When his eyes met hers, there was no irritation or anger. "I can give you an initial range now, as long as you understand that given more time I can give you a more exact window."

"I'll take it." Leigh spoke so quickly she nearly cut him off, making his lips twitch in response.

"If you remember, I estimated the most recent set of remains at fourteen to sixteen months old, taking us back as far as late spring or early summer of last year," Matt stated. "Now the other two 'B' graves are both older burials than that. Over the last day, we've tried to move as quickly as we could to get you anything that would help narrow the range. We've done some macroscopic and microscopic testing and I've got some preliminary findings."

215

Leigh crooked her fingers in a "give it to me" gesture.

"I'd estimate that 'B1' is thirty-six to forty-eight months old and that 'B2' is eighteen to twenty-four months old, but I'm leaning closer to twenty-four than eighteen. The 'A1' grave I'd estimate at five years, give or take six months on either side. I can do better than—"

"Wait."

Matt stiffened at her tone, his expression wary. "What?"

"You said eighteen to twenty-four months?"

Matt closed the notebook with a soft snap. "For 'B2,' yes. I have somewhat more confidence in that estimate because . . ." His voice trailed off as her eyes narrowed. "What's wrong?"

"Do you remember I said that John Hershey was convicted of a B&E? Well, he did one year in the Connelly Youth Detention Center in Roslindale. Matt, he was essentially behind bars during the killing of the two victims in 'B2.' It's a youth detention center, but those kids are locked down. He didn't get out at any time or it would be in his record."

"But then he couldn't have participated in the killings," Paul stated. He glanced from Leigh to Matt and back again. "Are you suggesting that up until this killing the other suspect worked alone?"

"That's hard to believe," Leigh said. "Killers don't usually change up their MO that much. There can be subtle differences or escalation, but taking on a partner in crime at that point would be very unusual." She looked over to find Matt standing motionless by the gurney. "The pairs in the graves . . . does the method of death seem consistent?"

"Across the 'B' graves, yes. Extensive trauma for the female victims. Single gunshot to the head for the males."

"What about the 'A1' grave?"

"Similar trauma to the skeletal structure as the 'B' female victims. And if we recall the interment we interrupted at the 'C' burial site, we have another woman who died of traumatic injuries."

Paul pulled out a rolling lab chair to straddle it backwards, resting his arms along the top of the seat back. "So isn't the question really what are the differences between the graves? 'A1,' the oldest grave, is a single burial. Then we're roughly looking at one new grave a year, and all of those are double burials. Then this year's burial is a single victim again."

"So he murders once a year? Like it's some kind of annual ritual?" suggested Kiko.

"Why does it necessarily have to be something so formalized?" asked Juka. "Perhaps he picks his time to kill based on something as practical as knowing when the ground is soft enough to bury a body. He doesn't kill during the winter because then he would have to find a location to store the body."

"There was no sign that the bodies were stored and then moved," Matt said. He ran his hands distractedly through his hair. "Maybe there's something in the pattern of the victims. The women are of varying ages, so he's not selecting them based on that characteristic. The men are practically boys, some not even out of their teen years. Maybe he's selecting the men first and then—"

Suddenly Leigh understood the awful possibility, and it stopped her cold even as a soft gasp of surprise broke from her lips. She stood frozen, staring into space until Matt stepped into her field of vision.

"What?" he asked softly.

"What if—" she broke off, trying to organize her rapidly tumbling thoughts and explain her flash of inspiration coherently. "We've been going on the assumption since we saw that surveillance tape that we didn't just have one murderer, but two, working together."

"Right," Matt said slowly.

"You may have just hit on the key. All the male victims in the grave were young, barely out of their teenage years, if they were out of them at all. *Just like John Hershey.* Maybe you're right when you say he's picking the men first." She locked gazes with him. "But what if they weren't picked as victims? Not to start."

Matt's eyes suddenly went wide as understanding hit.

"Wait," Kiko said. "I'm not sure I'm following. What does John Hershey have to do with the other male victims? He was killed in his house. He was never buried."

"Follow along with me here," Leigh said. "Each of the 'B' graves has a male and female victim in it. The female was tortured to death, the male was a head shot to end his life quickly. The oldest and newest graves, 'A' and 'C,' only had the female victim, no male victim. But we know John Hershey helped with the abduction of Tracy Kingston and—we're assuming—with her death. And yet our remaining suspect was out on the island alone that day. He had no helper with him then."

"Follow the connection, guys," Matt said. "All of the male victims were young, *just like John Hershey.*"

Kiko's brows drew together. "Are you suggesting John Hershey wasn't his partner for all the killings? I mean he couldn't have been for one of them as he was in Juvie, but . . ." Fleeting expressions of surprise, astonishment, and horror flitted over her face in succession. "You're suggesting each time he had a *different* partner in the abduction, torturing, and killing of the girl, but when they went to the island to bury the female victim, he killed his teenaged partner and buried them together?" She looked to Leigh for confirmation.

"It makes sense doesn't it? We don't know why he's killing but for some reason he feels he needs a partner in crime. But after the murder is done, if he kills the partner, then there's no one to tie him to the murder, no eyewitness to the crime."

"Think about the orientation of the bodies in the graves as well," Matt suggested. "In two out of three of the graves, the male remains were found on top of the female remains as if they'd been added last. In the 'B2' grave, the remains were side-by-side so burial order isn't clear, but the female victim could have gone in first."

"That makes one wonder why the first burial in the 'A' grave-site was different," said Juka. "Perhaps he didn't find it satisfying as a solo act? Or maybe he found it too difficult to transport and bury the body on his own?"

Leigh shrugged. "Crimes aren't static acts. Criminals develop a style as they go and they escalate, both of which could explain why the oldest grave only has a single victim. The more important question is—why does the newest grave only have a single victim?"

"Maybe Hershey suspected that his death was imminent and bolted," Matt suggested. "Maybe he was supposed to come to the island and help to bury the body, but he suspected something and took off. That would explain why our suspect was still burying the body in daylight when we got there. Maybe his grand scheme was falling apart around him." He glanced over at Leigh. "We still don't know where the killings took place."

"But we may know how they met—'Death Orgy.' That seems to be the connection between them. And if this theory is correct and that's how he's been meeting his 'partners,' then there must be past players who have disappeared from the game. The other players or the group that runs the game could tell us that."

"But that's not going to help us find him," Kiko said.

"And who knows how desperate he'll be." Paul shook his head. "He might grab someone else."

"Unless he's confident we can't track him," Leigh suggested. "Then he may just lay low until next summer. He may consider this round done now. The female victim was killed, and now his male partner is dead. Not by the usual method, but this method actually speaks more of anger and revenge. A gunshot to the head is quick. You're no longer useful to me—bang: you're dead. But Hershey's death . . . that was more like the women. Drawn out and painful." She met Matt's eyes. "He wanted Hershey to pay."

Matt nodded in agreement. "There's no doubt Hershey suffered in the worst way possible."

At that moment, Leigh's cell phone rang. She pulled it out of her pocket. "Abbott. Tucker! What have you got for me?"

Four pairs of eyes stayed fixed on her as she listened. "You do? How fast can you track it down? No, I'll find a judge to sign the warrant, just find me someone at those companies to talk to. Right." She hung up and turned to the team. "Rob Tucker says he's on the trail of Orcus." The smile that curved her lips was triumphant. "He's picked up the scent. We're closing in on him."

CHAPTER TWENTY-FOUR:
YELLOW GRUB

Yellow Grub: Clinostomum marginatum, a common fish parasite. Through the course of its life cycle, the Yellow Grub uses snails, fish, and herons as hosts as it moves from egg to larva to adult flatworm.

Monday, 10:19 A.M.
Essex Detective Unit
Salem, Massachusetts

Leigh shifted restlessly in her chair, checking her wristwatch for the fourth time in ten minutes.

What was taking so long?

She knew Tucker was working as fast as he could, but she was getting impatient. She didn't want to sit in her cubicle. She needed to *do* something.

The tip of her pen tapped in a rapid staccato against her paper-strewn desk as she surveyed the flurry of forms spread out in front of her. She picked up the original death investigation form, reviewing the scant details she'd noted about the single bone that began their journey. A week ago, they'd had so little to go on, but Matt and his team had led them to the brink of discovery.

"Now, if Tucker would only call me back . . ." she muttered under her breath.

Tucking a loose strand of hair behind her ear, she bent over the paperwork once more. She'd go over it again. Maybe she missed something; something that could be the clue they were looking for—

"Hey, Abbott! You there?"

"Right here." Leigh got to her feet, rising above her divider to see Riley striding toward her through the cubicles.

"This just came for you." He extended a standard, slim white business envelope.

"Came how?"

"Same day rush courier. It was just dropped off at the front desk. Charlotte flagged me down as I was going by and asked me to bring it to you." He held it to his ear and gave it a brief shake. "It sounds like there's something in it."

The back of Leigh's neck prickled with alarm. "Put it down."

Riley looked puzzled, but promptly set it down.

Bending, Leigh rummaged through the messenger bag beside her desk and pulled out a pair of latex gloves. Riley's eyebrows shot straight up but he remained silent.

After gloving, Leigh examined the envelope. The address was neatly laser-printed directly onto the securely sealed envelope. Then she read the return address and swore softly. "Do we know who delivered this?"

Riley nodded. "You know Charlotte. Nothing comes in here without a way to trace it. She's got the name of the company and the delivery boy."

"I have a feeling we're going to need that information. Look at the return address."

"One Schroeder Plaza, Boston." His brows drew together. "Why does that seem familiar?"

"Because it's Boston P.D. headquarters, that's why." Leigh ran her fingers over the envelope, feeling the outline of something solid inside. "I need a letter opener. Charlotte has one." She looked at him expectantly.

"Uh . . . right. How about I go get that for you?" He ran from the room and was back in less than a minute, a wickedly sharp letter opener clutched in his fist.

Leigh took it from him and slipped it under the edge of the envelope, neatly slicing it open before peering inside.

A single sheet of tri-folded paper lay inside; cradled in the folds of the letter were the tangled links of a silver chain. She laid a clean piece of paper on her desk and carefully tipped the envelope sideways. With a metallic slither, the necklace slid free to puddle on the paper. Leigh picked up the necklace in her gloved hands, letting the pendant fall free, straightening the links.

She heard Riley's sharp intake of breath.

The chain was blackened with dried blood.

Her gaze flicked up to meet his.

"Do you think this is from your guy?" he asked.

"I'd be willing to bet money on it." Hanging from the delicate silver chain was a silver Gothic cross, beautifully inlaid with onyx and overlaid with silver filigree. She turned it over to find the name *Harcourt Jewelers* inscribed on the back.

Leigh sealed the necklace in an evidence bag and set it aside. Then she carefully extracted the single piece of paper. As she unfolded it on the desk, Riley moved so he could read over her shoulder.

Trooper Abbott,

How does it feel to be the public face for your department's failure to find me? Or to even know that I was out there? All those women gone and not a single lead.

Failure can come in many forms. Being fired from the case would be the easiest one for you. The most painless.

Staying on the case will only bring you pain and misery. Be careful, or rather than leading the case, you'll be the next victim.

Have you ever noticed that sometimes it's the things that we don't suspect that can wound us mostly deeply? Reach into a jar of sea glass, for example, and you never know what you might find. If you're not careful, perhaps instead of all those softly rounded pieces, an unexpected sharp edge will pierce your flesh, perhaps to the bone.

Never assume something is as innocuous as it looks. That kind of mistake could get you killed.

Until we meet again, a little token to remember me by . . .

The letter was unsigned.

At first, all was silent in the bullpen. Then Leigh exploded. "Son of a bitch! That bastard knows where I live. He was in my yard."

Riley stared at her in confusion. "What? Who?"

Leigh shook the letter under Riley's nose for emphasis. "Our serial killer. He wrote this note."

"Well, I figured that." When Leigh whirled on him aggressively, Riley took a nervous half step backwards.

Leigh struggled to pull herself together. It wasn't Riley's fault that it was all snapping into place for her just now. "Sorry. It's been a tough week."

"No problem. What makes you think he was in your yard?"

"Several days ago, after shift, somebody hurled a rock through my kitchen window while I was making dinner. At the time I chalked it up to some teenaged punk pulling a prank." She rapped at the letter with her index finger, the paper snapping under each sharp blow. "But he's telling me here that he's the one who did it."

Riley searched the letter again. "How? I don't see that."

Leigh lay the letter back down on the desk and pointed to the third paragraph. "That's because no one is supposed to get it but me. My kitchen is at the back of my house. You can't even see it from the road. The only way that someone could throw a rock through that window in particular would be by standing in the yard that runs along the side of my house. The relevant point here is there were three Mason jars on my kitchen windowsill that were filled with the sea glass I've collected walking the beaches over the years. When the rock came through the window, it shattered one of the jars and spilled bits of broken jar and sea glass all over my floor."

"You didn't see anyone in your yard when you were inside? Before the rock hit?"

"No, I had my back to the window. But it's a narrow galley-style kitchen so I would have been clearly visible to anyone out there. I ran out to my yard right after, but he was already gone." She leaned back on the edge of her desk. "Clearly I was a bit rattled because I didn't think it through at the time. Had it truly been a random hit, no teenager would pick that window when the front windows are right on the street and would make for a much easier getaway. He went to the trouble of actually entering the yard. *It had to be him.* I've been in the public spotlight. All he had to do was follow me home from the Detective Unit."

"It makes sense, once you filled in the blanks."

"Any cop worth his salt should have been able to figure that one out. This isn't rocket science." She fixed him with an unblinking, icy stare. "Don't believe everything you hear, Riley. I'm a better detective than some people say."

Riley flushed bright red but had the courage to not look away. If she'd had the luxury of time, she might have felt sorry for him since he was clearly sensing a disconnect between what he'd been told and the flesh-and-blood woman who stood before him. But there was no time for such niceties now.

Riley's gaze dropped back to the letter. "He really doesn't like you."

"I don't think it's just me that he doesn't like. Look at how he treats his female victims—he doesn't like women in general. In fact, I bet he's insulted that a woman is leading this investigation." She tapped the letter again. "He's threatening me and insinuating what might happen to me if I stay on the case. He's trying to scare me off, trying to throw me off my game. It's not going to work."

Riley grinned with approval. "You know, Abbott, if you need any help on this one, I'd be willing to toss in some overtime for you. I know we've never worked together but it's a big case, so if you need a hand . . ."

"Thanks for the offer. I'll keep it in mind. Due to the expanding scope of the case, Harper's going to be putting together a task force in the next couple of days, so maybe there might be a place for you there." She glanced down at the letter. "Actually, you could do something for me. I'd like Kepler to see this. Can you see if he's in his office?"

Riley grinned at her. "Sure."

Leigh watched him jog from the bullpen, a pleased smile curving her lips. Perhaps there was a kindred spirit in this room after all.

As she sealed the letter and envelope in an evidence bag, she considered her new evidence. Everything from the generic envelope to the plain paper to the laser-printed ink could be found at any big box office supply store by the gross, so they were unlikely to generate any new information there. But while the necklace might not point directly to the killer, it definitely would help in the identification of one of the missing victims.

Every step forward was a step in the right direction.

She gave a small start when her phone rang. Picking it up, she checked the caller ID. *Finally.* "Tucker, what have you got for me?"

Chapter Twenty-Five:
Marsh Hawk

Marsh Hawk: Circus cyaneus, also called the Northern Harrier, is a raptor that flies close to the ground over marsh and grasslands, hunting for small rodents, fish, and amphibians.

Monday, 1:03 P.M.
Boston University, School of Medicine
Boston, Massachusetts

Dodging pedestrians, Matt hurried down the sidewalk, a hot coffee clutched in one hand. He glanced at his watch, wondering once again how long it could possibly take to get a warrant. Agitation made him pick up his pace as he cut through Boston University's Medical Campus Park and past the few lunchtime stragglers still sitting at the picnic tables under a spreading ash tree.

After a morning spent in Rowe's lab examining the last two victims and still with no word from Leigh, Matt gave himself fifteen minutes to run down the street for coffee, some fresh air, and a chance to stretch his legs. The suspense was killing him. They were so close; it felt as if they were standing at the edge of a precipice, just one step away from free-falling toward either glory or certain death.

When Leigh's ringtone finally sounded, he didn't even take the time to utter a greeting. "How are we doing on the warrant?"

"Hello to you too," Leigh said. "I'm at the Essex Courthouse. Justice Connelly is in chambers right now, but his admin promised that I can get twenty minutes with him as soon as they're done."

He walked over to a nearby vacant bench, dropping into it and setting the coffee beside him. "You have the address? You're sure?"

"Yes. Tucker worked damned hard yesterday, tracking down the Internet service provider. We served the warrant on them this morning and that lead us directly to him." Excitement made Leigh's words come quickly. "We've got a name, Matt. We've got *his* name."

Matt fist pumped the air and grinned at the students who stared at him curiously. "Finally. Who is he?"

"Neil Bradford. He has no record and we've never looked at him before for any reason. But he has both a motorcycle and motorboat registered in his name."

"Bingo," Matt said. "We know he's got both. Where does he live?"

"Gloucester. He works in town as part of the maintenance staff at the Riverdale Community Health Center."

"You're going there?"

"Yes. I've got the Special Tactical Operations Team—STOP— standing by. After what happened at the Hershey house there's no way I'm going in there without STOP, and Detective Lieutenant Harper is one hundred percent behind me. Sergeant Kepler also wanted in on the search, so he'll be there too." She paused for several seconds, long enough to quench his euphoria and raise the hair on the back of his neck. "There's something else. Something that makes me think that tactical backup would be a good idea."

"What's wrong? What's happened?"

"I'm pretty sure Bradford's been watching me."

"What?" When she remained silent for a fraction of a second too long, Matt pressed again. "What's going on, Leigh? Don't keep me in the dark on this. I'd like to think you'd tell me even if it wasn't case-related."

"It's nice to know I've got you standing behind me."

"Then tell me what happened."

"Remember the window? I was chalking that up to a teenage prank until I got a package at work this morning."

"What kind of package?"

"A letter and a blood-stained necklace, likely from one of the victims. The letter was unsigned, but was clearly from our killer. He warned me off the case and made reference to being in my yard that night. It would certainly be consistent with his psych profile. I mean, inflicting terror is his goal, right?"

Matt sat frozen in place, every instinct screaming that she was putting herself directly in harm's way. "Damn it, Leigh. I don't like this. He could have you in his sights right now and you're just going to stroll right up to his front door?"

"He's not going to stop me from doing my job. That's exactly what he wants, but it's not going to happen. I'm taking the necessary precautions."

"He's a dangerous man."

"I'm taking his threat seriously. We'll be heading out just as soon as the warrant is signed," Leigh continued. "I'm throwing the net wide and asking the judge for the warrant to cover all three-and-a-half acres of land and all of the associated outbuildings, including a detached garage and a boathouse. Considering we're looking for the kill room as well as the weapons used on the victims, I'm confident he'll sign it as is. If we bring Bradford in, Kepler will join me in the interview room. We want to nail this thing shut, and, truthfully, I could use his experience on this one. There's no room for any mistakes."

Matt weighed his options quickly, finally going with his gut.

"I'd like to come with you."

When Leigh finally spoke, her voice was full of resignation. "Matt, that's not a good idea. I should never have gotten you involved at the Hershey house." She sighed. "Is this because of Bradford's interest in me?"

"No, you've got more than enough protection if he decides to go after you today. You've got a whole SWAT team and an experienced cop on hand to watch your back. I'm not asking to go in with you, guns blazing. I know you can't have me underfoot for that."

"You do realize you're making my point for me," she said wryly.

Matt raised his fist to rap it softly against his forehead in frustration. When he finally spoke, it was calmly and with care, but he suspected he wasn't doing a good job disguising his unraveling patience. "I'd like to be there so I can evaluate the evidence as it pertains to our victims if you find the kill room. And then there's—"

"Time-out." There was a bone-deep exhaustion in her voice as she cut him off.

The silence dragged on for several seconds, but he didn't dare interrupt it. He knew she was wavering and he needed her to decide in his favor. He'd go crazy if he had to sit in the lab, waiting for word of the raid.

"What about that examination with Rowe?" she finally asked. "I thought it was supposed to happen today?"

"Already done. He said he'd send you a report, but our findings were totally in line with what we've seen and identified in our skeletonized victims. I'll tell you all about it later when you're not so squeezed for time. I'm clear for the rest of the day. I won't even get out of the car until you give the okay."

A long gusty sigh came down the line, and he knew he had her. "All right, but you have to get up here. As soon as this warrant comes through, we're moving out. If you can get to the Detective Unit before we go, then you can come with me. But you will stay in the car," she insisted, "until I give the all clear."

"Done," Matt said quickly. "I'm leaving now. I'll call you when I get into town and you can tell me where to meet you. See you in about forty-five." He ended the call abruptly.

He grabbed his coffee and shot to his feet, heading for East Concord Street and the parking lot where he'd left his SUV. He'd call the lab and let them know the change in plans. But first, he had a little side trip to make. If they were going to walk up to Bradford's front door, Matt needed to stop by his own house first.

Monday, 3:16 P.M.
Bradford residence
Gloucester, Massachusetts

Matt impatiently drummed his fingers on his knee as he sat in the passenger seat of Leigh's Crown Vic and refrained from checking his watch for the third time in under five minutes. Looking up at the house, he scanned it for signs of movement.

Nothing.

The house looked innocuous—it was a traditional New England two-story clapboard, perhaps a little shabby and in need of minor repairs, but it certainly didn't look like a place of misery and death.

It had been over forty-five minutes since Leigh, Sergeant Kepler, and a team of eight tactical officers had swarmed the house and grounds. And still Matt waited for news.

After what seemed like an eternity, the tactical team poured from the front door, jogging toward the van parked down the street. Leigh appeared on the front porch behind them.

He knew immediately from the set of her shoulders that they'd failed.

She strode down the driveway, her fists clenched and her body tight, reaching the Crown Vic just as the STOP van pulled away from the curb, leaving the scene. Opening the back door, she pulled off her bullet-proof vest, tossing it with more force than required onto the back seat.

She ducked her head below the roof of the car to peer inside. "We've got nothing. Bradford's not on scene and we didn't even find the kill room."

"Nothing new at all from the search?"

"Well, no . . . not exactly. There's a boat moored down the hill on the river that Kepler is checking out right now. At least that's something. But the house is clear and so are all the outbuildings."

"The motorcycle?"

"Not here." Her fist came down hard on the roof of the car. "Goddamn it! I was so sure this was it." She reached in to grab her blazer off the back seat, shrugging into it. "I've called in Crime Scene Services to go over the house anyway."

"Maybe they'll find something. Leigh, you did the best you could."

"Tell that to the next vic he grabs if we don't catch him." She tipped her head down to rest it briefly against the edge of the doorframe before looking up to meet his eyes. "I want to go through the house again, even though I don't think those women were ever there. Want to come? Two pairs of eyes are better than one."

Matt was already climbing out of the car before she could change her mind. "Let's do it."

Monday, 3:50 P.M.
Bradford residence
Gloucester, Massachusetts

Sunlight sparkled on undulating dark blue water as Matt and Leigh trudged down the gravel path leading to the boathouse and dock at the river's edge. In the distance, rows of boats bobbed in neat lines at the Heron Way Marina. The sound of a motor ripped through the quiet, and suddenly a white boat speared into the water, the roar of its engine rising and then fading off into the distance.

Sergeant Kepler had left thirty minutes before and now two state troopers kept watch in Leigh's unmarked car as they waited for Crime Scene Services to arrive. Together, Matt and Leigh had done a second sweep of the house, leaving no corner unchecked. The only new discovery was a computer in the den; Leigh had already called Rob Tucker in to go over it with a fine-toothed comb.

"There she is." Matt pointed to the sleek white boat moored to the short, battered plank dock. "Pretty nice. Not new, but in mint condition."

"A lot of people who have lived by the sea all their lives consider their boat to be more important than their car. It's their ticket to freedom or to life out on the water."

Matt glanced sideways at her. "I think you were right the first time—it's his ticket to freedom. And his transportation for the bodies."

"I wonder if Bradford's had it since the first killing."

"That would be my guess," Matt said. "He had to have something to get him out there to bury his first victim. It's easier to get to the burial site by boat than over land. From here on the Annisquam, it's a straight shot north to go upriver and right out into open water. And did you notice the lamp?" He pointed at the silver halogen spotlight attached to the forward tip of the boat's handrail. "To light his way in the dark."

Leigh nodded. "Yeah, I spotted that little feature."

They stepped from the path onto the wooden dock, their boots thudding against the worn, weathered wood as they moved to stand near the stern. They both peered in to scan the interior.

Mud and bits of marsh grass smeared the deck and dirty fingerprints marked the dash.

"Just as I thought. He hasn't had time to clean it out." Leigh pointed toward the bow. "Kepler said it was a cuddy with a closed cabin. If there are going to be any traces of blood, skin, or hair, I'll bet that's where we'll find them. We'll get the techs out here as soon as they arrive." Her phone rang from inside her blazer pocket. "Sorry. Excuse me for a minute." She stepped away to take the call.

Matt wandered to the end of the dock to look out at the houses opposite, easily five hundred feet across the Annisquam. This really was an ideal place for a secret life: shielded by leafy trees in the summer with a driveway that curved around the back of the house, bodies could easily be moved on and off the property.

He turned around to consider the house up the hill. If he was loading the boat at night, where was he holding and killing the girls? The house had been checked twice. The garage had been cleared. They hadn't personally examined the boathouse yet, but STOP had reported it empty and Kepler had confirmed.

Where was the kill room? Something simply didn't add up.

An exclamation from Leigh had him spinning toward her. She was standing with her back to him, talking animatedly. As soon as she hung up, she turned to him, smiling brilliantly.

"What happened?" he asked.

"They just picked up Bradford."

"Whoa. What happened?"

"We've got a statewide APB out on his motorcycle and a sharp-eyed trooper in an unmarked car spotted a man with that distinctive helmet on a bike going south on Highway 128 outside of Waltham. He called it in and followed at a safe distance so he wasn't spotted. Once there was enough support, they boxed him in and pulled him over." She grinned at him.

"They've got him in custody and are bringing him to Salem for questioning."

"He was out by Waltham? Do you think he was going south, trying to leave the state?"

"Possibly. Or maybe he was heading to Logan to get a flight out of Boston. Maybe things were getting a little too hot for him here."

"I guess it doesn't matter because we've got him." Relieved laughter unexpectedly burst from Matt. "Wow . . . could this really be the end of the case?"

"If we're very lucky. We've got him in custody. Now the crucial thing is to keep him there because he'll be a flight risk."

"Then we need to find his kill room to really nail him. He's not going to just hand it to us."

"No, not a chance of that," she agreed.

"Let's take a look at the boathouse then," Matt suggested. "There has to be a place where he's holding and killing these women. It's not in the house. It's not in the garage. By process of elimination, it has to be in the boathouse. It makes sense. He could bring the boat right into the boathouse to load the women on board."

"Fine with me. It's been cleared, but I won't believe it until I've checked it out for myself." She glanced at her watch. "I've got about half an hour before I need to be on the road back to Salem for the interview with Bradford."

They stepped off the dock and started toward the boathouse at the edge of the water.

"I think—" Matt froze as a faint, high-pitched squeak reached his ears. He reached out to grab Leigh's arm. "What was that?" he whispered.

They both looked around wildly—from the boathouse, to the boat, and back around to the house behind them.

No movement. No sound.

236

But what drew their attention hadn't come from the boathouse, the boat, or the house up the hill. It had come from their left.

They both swung around to face the sound, but all they could see was a grassy hilltop.

The sound had definitely been metallic and man-made.

They glanced at each other before moving forward in unison, climbing the hill in search of the source of the sound.

Then they saw it—the trench cut into the side of the hill. It was narrow, only a few feet across, and the sides and the back were grass covered.

Leigh went first, stepping into a short passageway behind a false front wall cut into the hill. The path angled steeply downwards, the walls of the passageway quickly rising above their heads with open sky still bright above them. Six feet in, the path abruptly veered right and Matt suddenly realized what they were looking at.

A doorway was carved into the side of the hill, with a weathered, scarred metal door hanging on ancient, rusty hinges. The metal sign riveted to it was still legible, even if faded. He'd never seen one in real life, but he remembered hearing about structures like this in school during history lessons about the Cold War.

The three yellow triangles arranged like fan blades on a black circle. Bright yellow block letters on a black background: "FALLOUT SHELTER."

It was an old underground fallout shelter from the 1950s, built when Americans feared the Soviets would attack them with nuclear weapons. When those along the East Coast were convinced they would be the first to die.

The door was slightly ajar.

Darkness beckoned from within.

Chapter Twenty-Six:
Crab Burrow

Crab Burrow: A sand-covered burrow, usually found at the border of tidal creeks; it contains an air bubble that allows the crab to breathe while submerged at high tide.

Monday, 4:02 P.M.
Bradford residence
Gloucester, Massachusetts

Leigh's hand clamped over Matt's wrist, squeezing tight. "They didn't find this when they searched the property," she breathed. "The way it's built into the side of the hill with the grass growing over the entrance, you wouldn't see it unless you were literally standing right in front of it. You could walk right past it and never see the entrance because it blends into the hillside. And it certainly wasn't on any of the maps."

"This thing was probably built in the nineteen-fifties. I bet there was no need for a permit back then, so there's no record of it. Leigh, think about how soundproof a structure like this would be." Matt pointed at a series of horizontal wooden slats just to the left of the door. "Except for ventilation so the occupants don't die of oxygen deprivation, this place was built to be able to withstand a nuclear holocaust. The walls could easily be several feet thick." Grasping her left hand tightly, he started to pull her forward. "Let's take a look."

"Wait." She tugged him back. "We need to do this by the

book. We can't risk contaminating anything. Our entire case could rest on what we find in this room. I go first." Matt gathered himself to argue. "I go first," she repeated insistently, "and we only go in a few feet. I know you're anxious to get in and start matching tools, but you need to be patient." She poked his chest with an index finger for emphasis. "We do this right." She pulled her gun from its holster, the familiar weight comforting in her grip.

"You think we need that? Bradford's already in custody."

"In this case I'm going to go with 'better safe than sorry.' I don't trust anything when it comes to this case."

"Fair enough." He held out his hand for her to precede him. "Ladies . . . uh . . . officers first."

She gave him a pointed look, but moved past to stand in front of the door. Bracing her free hand against the cool, weathered metal, she gave it a hard push. It gave way with a low grind of disused steel hinges. The door swung wide to *clang* against something metallic behind it before bouncing back slightly.

Light flooded into the darkness inside.

They stood motionless for several heartbeats, waiting for some sign of movement from within the room. But there was only the sound of the wind blowing through the treetops around the house and the mournful cry of a seagull out over the open water.

Leaning forward slightly, Leigh peered into the space, now illuminated slightly by daylight spilling through the doorway.

In the shadows, she could see part of the top of a metal table and a single leg. A dark metal chain dangled from the table to the floor. She squinted, trying to see it better. Was that rust?

Her mouth went dry.

Not rust. Blood.

They'd found the kill room.

Taking a deep breath, Leigh stepped into the dim space slowly, cautiously, her eyes adjusting to the low light. The main area of the shelter appeared to be a single large room. The metal table sat in the middle, the top dark with dried blood. A wooden worktable covered with bloody rags and weapons stood against the far wall near a tall roll of plastic sheeting that leaned into the corner. There was a blood-splattered sink in the opposite corner beside shelves stacked with canned goods and wooden crates. One wall held a collage of newspaper clippings. Two doorways to the right opened into darkness.

The air inside the shelter was damp and cool but Leigh knew the shiver running along her spine was due to more than the sudden drop in temperature. The hair along the back of her neck rose in response to something unseen but still sensed. Eyes darting, she searched the shadows to find nothing tangible to explain her sudden nervousness. Perhaps it was just a response to the atmosphere inside the shelter—the air was thick and stale, almost wet, but heavy with the metallic smell of dried blood, acrid sweat, and human waste.

It was the scent of fear.

She took another two steps inside, sensing Matt's presence close behind her when everything suddenly went to hell.

With an ear-piercing shriek followed by a heavy *clang*, the door slammed shut, trapping them in suffocating darkness. Behind her, Leigh heard a hard blow and a ragged exhalation from Matt, followed by the sound of a body falling heavily to the floor.

Leigh spun toward the door ready to shoot at anything she could see. But all she could sense was darkness and silence. She cursed herself for leaving her flashlight in her car.

What just happened? Who else was in here?

Clearly, Matt was down. Was he unconscious? *Was he dead?*

For a moment, Leigh heard only the roar of her heart pounding in her ears as adrenaline flooded her system. Then she heard a low satisfied chuckle to her left. Gooseflesh rose as if an icy finger stroked over her skin.

Leigh knew that laugh. The last time she'd heard it, it had floated over a fence as the man she pursued had evaded capture. She knew with certainty that the man in custody was not Neil Bradford. Neil Bradford was here with her in the dark.

She swung toward the sound, but it faded into the blackness. She pulled her cell phone out of her jacket pocket and, shielding the screen to block the light, started to call for backup.

No bars. Her cell phone wasn't getting a signal so far inside the fallout shelter.

There would be no backup. They were on their own.

She dropped to a crouch and quickly jammed the useless phone back into her pocket. Still clutching her gun in her fist, she reached out with her left hand in the direction she'd heard Matt fall. Her fingers touched flannel. *His shoulder.* She shook him hard, but he didn't respond. She reached over further, found his hair. Moving her fingers toward his face, she felt the wetness of blood. She jerked her hand back from the wound.

If he was dead, he was beyond her help, but she wouldn't even consider that. It was up to her to protect him.

She had to save them both, trapped in the dark with a man who'd proven time and again that life meant nothing to him and human suffering was a thing to savor. The words from his letter echoed in her head—*Be careful, or rather than leading the case, you'll be the next victim.*

She crouched down low, making herself as small a target as possible. "I know you're here, Bradford," she called out.

Another low laugh. "Very good, Trooper Abbott. I knew even you'd figure it out eventually."

Even though Leigh expected to hear his voice, she still flinched at the venomous tone. She forced her whirling thoughts to settle. *Focus.*

241

She looked back toward the door—no light was visible around the edges. Then she realized she could see faint horizontal lines in the wall to the right. *The ventilation system.* Using it to mark her orientation, she concentrated hard, mentally going over the room as she had seen it in that quick flash of dim light before everything went dark.

Metal table with restraints. Wooden crates. Shelving. Worktable . . .

There were weapons on that worktable. She had her gun, but she didn't have a backup weapon. And if this came down to hand-to-hand fighting, an extra weapon for close-quarter use would come in handy. She had no idea what weapons Bradford might have. So far, he hadn't tried to shoot her, but he owned a gun. And with all these sharp implements at hand, he must have something. The question was . . . what?

Staying low, she started to inch toward the far wall.

"I told you to stay away." The taunting voice floated toward her in the dark. "I told you what would happen to you if you kept going." The voice went cold and flat. "You were warned."

The sudden absence of all emotion in Bradford's voice gave Leigh pause, solidifying her gut instinct that he wasn't going to think twice about killing her the moment she was in reach. If she couldn't subdue him, it was going to be a fight to the death.

She forced the fear down, knowing it distracted her, but her hands still shook. She continued across the room, crouched down, her left hand outstretched. She breathed a sigh of relief when her fingers touched the rough wood of the worktable.

She laid her gun on the floor in front of her and shimmied out of her blazer, stuffing it under the worktable before picking up her weapon again. She stretched out her hand, her fingers searching over the table.

She touched metal and closed her hand over it. She bit back a cry of pain, jerking her hand back as the razor sharp edge of a knife bit into the pads of her fingers. She clenched her hand into a fist, feeling the warm dampness of blood against her palm. Stretching her hand out again, she explored the weapon carefully—a knife: straight blade, wicked point, jagged serrations near the hilt. She ran her fingers over the handle and a small button depressed under pressure. A spring-loaded folding tactical blade. *Perfect.*

She picked up the knife and quickly closed it, bracing the back of the blade against her thigh, hearing the quiet *snick* as the blade folded into the handle and locked into position. She hesitated for a moment, unsure where to put the knife since neither her dress pants nor shirt had pockets. Inspiration hit, and she tucked it up the right sleeve of her shirt, under the cuff where a quick shake would have it sliding into her hand if she lost her gun, or she could pull it out with her left hand for a two-fisted approach.

Time to get him talking. She was helpless in the dark if she didn't know his location. But she knew with certainty this was risky for both of them. Bradford's voice gave away his location, but she would be giving hers away as well.

"Nice place you have here, Bradford." Her voice sounded suddenly loud in the silence, carrying more bravado than she felt. "I love what you've done with it."

"It suits my needs." The voice came from directly across the room and Leigh realized he must be further inside the shelter, beyond one of the two doorways that she had previously seen.

Keep him talking. "Let's talk about those needs, Bradford. Why did you torture those women?"

The laugh that answered her showered over her flesh like icy barbs. "You really don't understand, do you? You don't understand at all."

"Then explain it to me. I want to understand."

Closing her eyes against the near total darkness, Leigh tried to imagine the room again. Light would even the playing field and a switch would logically be located near the door. She started to inch back across the room, trying to avoid giving herself away.

"I wanted to influence them. I wanted to see if I could make them do something that even they would normally never do."

Leigh froze in place, confused by his words. "The women?"

Another laugh, this one full of derision. "Not the women. They were simply a means to an end."

Fury filled Leigh at his careless tone. She knew that he considered women to be beneath him, but the proof that the victims really hadn't mattered to him at all infuriated her. They were simply tools in his eyes.

"It was the men I tested." It was almost a hiss.

Pieces of the case, pieces that hadn't made sense before were starting to fit together in her head. As she crept further across the floor, the toe of her boot suddenly hit something solid and she stopped to feel what was in front of her. She caught Matt's scent, that now familiar hint of spice, just before her fingers touched his outstretched hand. Her gut clenched in fear again. He seemed so cold and he hadn't moved. But the door had to be close now and with it the hope of light. She moved to the right to avoid stepping on Matt, placing each foot carefully to avoid tripping, keeping her left hand outstretched.

She was rewarded seconds later with the cool metal door suddenly beneath her fingers. She ran her fingertips over the door, quickly moving past the frame. She ran her hand up the wall and quickly found a switch plate. *Bingo.*

As her fingers found the switch and she started to push it upwards, she had the brief thought that she didn't know where Bradford was. But it was already too late.

Leigh swung around, gun extended as light flooded the space, but Bradford was already in mid-air. She had a brief glimpse of angry blue eyes in a thin, pale face before he hit her mid-body, sending her sprawling to the ground under the ventilation unit, her gun flying from her hand and sliding under the wooden shelves against the far wall. Air whooshed from her lungs as she was pinned to the floor by his weight. She wedged her hands between them and shoved as she rolled left, throwing him off.

She rolled to her feet, crouching in a defensive stance just as Bradford got up. They eyed each other, well out of reach, both breathing hard. Her gun was gone, but his hands were empty too. Leigh kept the knife hidden. She wanted the aspect of surprise in close quarters. By the time he spotted the weapon, it had to be too late for him.

She had to keep him talking, keep him distracted. "So you were testing the men? Why?"

His smile was one of pure malice as he rocked on the balls of his feet. "I chose them because they were weak. Then I molded them to my will. And in the end, they all killed for me." His eyes narrowed, dark anger filling his face. "Except one."

And there it was—the lever she could use to keep him off balance. "John kind of messed it up for you, didn't he? Was he just not good enough?" Leigh taunted. "You picked badly, Bradford. You were the one in control. You're the one who's responsible for your own failure."

As Bradford bared his teeth and opened his mouth to respond, Leigh took advantage of his momentary distraction, launching smoothly into a low kick, moving between his braced legs to strike the inside of his left knee. The knee buckled and he went down hard, landing on the blood-stained floor only inches away from Matt's head.

Leigh firmly planted her left foot and drove her right knee into his solar plexus, hearing his breath forced from his body by the blow. But Bradford recovered quickly, grabbing her knee and twisting her off balance. Leigh tumbled hard to the floor, rolling away from his grasping hands into the leg of the worktable.

An ice pick rolled off the table, just grazing her hip.

Leigh grasped the pick as she scrambled to her feet, sizing up her opponent. He was tall and lanky with short hair, wearing worn jeans and a faded black sweatshirt. He didn't look very strong, but he moved surprisingly fast. And the light of insanity in his eyes made him look terrifyingly reckless.

Bradford was shifting his weight from foot to foot before her, his eyes fixed on the ice pick. Then he charged, head down, ramming into her stomach. Leigh managed to partially step aside, but the blow was still brutal. As the air left her lungs, she brought the ice pick down, feeling it sink cleanly into the flesh of his shoulder, hearing his roar of pain. But he wrapped his arms around her, carrying her down with him to the floor as the ice pick spun away across the floor.

Leigh fought free, then took advantage of his face-down position to get her knee into the small of his back before punching him in the kidney. Bradford reached over his shoulder to grab her arm, using her inertia from the next punch and her already unbalanced position to yank her over his shoulder.

With a crash, she landed against the legs of the metal table, unable to stifle a small cry of pain. Struggling to her feet, she staggered upright just in time to see his right fist coming toward her face. He clipped her hard on the lower jaw and she staggered backwards, arms outstretched. She almost had her balance but then one last step had her tripping over something on the floor.

Her last thought as she fell backwards was *Matt . . .*

Then pain exploded in her head and everything went black.

Leigh blinked rapidly in the bright light, momentarily stunned. Then a dark shape eclipsed the light. She forced herself to focus on him. *Bradford.*

He grinned at her. "Comfortable, Trooper Abbott?"

Leigh suddenly became aware of her body. She was flat on the table and when she tried to sit up, she found herself strapped down. Frantically turning her head, she found her wrists bound by bloody chains. More restraints bound her ankles. She was gagged, a length of material jammed brutally between her teeth and tied tightly behind her head.

She struggled against the chains, but while there was some play in them, the ends were secured firmly. Closing her eyes, she pictured the table and the attached chains as they'd looked from the doorway. The chains were bolted under the tabletop, near her shoulders. Her arms had about six inches of play up or down the table from breast to just above her shoulder, but she couldn't lift her hands more than an inch off the table. She pulled against her restraints again, trying to free her wrists, but only succeeded in digging her own handcuffs into the small of her back as she struggled. Craning her neck at a painfully awkward angle, she tried to look for Matt. She finally found him, still motionless by the door.

"You should stop struggling," Bradford said mildly. "You're mine now." He grinned. "I always let the others take the lead when it came to killing. But this might be fun. Now I get to try it." He held up a Walther P22 pistol, molded of dark carbon fiber except for the bright nickel slide on top. *The gun Matt saw . . .* Grinning, he rubbed the barrel against her cheek. "I could have just shot you in the dark, but what would be the fun in that? That would end the game too quickly. This way we get to play together for a while. That will be much more satisfying." His eyes suddenly filled with fury. "That's the least you owe me after spoiling my fun with John. I was just getting started. You made me stop much too quickly." He took a deep breath, and gained control of his anger. Leaning forward, he tapped the gun lightly against her gag. "Too bad I can't take this off you, but we wouldn't want the neighbors to hear. We never want the neighbors to hear." He smiled again, and pleasure lit his eyes with an almost unearthly glow.

Neighbors? *Not likely,* she thought, then wondered about the Crime Scene techs. *Had they arrived and would they be able to hear anything from inside the bunker?* Leigh futilely pulled against the restraints again and tried to speak through the gag, but all that came out was a low, unintelligible gurgle.

"I like your spirit, Trooper Abbott." He cocked his head to look at her, considering. "But maybe I should call you 'Leigh.' We're going to come to know each other very well, so we shouldn't stand on formality. If you're as good as some of the other girls, we're going to play for hours. Maybe even longer. So, I'll call you Leigh. And you can call me Neil." Suddenly he laughed, a sound full of cruelty and sadism. "Or you could if I took off the gag." He leaned forward, his breath rushing hot over her face, making her lip curl with distaste. "Which I won't."

He straightened and casually walked around the table. "No one will find you, you know. The police from earlier are gone. And they never found this place anyway. I heard you say that techs are coming, but we're practically invisible in here. You wouldn't have found me if I didn't want you to. If anyone else comes by, we'll just be very, very quiet." Her expression went mutinous and he leaned in low again. "You *will* be quiet," he insisted, suddenly pivoting to point the gun directly at Matt's head. "Or he will die. I have no problem with killing him." He curled his lip. "He's road kill, totally disposable. And I have a silencer, so they won't even hear the shot." He spun back to look at her with half-wild eyes. "But you will. You'll hear him die."

Leigh latched on to his words with a frenzied hope. *"You'll hear him die." Maybe Matt was still alive.* Then harsh reality set in, hope dying away to leave her even emptier than before— Matt was still on the floor by the door; he hadn't moved. If he was alive, Bradford would have tied him up. He was simply using Matt as leverage to ensure her cooperation.

She was going to die with him.

"Now . . ." Bradford wandered over to the worktable. "Where to begin? So many choices . . . I could break both your arms to start like John did with the last one, but that took too much of the fight out of her. I like the fight." He sounded thoughtful, like a man who was serious about his work. The man was a psychopath, and she was completely at his mercy.

While his back was turned, Leigh frantically scooted to one edge of the table, extending her left arm as far as it could go so that she could drop her right arm off the edge of the table. Giving her arm as much of a shake as she could manage, she felt the folded knife in her sleeve shift and then stop, butting up against the restraints. *Damn it, come on!* She shook again, hard, and the knife started to slip. It slid out of her sleeve, skittering off the outside of the chain and she desperately caught it, nearly losing it as the chain redirected the forward motion almost out of her grasp.

"Ah, yes," she heard him say, almost reverently. "Let's start with this one."

Breathing a desperate sigh of relief, she clenched the knife in her fist and shifted back to the middle of the table, positioning her right hand down as close to her waist as she could manage until the chain tore painfully into the skin at her wrist. She buried her fist against her side hoping that would keep him from spotting the knife. She continued to rock back and forth, so when he turned back, it simply looked like she was still struggling against the restraints.

"Fighting won't help, you know," he stated. Her eyes fixed in horror at the knife in his hands. The five-inch blade was razor sharp and dark with old blood. He held the knife up, turning it back and forth, admiring the curved blade in the light. "This is one of my favorites. I didn't have it for John, so I had to make do." He looked down at her, and his eyes were full of malicious glee. "This is my best skinning knife. It's so sharp, you'll hardly feel it." He started to laugh. "Well, maybe only for the first second or two."

Terror swept through Leigh and the palm that clutched the switchblade went damp. She forced herself to stay calm, knowing she'd only have one chance.

"Let's give it a try shall we? This will give you insight into what my victims suffered that you'd never get otherwise. Think of it as a chance to share what they experienced. You said you wanted to understand." His voice was an intimate hiss, as if he was sharing a secret with her.

As he leaned over her, his fingers moving to the buttons of her shirt, Leigh pulled her hand away from her side, turning it over and twisting the knife hidden in the palm of her hand to find the release button. The blade snapped into position with a sharp *click*. Thrusting upwards, she buried the knife in his forearm, feeling it thrust cleanly through flesh, then stutter as the serrated edge of the blade dragged over bone. Bradford gave a scream of agony, pulling desperately away from the knife, his own knife landing lengthwise on her chest and then rolling sideways to clatter onto the table.

Suddenly the explosion of a gunshot filled the room. Leigh jerked away in shock as Bradford gave another scream and dropped to the floor.

Craning her neck to see behind her, Leigh looked around frantically, her eyes finally alighting on Matt as he rose shakily from the floor, his Glock gripped tight in one hand. He held onto the edge of the table as he steadied himself. Rivulets of blood ran over his right temple and ear and dripped down his neck to stain the collar of his shirt. He was ashen and covered in blood, but he was alive. Bradford must have been too quick when checking to make sure he was dead.

Matt circled the table, his Glock fixed steadily on Bradford, who writhed on the floor, whimpering pathetically and clutching his ruined knee. "For someone who likes to dish out pain, you certainly can't take it." He set his boot down on Bradford's shin and Bradford howled at the pressure. "Not that you're in any shape to run, but I'm just going to make sure you stay down." He twisted to look at Leigh. "You wanted him taken alive so I shot him in the knee from under the table. We have to restrain him. Where are your cuffs?"

Leigh managed to gurgle from behind the gag.

He turned and squinted at her as if trying to focus on her face, his gaze sharpening when he saw the gag. "Sorry, couldn't see that from the floor." Keeping constant pressure on Bradford's leg, he set the Glock down by her shoulder, struggling with the knot behind her head as his unsteady fingers kept fumbling. "Son of a bitch, this is tight." He eyed the bloody knife still clutched in her fist, before reaching across her to pull it from her grasp. When her hand stayed in a death grip around the handle, he closed his fingers over hers, stroking lightly. "Leigh, you can let go now. It's safe." But she still didn't release the blade. "Leigh!" She blinked once, focusing on his face. He gentled his voice. "I need you to let go of the knife."

Her fingers instantly loosened and he pulled it from her grip. He stared warily at the bloody blade and then bent out of Leigh's line of sight. After a few seconds, he straightened. "I'm sure you don't want his blood smeared on you, so I wiped it off on his sweatshirt," he explained, grinning, a flash of white teeth in a blood-streaked face. "Sorry, I probably shouldn't be enjoying this, but a tiny part of me is. Don't worry, it'll pass. Probably around the time my head stops throbbing." He bent over Leigh, deftly sliding the blade in between her cheek and the gag, careful to keep the serrated backside of the knife below her jaw to avoid cutting her. It only took gentle pressure and the cloth sliced apart cleanly over the razor-sharp blade.

Matt set the knife down beside his gun and pulled the gag from between her teeth.

Leigh made a small sound of relief. "Thanks." She spit out bits of thread and lint, glancing at the blood-stained length of material that Matt held. She winced. "I don't want to know what was on that."

Matt carelessly tossed it onto the worktable against the back wall. "Good thought." He glanced down again, but Bradford hadn't moved even an inch under his boot. "Cuffs?"

Leigh arched her back off the table. "Under me. At the small of my back."

"I'll get you free in a second." He smiled sheepishly before slipping his hand behind her back to free her cuffs from the small pouch. He unsnapped the cover, dragging them from under her. "Sorry."

"Don't be. Get him secured and then worry about me."

Matt dropped from view. She shifted sideways on the table as far as her restraints would allow so she could see. Matt flipped Bradford face down on the ground binding his arms behind him, before rolling him over to lie on his bound arms. Blood soaked one of Bradford's sleeves and one pant leg was tattered and splattered with blood and tissue.

Bradford started to swear and Matt bent over him. "Shut up," he snarled, but then looked thoughtful, as if reconsidering. "Or maybe you'd like to keep talking. Then I'll have one more go at you and I'll make sure it ends up in the report that it was all part of the initial struggle." He reached over to the worktable and picked up the baseball bat that lay at one end, the end darkened almost black with dried blood. "You used this on your last victim. How do you think it would feel? Want to give it a try?"

Bradford glared at him, but went quiet.

Matt set down the bat and quickly moved around the table, winking at Leigh to let her know he never intended to use the bat. He made fast work of unfastening her restraints, first her hands and then her feet, showing her the small, sturdy carabineer clips that had been used to lock the sections of chain together. Leigh pushed herself into a sitting position, rubbing her wrists. Her fingers and left palm were smeared with her own blood. She hurriedly wiped it off on her pants.

"You okay?" Matt's eyes shifted from her abraded wrists to the large purple bruise that was spreading across her jaw.

"Yeah." She reached up and rubbed her fingers along her jaw, wincing. "For such a skinny guy, he hits like a sledgehammer." She eyed Matt's gun. "Where did that come from?"

He shrugged. "Hidden under my shirt. You didn't tell me not to bring it this time."

"Thank God for small favors." She jumped off the table and then retrieved her own gun from under the shelf.

She returned to stand by Bradford's head, quickly taking in his injuries. "We're going to need an ambulance." She glanced over at Matt. "How bad is he?"

Matt squatted down beside Bradford's bloodied knee. "The arm wound is deep, but you missed both the ulnar and the radial arteries. Not enough blood loss for that. But the knee . . ." He took in the damage from his own shot with clinical detachment, clearly feeling no remorse. "If the blood flow to his foot isn't good, he might lose the limb."

Bradford made a strangled sound.

"It would be the least you deserve," Matt snapped. "Call it in. I'll keep him covered." Matt moved to stand at Bradford's head, holding his gun steady on his forehead. He met the cold hatred in Bradford's eyes and smiled back brightly. "Damned frustrating to be at someone else's mercy, isn't it, Bradford?"

The smile died. "Get used to it."

Moving to the worktable, Leigh bent to retrieve her jacket before dragging the heavy door open. Late afternoon daylight flooded through the open doorway. She hurriedly called in her request for backup and a full paramedic team with a second team kept on standby.

She turned around to see the disgruntled look on Matt's face and couldn't help but smile.

"He may need the paramedics but I don't," he said stubbornly.

She gently clasped his head in both hands, tipped it sideways so she could see the wound better. The gaping dark gash was inches long and steadily oozing blood. Blood matted his hair and continued to drip down over the side of his face. She tilted his head back up and met his eyes. "Yes, you do." When he started to protest, she cut him off. "You can't see it. I can. You need stitches. They'll want to send you to the ER for that. And you lost consciousness, so they might want to keep you overnight for observation." She turned away so he couldn't see her lips twitch, but she could imagine the outraged look on his face. "Keep watching him. I want to take a look around."

She crossed to the worktable. She had caught a brief glimpse of a collage of photographs and newspaper articles before. She stood before it, trying to take it all in. The wall was covered with newspaper articles from local papers about the missing women. The most recent articles concerned the discovery of Tracy Kingston's body and the multiple graves.

But the picture Leigh focused on was of the press conference. Law enforcement and legal personnel were grouped outside of the Essex Police Department, the press officer in front speaking to the media. What drew her attention was the hand-drawn circle in red ink around her own face.

She turned to find Bradford watching her. "Is this how I

caught your eye, Bradford?"

"You ruined everything," he sneered. "You stopped the game. I would love to have added you to my collection." His gaze flicked to the wall of newspaper articles. "You deserve to die slowly and in agony."

"Hey." Matt forcibly rammed the toe of his boot into Bradford's shoulder, smiling in satisfaction at his grunt in pain. "That's enough."

Leigh held out a hand. "No, that's okay, Matt. Let him talk." She turned back to the trussed man on the floor. "Was that all it was to you? A game?"

"I wanted to make them do my bidding. And in the end they were almost all malleable. Young minds can be bent so easily. They even thought it was their own idea."

Leigh looked at him in disbelief. "You're insane, Bradford. But not insane enough to make a plea of it. You blew it when you had someone else pose as you today. That shows a level of forethought that a crazy man simply doesn't have. So, who was it? You might as well tell us. I can guarantee he's currently singing like a canary to anybody who will listen."

"He's a guy I work with," Bradford spat. "I told him I sold my bike to someone down in Plymouth, but the buyer wanted the bike right away and I couldn't get it to him because I had to work the next few days straight. I paid him one hundred and fifty dollars to ride the bike down there and then to take the bus back." He laughed cruelly. "He's an idiot and had no idea what he was getting into. I was hoping that the cops would take him down the minute he was spotted."

"Let me assure you he's alive and well and in custody. You knew I got a good look at your helmet and had reported it. Anyone caught with that helmet riding the bike with your license plate on it had a big red bull's-eye on his back. Considering the current body count, any cop would simply pull him over and ask questions later, once he was back at headquarters."

"I fooled them long enough to catch you off guard," Bradford crowed.

"Not well enough though or you wouldn't be the one lying cuffed on the ground," Leigh said easily. She turned back to the wall. "And you know what you've done here with your 'trophy wall'? You're going to help us identify your victims. Help us bring them home to their families."

She leaned down over Bradford, feeling a kick of satisfaction as she made eye contact with him. "We've got you, you son of a bitch. And if I have my way, you'll never see freedom again." She smiled when he started to struggle against his restraints again in fury. "You have the right to remain silent . . ."

Chapter Twenty-Seven:
Salt Marsh Mosquito

Salt Marsh Mosquito: Aedes sollicitans; a common marsh insect that lays its eggs in the high marsh. The female *Aedes* requires a blood meal for egg production and can spread disease through its bite. Mature eggs require an extremely high tide or heavy rains before hatching.

Monday, 10:54 P.M.
Abbott residence
Salem, Massachusetts

With a low sigh of pleasure, Leigh sank down on the edge of her bed.

The day was over. The case was closed and the real Neil Bradford was safely in custody.

She swirled the pale liquid in her glass mug, the scents of cinnamon, ginger, and cloves wafting into the air. She took a long, slow sip of the mulled wine before setting the mug down on the bedside table. She stood, pulling back the duvet to crawl into bed. All she wanted for the next half hour was to unwind in the soothing quiet of her bedroom with the book she'd been ignoring for two weeks while—

Her cell phone rang and she groaned at the interruption. She glanced at the number, but didn't recognize it. "Leigh Abbott."

"It's Tucker."

Her heart sank. "Tucker, I just got home after one hell of a day and it's late. All I really want to do is have a drink to celebrate the end of the case, relax for a few minutes, and go to bed. Do you really need me tonight?"

"Kicking back with a beer?"

"No. Mulled white wine with pear brandy. It's quite lovely."

Tucker made a mock retching noise. "What are you, some kind of girl?"

"I'm hurt that you never noticed. Now, if you're done insulting my celebratory beverage of choice, why don't you touch base with me tomorrow—"

"You need to see this now." All trace of humor vanished from Tucker's tone, making Leigh snap to attention.

"What have you got?"

"You remember how we got the warrant for Bradford's ISP and that I've been tracking his Internet traffic? Well, I found something. Something that's going to make you wish that your mulled wine was Jack Daniel's because you're going to need it to read this."

"What is it?"

"The sick bastard kept a personal blog. An online journal of his activities."

Sitting back down on the bed, Leigh stared blankly at a watercolor of a wind-swept ocean view on her bedroom wall. "That doesn't make any sense. Why would he take such a risk? It's not a diary he kept under his bed. A blog is something that's out there on the Internet for public consumption. What if someone else read it and turned him in?"

"I think that was part of the thrill. 'Look at me, getting away with all this torture and death and mayhem, and no one can catch me,' " Tucker mimicked in a sneering tone. "Some of these guys even get off on going back and reliving their kills, so he might have done it for that as well. Also, if it's out in the 'cloud,' he can access it from anywhere to add to it or savor past posts. But he was smart enough to take some precautions. For starters, he was careful to have his domain hosted outside of the U.S. In this case, the server is in Russia. Whether there are connections there to the shady side of Russian crime, I'm not sure, but I'll be looking into it. He had the site locked down, but not so well that I couldn't hack in. And no one else accessed it but him, probably because only he knew about it. You definitely need to read it before you interview him again."

"I haven't interviewed him at all yet. Kepler and I are going to do that tomorrow morning. Bradford just came out of surgery. Nothing we got out of him today would be allowed in any courtroom because he would have still been under the influence of the drugs they gave him."

"Then make sure you read it before you talk to him. Have you got a pen and paper to write down the URL? I've changed his password, so you'll need that too. For security's sake, I don't want to send this information to you electronically."

"Hold on." Leigh opened the drawer of her bedside table and pulled out the small pad of paper and pen that she kept there. "Okay, go ahead."

Tucker rattled off the website, screen name, and password. "If you have any problems logging in, give me a call. Otherwise, happy reading."

"Thanks." Leigh's body sagged, her head bent, and her shoulders stooped in exhaustion. She glanced regretfully at her mulled wine and the book sitting beside it on the bedside table. Apparently, her day wasn't over quite yet.

She retrieved her laptop and settled into bed, propped on pillows against the wrought iron headboard while her computer booted up.

Maybe it was because it was late and she was impatient, but her computer seemed slower than usual. She glanced at her clock, then, on a whim, she picked up her phone and dialed.

Matt picked up on the third ring. "Hey."

"Hey. I'm not calling too late, am I?"

"It's okay. I'm not settled in yet."

Concern rose. "Is it your head? Are you in pain?"

He chuckled. "It's kind of achy but it's not that bad."

"You should be in bed already. I shouldn't have called."

"If I was ready to be in bed, I'd be there. I'm just lying on the chaise, doing a little stargazing. It's soothing."

She could picture him lying stretched out on the padded chaise in his darkened room, the shutters thrown open and a beam of moonlight falling over his body. "You had a tough day. I'm sorry I didn't see you earlier. I didn't want to leave Bradford unguarded for even a second and by the time I could get away to check on you, you'd already been released."

"Don't worry about it. I actually came up to find you before I left, but I saw you down the hall in what looked like a serious conversation with Kepler, so I didn't stay. You had a job to do and I knew we'd hook up when you got free." Matt's tone was easy and it soothed some of Leigh's remaining tension.

Leigh tipped her head back against the pillows and closed her eyes, giving herself a moment to relax. "A doctor checked you out? There's no risk of concussion?"

"No, Mom. It's all good. What about you? You blacked out for a while there too."

"I'm fine. I don't even have a headache."

"Glad to hear it. Did you interview Bradford today?"

"No. He was triaged and then went almost immediately into surgery. And he was in no shape afterwards to be interviewed. Kepler and I have that booked for first thing tomorrow morning in his hospital room. In the meantime, Gloucester P.D. will have a man stationed at his door 24/7. Not that he could run far on that leg."

Matt gave a snort of laughter. "You're welcome."

"Which reminds me, I haven't actually thanked you for your help in the fallout shelter. You saved my life."

"Nah . . . You were already fighting him off. You can take care of yourself."

"But I was still restrained. There were no guarantees that I would have been able to fend him off. You took him down."

"I couldn't see what was going on from the floor, but from what I saw later, you pretty effectively took out his right arm. He would have had a lot more trouble doing damage to you just from that single strike, and you still had a hold of that knife so the fight wasn't over yet." When she remained silent, he capitulated. "Okay, let's say we did it together. And no thanks are required."

"Deal." Leigh opened her eyes to check her computer's progress. "Finally."

"Finally . . . what?" Matt sounded confused.

"I was waiting for my laptop to boot up. Tucker just called me. Apparently Bradford kept an online blog about his activities."

"No way." Suddenly Matt's relaxed voice was full of tension. "That's insane. What if someone read it and reported him?"

"That was my first thought too. But Tucker said that it was password-protected and no one had visited the site but Bradford because no one else knew that it was there."

"He certainly wasn't going to tell his partners," Matt reasoned. "They'd have run for the hills or turned him in for sure if they thought their lives were in danger."

"You'd think so. Well, I'll let you go. I just wanted to make sure you were okay. I've got to take a look at this site and—"

"Don't even think about it," Matt growled. "You think you're going to hang up and read that blog on your own?"

"Yes, I—"

"Well, you thought wrong. Don't cut me out now. This is my case too."

"Did you join the force when I wasn't looking?" she asked dryly.

"You're funny. Look, Leigh, if that blog is the key, I want to know what's in it."

Leigh didn't need to think it over for long. "You're sure? This could be some pretty awful stuff."

"I'm sure. Let's do it."

"Okay. Give me a second. I have to log in first." She followed Tucker's detailed instructions, navigating to the site and then using the user ID and password that he provided. "Okay, I'm there. The latest entry is a week ago Saturday."

"The day after Tracy Kingston was kidnapped," Matt said, "and before it all went to hell. He hasn't had time to blog since then, I'd bet."

"No doubt." She started to scan through the post, then gave a sharp gasp.

"What? What's he saying?"

Her lip curling in distaste, Leigh leaned forward to more carefully study the screen. "It's not what he's saying. I'm not even to that part yet. He posted photos."

There was a moment of silence. Then, cautiously, "Photos?"

"Yes, exactly the kind of photos you're imagining. They're of Tracy being tortured." She made a sound that was a mixture of anger and pity. "There are several pictures of her, restrained on the table. Some of the tools they used are clearly visible and some of the shots include John Hershey."

"Guess you'd be able to recognize him after this past week," Matt muttered.

"Bradford also writes about everything they did to her. Hershey is named specifically." She swore quietly. "I think Tucker might be right. He's putting so much detail into it so that he could come back and experience the rush again through both words and pictures."

"That's sick. Okay, how about we do this in logical order. What's the oldest entry? It would make more sense to start at the beginning and work forward."

"Hold on." She scrolled down the page. "There's an archive calendar here. Dates with entries are bolded. Let's see how far back this goes . . ." She quickly flipped through consecutive months.

"So . . ." Matt pressed when she had been silent for a full thirty seconds.

"Sorry, hang on, still looking. Okay, I think this is it. He started it about three years ago. The entries are kind of spotty in places and then they come in bunches."

"Probably clustered around the killings." Matt's voice was harsh. "So, going back three years, we're looking at the 'B1' grave then."

"Yes." Leigh scanned the entry. "He's hunting."

"For a partner or a victim?"

"In this entry he's discussing possible partners." She gave a low whistle. "He wrote it."

"Wait. Wrote what? The blog?"

"No, 'Death Orgy.' He wrote the game. Based on . . . no way . . ."

"What? *What?* Damn it, what's the address of this site? I need to see this too."

"You've got your laptop handy?"

"On my dresser. When I got home I emailed my students to update them on what was going on. It was faster than individual calls and they're all connected all the time anyway." Leigh heard him shift position, and then give a short hiss of pain.

"Are you okay?"

"Just moved too fast. The ache became a chorus of hammers."

"You shouldn't—"

"I'm fine." Leigh couldn't see his face, but she could imagine the stubborn set to his mouth. "Can you email me the link?" She heard a soft groan as he resettled himself, followed by the musical tones of his computer booting up.

She sighed. There was no point in fighting with him. He'd hear about it soon enough anyway and she'd like his opinion. "Tucker doesn't want this to go out electronically. Boot up and I'll walk you through it verbally."

"Thanks. While I'm waiting, go back to what you were saying. The game is based on . . ."

"Seven years ago, I was just finishing my undergrad degree before joining the force. The department encourages post-secondary education for its officers, either before joining the force or part-time afterwards, so I got my degree before applying to the Academy. I haven't told you about my father, but he was the sergeant for the Detective Unit until he died in the line of duty four years ago."

"Leigh . . . I'm so sorry. That must have been terrible for you."

"It was. Dad was all I had left because we lost Mom to cancer when I was just a little girl." She cleared her throat when she heard emotion start to creep into her voice. "Anyway, back then, Dad would discuss current cases with me as teaching material because we both knew that I was heading for the Academy. One of the department cases involved a man named Ray Nesbitt who was convicted for the brutal torture and murder of his wife. Bradford writes about the Nesbitt case and the way he talks about it here, so full of admiration and envy, it's clear this was his inspiration for 'Death Orgy.' "

"He used a real-life torture scenario as a jumping off point for coding a video game? That's horrible. Okay, I'm ready. Where's the blog?"

Leigh took him through the steps to gain access to the site.

"I'm in," he finally said.

"Start by checking out this blog post." Leigh specified a date. "He's talking about selecting his partner."

There was a pause. Then, "Son of a bitch, do you see that?"

"What? What are you reading?"

"That same post, but I'm scanning and may be further along than you. He used his position at the Riverdale Community Health Center to pick his targets."

"That doesn't make any sense," Leigh said. "He wouldn't have access to patients. He worked three to eleven P.M. cleaning offices and patient rooms after hours. He wasn't part of the medical staff."

"He didn't need access to patients, just their records. According to this, he had the run of the place at night and full keycard access to every office so he could rifle through the unlocked desks of the medical staff. One worker had her password on a Post-it note in her desk drawer. Once into her account, Bradford had access to the system that includes every mental health clinic that Massachusetts Health oversees. He reviewed patient records at his leisure and chose his partners from there. He could find exactly the type of person that he was looking for—someone who was young and immature, with a trend toward violence and anger-based tendencies."

"And Hershey was in the system for behavior modification," Leigh said. "That's how Bradford cherry-picked his partners. Hershey's file likely would have noted his love of violent gaming."

"That's really low—picking on the young and mentally vulnerable."

"Look at the next entry. He's made a list of potential targets and he's sent them invitations to play 'Death Orgy.' He must have been casting the net wide and then picking the weakest of the pack."

"Pretentious bastard. I'm skipping forward a few entries. He's got comments on all the potentials. He's outlining all the weak points of these kids and zeroing in on the one who will be the most easily swayed. That's what he was doing—he wanted to see how he could take an unstable mind and twist it. He was essentially brainwashing these kids." Matt blew out a long puff of air. "This is really pissing me off."

"I know how you feel. It's a mixture of anger and disgust with some pity thrown in for these kids."

"I'm not feeling sorry for these kids. They may have been weak, but they were brutal to their victims. Mental health issues might be an explanation, but they're not an excuse. Now the question is how did Bradford and his partners go from online gaming to real-life murder?"

Leaning back against her pillows, Leigh started scanning through entries more quickly. "He's included a lot of information here. I'm going to have to come back to this and make detailed notes before I talk to Bradford tomorrow, but . . ."

Matt waited a few beats before speaking. "Got something?"

"Yes. Check out the post dated August sixth. The partner this time around was a boy named Lawrence. Not sure if that's a first or last name. They'd just had their first face-to-face meeting."

"So he was wooing them in the game and them meeting them in person? I mean, we knew that had to happen at some point because they kill together, but what prompted the change from virtual interactions to a real-life meeting?"

"Look at the entry. He's mocking these boys. Says that this one, Lawrence, is mentally defective and he had to lead him along every step of the way. It sounds like he wanted the boys to think they're coming up with the idea to kill the women on their own, and then he played the role of cheerleader by saying 'Wow, that's cool. We should try that together.' "

"He thought it gave the boys ownership in killing and made them less likely to bolt. He was stroking their egos and counting on that to keep them in the game. And they might have been flattered to have an older man interested in them. I'll bet a lot of these boys didn't have a dependable father figure growing up, so Bradford may have felt like he was filling that role for them."

Suddenly chilled, Leigh leaned back against the pillows and picked up her mug to take a long sip. The brandy burned a trail down to her stomach, warming her. Her hands cradled the mug, the heat a comforting balm against her injured fingers. "You realize how smart this whole plan is though, don't you?"

"I'm not sure I follow you."

"Because of his partner selection, victim selection had no common factor. If he was using the medical system to pick the boys, then he was likely choosing from multiple clinics all over Essex County. So there was never any localized pattern of victim disappearance."

"Ahh . . ." Matt's voice was a quiet whisper across the line. "I see what you mean. And if he was smart, he let the partners contribute to the victim selection so he was never a common denominator in either location or victim type."

"So law enforcement never put two and two together because there was no commonality between any of the disappearances and they occurred so rarely." Leigh set the glass down again. "It was damned smart."

"He was a careful planner," Matt agreed. "Right down to the location of the house. It's isolated from the neighbors, but convenient to the river for easy transport of the bodies. It has a soundproof, hidden structure right on the property. And because Bradford owned a motorcycle and not a car, he must have picked partners that had a car to use for the kidnappings. If they were spotted, like they were at the Cummings Center, then the vehicle couldn't be traced back to him personally." He made an odd humming noise. "Now, look at this."

"What?"

"Look at the entry for January twenty-third. He must have been biding his time between killings as he was grooming a new partner over the winter while the ground was frozen. He did an actual comparison between the two partners he'd had so far. So, 'Lawrence' is Tyler Lawrence. The other partner was Luke Simons."

"Hold on." Leigh quickly scrolled up to the post. "Two partners? He had a partner for the 'A1' grave? Then why is there only one body? I assumed he did that one solo and then picked up a partner the second time round."

"Apparently not." Matt let out a harsh, humorless laugh. "This is immensely cocky. He did a comparison chart, right down to a 'lessons learned' column."

"Do you see how he refers to the boys? As 'subjects'?" Leigh couldn't keep the outrage out of her voice.

"And now we see what happened to Luke Simons. Keep scrolling down. You'll find it." He waited a moment for her to catch up to him. "It was never in his initial plan to kill him. But they were in the boat on their way back from burying their first victim when the kid started to mouth off about taking a second victim, this time someone that he knew. Bradford panicked. It was one thing to take an anonymous woman who had no connection to them. It was something else entirely to kill someone who could be traced back to either of them. Bradford had his gun with him just in case anyone caught them burying the body, so he shot Simons in the head and the force of the gunshot toppled his body overboard. Then he went to Simons' apartment and broke in to steal his computer so Simons couldn't be traced back to him. He took the TV and some other items so that it would look like a run-of-the-mill burglary."

"I'll check the Missing Persons database, but depending on how far out they were, there's a good chance that the body was simply washed out to sea and never found." Leigh suddenly stifled a huge yawn.

Matt chuckled. "Ready to call it a night?"

Leigh stared at the entry on her screen. She had hours of reading still to do, but felt completely drained. "I think so. I need to go over all of this information before talking to Bradford tomorrow, but I'm really tired."

"You had a tough day too, you know. Give yourself a break. Go to bed now and start fresh in the morning. You did a great job today."

"*We* did a great job," she corrected. "But you're right. It's time to quit for the night."

"Can you come by the lab tomorrow after your interview with Bradford and let us know how it went?"

"Yeah, I'd like that. I want to thank your students again. They were really fantastic through this whole case."

"Yeah, they really were." Leigh could hear the pride in Matt's voice.

"You're packing it in too?"

"Oh yeah. I think the only thing that is going to make this pounding go away is unconsciousness."

"Have a good night then. Sleep well."

"You too. I'll see you tomorrow." He ended the call.

Leigh stared thoughtfully at her monitor for a few seconds. Then she shut down her computer, putting the case away for the night.

Chapter Twenty-Eight:
Killifish

Killifish: Fundulus majalis; an omnivorous fish, commonly found in the salt marsh; an important food source for wading birds.

Tuesday, 3:40 P.M.
Boston University, School of Medicine
Boston, Massachusetts

Matt ended the call and laid his phone down on top of the haphazard stack of journal articles on his desk. "Leigh's on her way up," he told his students. "She managed to get free for a few hours to come down to let us know how her interview with Bradford went." He reached up with one hand to rub his head carefully just below the stitches where the skin felt tight and itchy.

"How's your head?" Kiko asked.

"The headache's mostly gone at this point. But the skin pulls a bit."

"You really didn't do very well at coming through this case in one piece." Kiko set down her sketching pencil to pin him with a level stare. "If we ever do this again, you need to try harder *not* to be a target." She laughed at the shock that flashed over Matt's expression at her suggestion. "Do you honestly think after the job we did this time Leigh wouldn't want us to help out again if they ever needed our particular skills?"

Matt moved to one of the sets of remains, leaning over to

examine one of the kerf marks in an attempt to hide his sudden wave of uncertainty. "Maybe . . . I don't know. Anyway, we'll be busy with this case for a while yet. They may have the perp essentially behind bars, but we need to build a court case and that's going to take us weeks to complete."

"Would you be willing to do it again?" Juka asked from his workstation.

"Willing to do what? Work another case?" At Juka's nod, Matt shrugged. "Two weeks ago the answer would have been 'Hell, no!' Now . . . I'm not sure. It didn't turn out at all like I expected. It wasn't anything like the last time I worked with the police."

At the sound of a quiet knock on the door, Matt turned away, grateful for the interruption. He opened the door to find Leigh holding a takeout tray with five coffees precariously balanced over two brown paper bags. "How are—Whoa . . . let me take some of that." He reached out, easily lifting the tray of coffees from her hands.

Paul's head shot up. "Do I smell coffee?"

Matt laughed at Leigh's startled expression. "It's his special talent—Paul can smell coffee from miles away."

"I hit the bakery around the corner on my way here and got coffee and cookies for my team," Leigh explained, her smile including the whole group.

Paul elbowed Juka. "Did you hear that?" he asked in a clearly discernible whisper as he shed his lab coat. " 'Her team.' "

Juka grinned back. "I'm quite happy to be a part of her 'team' if we get paid in coffee and fresh baked goods."

"All right you two," Matt interrupted, shaking his head at their antics. "If you're done fawning, why don't you take this stuff down to the lounge? We'll be right there."

Paul grabbed the tray of coffees from Matt and headed out the door. Juka followed behind, neatly snagging the bags from Leigh's hands.

Kiko followed more slowly. "Don't take too long. You know those two—they'll eat everything if left alone too long." She grinned as she went out the door.

"No eating in the lab," Matt clarified, seeing Leigh's questioning look as her gaze followed Kiko out of the lab. She started for the door, only to stop when she realized that Matt wasn't following her. "What's wrong?"

"Nothing's wrong. I just wanted to thank you."

She cocked her head slightly in confusion. "For what?"

"For being so fair with my students during this case. They're young and they're just learning how science works in the real world. But you made this experience a satisfying one for them. You accepted them onto your team, you listened to what they had to say, and you never belittled any of their ideas. And you were patient and let me use this opportunity to show them what we can really do. There aren't many cops that would have allowed me that kind of latitude, especially on a case that exploded into such a high high-profile media circus."

"The San Marcos detective you worked with obviously didn't give you that kind of freedom, did he?"

"No," he said shortly.

"You know who showed me how to interact with them? You did. You don't treat them as equals, because they aren't. They know and you know they still have to grow into that role. But you treat them with respect. You draw out their opinions because they know it's a safe forum for discussion and because they know you'll listen. You don't belittle them either. Instead, you guide and encourage them. You're a very good teacher, Matt. I was simply following your lead at the beginning until I found my footing with them."

"A week ago, I wouldn't have thought you'd want to follow my lead anywhere," he muttered quietly under his breath.

But not quietly enough as she let out a quiet chuckle. "Okay, so we got off to a rough start. But we got to the end together and that's what counts." Her gaze tracked up and into his hair. "How's the head?"

"Not too bad."

"Can I see?"

He bent his head toward her and, reaching up, she gently swept his hair to the side, revealing the neat line of dark stitches that marched over the angry wound. "The doctor did a nice job. You'll hardly notice it's there once it heals."

Matt straightened, pulling away from her hands. "It's under my hair—and it's hardly noticeable now."

"Yes, but it's another scar for you. Two more if we count your arm. And that's added to what you already had before this case started." His eyes went wide when she boldly stepped forward to lay her hand against his scarred side. His breath caught in his lungs and hot color flooded his face. *Please don't do this . . .* To his surprise, he felt her fingertips stroke soothingly over him once . . . twice. She met his eyes unwaveringly. "Do you remember what I said before about battle scars and the fact that they mean something?" He clenched his jaw and gave a single jerk of his head. "Never, ever, be ashamed of them. They speak volumes about the kind of man you are. And no woman worth your time would ever think any less of you because of them." She let her hand drop from his side but didn't break eye contact. "I was surprised, Matt. Nothing more."

He stared at her intently, but when he saw nothing but honesty in her direct gaze, his body relaxed. His gaze dropped from her eyes to the dark smudge that marred her jaw. It had blossomed into a dark blackish-purple abrasion with an angry red border. He started to reach out to run his fingers over the mark, but suddenly felt awkward and unsure and instead jammed his hand into his jeans pocket. "How's your jaw?"

"Sore, but it's nothing serious. It's not going to look good tonight though. I'll have to try to cover it up."

"Tonight?"

Leigh sighed heavily, and her shoulders slumped fractionally as she turned away to pace toward his desk. "There's another press conference at seven-thirty tonight. It will be our official announcement that we've caught the man responsible for all these deaths."

"Did he confess?"

"Yes, once he realized that we'd found his blog and he was backed into a corner. Then, his whole attitude changed."

Matt cocked his head slightly. "In what way?"

"Suddenly he was trying to play the sympathetic victim. I'll tell you all about it when we brief the whole group, but we've got him nailed. Did you fill your students in on the blog?"

"I told them this morning so they're up to date as of last night. I hope that was okay."

"They've worked hard on this case. They deserve to know what happened. Come on, let's go join them before they eat all the cookies."

They started down the hallway toward the lounge. "By the way," Matt said, "that knife you used to defend yourself against Bradford? It's a perfect match for some of the injuries we've found on the victims. The kerf marks confused us at first but then we realized that it was a single-edged knife with a combination of straight and serrated edges on the front of the blade and an extra row of small even teeth near the handle along the back of the blade. So you could see three separate kerf mark patterns all from the same blade and sometimes the straight blade defects were obscured by the marks left by the serrated portion of the blade. That's going to help us identify a large number of the wounds since that seemed to be his weapon of choice."

They turned into the lounge. Paul and Juka were sprawled on the sofa directly under the window, their feet propped up on the same coffee table that held the tray with the two remaining coffees and two open paper bags. Kiko sat beside them in an armchair. After Leigh entered the room, Matt closed the door behind them and followed her over to the seating area.

Bending over, Matt looked into the cookie bag before glancing at Paul and Juka. "If you two ate all of the chocolate chip cookies, you're going to re-catalog every bone sample I have. Twice. That should take until the end of next month for you to finish."

Paul grinned. "Do you think we have a death wish? Of course we left the chocolate chips for you." He took another bite from the large, golden cookie in his hand and then spoke through the crumbs in his mouth. "Besides, I'm a peanut butter man myself." He grinned at Leigh. "Thanks."

Leigh smiled in return and positioned herself on the couch across from them. "You're welcome." She took a coffee, adding cream and sugar. Matt added cream to his before selecting a large cookie generously studded with thick chunks of dark chocolate and sitting down beside her. He took a bite and made an involuntary hum of pleasure in the back of his throat. She cast him an amused sidelong glance. He silently toasted her with his cookie and leaned back comfortably against the arm of the couch.

"I wanted to let you know where we are with the case currently," Leigh began. "You all have more than pulled your weight, so I wanted you to hear the outcome from me."

"We want to know one thing first," Paul interrupted, "because Matt's being really vague. Who took Bradford down?"

Leigh looked at Matt as if asking permission. He gave her a silent shrug. *Go ahead; you tell them.*

She turned back to the students. "We did it together."

Both men groaned and immediately dug into their pockets, pulling out crumpled five-dollar bills in unison and handing them to Kiko. She tried not to look overly smug as she neatly smoothed them and folded them in half before sliding them into her pocket.

Leigh glanced at Matt. "Are they always like this?"

"Always." But there was amusement in his tone.

Leigh shook her head, bemused at their antics. "Matt tells me that you're up to speed on Bradford's blog and its contents."

"I can't believe he was that cocky," Kiko said, shaking her head in disbelief.

"After talking to him today, I'm not sure 'cocky' even covers it," Leigh said. "But yes, he was. Let me give you a little background on him so you know who we're dealing with. Neil Bradford is thirty-three years old and was born and raised on Cape Ann. He lived with his mother, and they moved around a lot. He never knew his father. We know the father's identity because there was a restraining order out against him by Bradford's mother before Bradford was even born. So we suspect an abusive relationship there. Either way, Bradford was raised by his mother. He tells the story that she worked two and sometimes three jobs at a time to support them. As a result, he spent most of his childhood alone because once his mother felt that he was old enough to look after himself, he was on his own. That was *not* at an age that the state would consider ap-propriate, but there was simply no money to pay for daycare. Because she wanted to avoid Child Protective Services, he was kept very isolated as a child. If the neighbors didn't know he was there, then no one could report her. He started school late as a result, because she wanted to keep him out of sight."

Sympathy flitted across Kiko's face, but only for an instant. "So he was a neglected child."

"It's certainly the story he's trying to sell because he's in damage-control mode right now," Leigh said dryly. "You can rest assured that his lawyer is going to try to use it to reduce his culpability for these crimes, so we need to confirm his story. Anyway, his mother died shortly after he graduated from high school. Bradford had already enrolled at Salem State College in Computer Science and he finished out the year, but his marks were anything but stellar. He completed his sophomore year there as well, but left after that. He wasn't forthcoming as to whether it was because of his marks or because of a lack of money, but I suspect the former because he would have been eligible for financial aid since he was on his own."

"He's clearly not stupid," Matt said grudgingly. "He's planned and murdered for years. That level of organization indicates a minimum intelligence level that would be well above what was needed to graduate if he'd actually applied himself."

"I agree. But if you look at his personality, I'd say that he could be labeled as having Antisocial Personality Disorder." One of Matt's eyebrows cocked upwards in interest. "I took a course on personality disorders in order to better understand some of the suspects I might have to deal with. Bradford was classic Antisocial Personality Disorder in several ways—he was deceitful, he used charm to manipulate the people around him, he had no qualms about violating the rights of others, and he had a tendency toward violent behavior. He also showed absolutely no remorse." She glanced over at Matt. "Yesterday, he referred to 'testing' the men, like it was all a game to him."

"The next level of 'Death Orgy,' perhaps?" he suggested.

"Possibly. But what he may not have anticipated was how much he would enjoy the game. The power of selecting the perfect target, bending that vulnerable mind to do his bidding, assisting in the torture of the victim, and then the thrill of getting away with it. So he decided to do it again, but he decided to make one very important change."

"That one's obvious," Matt said scornfully. "Take out the target once he helped dig his own grave. That explains all three

'B' graves. It became a truly disposable and repeatable process for him this way and there was never anyone left who could directly link him to the crimes."

"And since he enjoyed the process, he could repeat it over and over again," Kiko added.

"He did do it over and over again. He would select one target at a time, training and molding them until he felt that they were ready. He was also careful to make sure that he only killed during warm weather when the burial conditions were right. He didn't want to have to store a body until spring thaw. He noted in his blog that he was careful to always use a silencer when he was killing his accomplices out on the marsh."

"Because a gunshot would echo in open air and he wouldn't want anyone getting curious and coming out to find a fresh grave." Matt lightly tapped his temple with his index finger. "He thought through every detail."

"Right down to the ketamine," Leigh said. "He confirmed that he used ketamine injections to disable his victims during the kidnappings. We saw that at John Hershey's death scene too. There was a discarded syringe on the floor."

"But where did the anesthetic come from?" Kiko asked. "That's not something that's going to be left out on a counter at the Health Center."

"That's a controlled substance," Matt said. "They would stock some parenterals at the community clinic, sure, but they wouldn't be allowed a controlled substance like that there. It would open them up to potentially dangerous drug seekers looking for a hit of 'Special K.' "

"It's still widely used in veterinary practices though," Leigh interjected. "He broke into a vet clinic in Salem and stole both the ketamine and the syringes. I still need to look into that because a report must have been filed from the break-in."

Matt nodded. "Smart plan. Much lower security at a vet

clinic and the break-in would be automatically blamed on the drug community. And ketamine would be perfect for their needs. It's a dissociative anesthetic but at lower doses it has sedative effects that make it a useful date rape drug. They just needed the victim to be sedated long enough to be restrained, preferably until they got her back to the fallout shelter. A sufficient dose of ketamine would accomplish that and would likely also have the added bonus of giving their victim some horrific hallucinations that would only add to her terror."

"Bradford said it would never knock the victim out all the way, but that she simply couldn't move to fight them or to escape. They gagged the women to ensure any screaming couldn't be heard, as sound like that might carry over the open water."

"Because of the ventilation system, the fallout shelter could never be totally soundproof," Matt said with disgust. "Just mostly."

"They waited until the victim was awake to get started. That was part of the fun and part of the challenge—to torture and kill while she was still conscious. They tortured her for several hours, stopping if she lost consciousness and then starting again when she came to." She glanced over at Matt. "From reading the blog, we know that what would normally happen is that when Bradford sensed that the end was near but that their victim was still aware of what was happening to her, he'd let the target carry out the final coup de grace as the victim was manually strangled."

"Smart guy," Paul commented. "If he was ever caught, he was never actually responsible for the death of the victim."

"Not directly, but indirectly he's still guilty as sin." Leigh took another sip of her coffee before setting it down on the table. "What Bradford personally did with each one was to carve the signature while the victim was still alive but weak enough not to struggle. That's why it's the only consistent marker on all the female remains. It was his possession of the act. Now, normally, once the victim was dead, they'd wait for nightfall, then they'd wrap the body in plastic sheeting and move it under cover of darkness to the boat. Then he and his partner would go up to the Essex coast for the burial."

"Why that particular spot?" Matt interrupted. "Why move the body so far away?"

"I wondered that too. But it makes sense when you know that Bradford was born in Essex and he grew up as a young child knowing that area and those salt marshes. They lived in an isolated house near the marsh, and Bradford used to roam for hours at a time because no one was there to wonder where he was. For him, the marsh was a place of safety and he chose that particular location because he knew it was close to a branch of the Essex River and because it was so isolated from the mainland."

"He was right," Paul muttered. "Those bodies remained undiscovered for years."

"And still would be if it wasn't for that storm surge," Juka added. "It does make one wonder though, why he didn't just unload all the bodies into the ocean. Matt told us about how he killed his first partner and the body never washed ashore."

"No guarantee it would work the next time though," said Kiko. "Tides can be unpredictable and bodies can wash up on shore months later and in another area altogether. If he was born and raised on the coast, he would likely know this and wouldn't want to take the chance. He probably considered burial safer."

"But what happened the last time?" Matt asked. "Not only did he not kill the target, he didn't bury the victim immediately. That body was days old."

"Everything went to hell for him the last time." She glanced at Matt. "As you saw last night, the entries stopped after they had taken Tracy Kingston but before they had killed her. We questioned him in detail about Tracy, so this is all right from Bradford once he knew we had him and he understood if he was helpful he might get a mitigated sentence."

"Mitigated from what?" Matt asked sarcastically. "Ten life sentences down to nine?"

Leigh smiled. "You're thinking more clearly than he is right now. We've got him, no matter what he tells us. But we didn't feel the need to tell him that and he never asked for a lawyer even after he was Mirandized again and one was offered to him."

"That was stupid. Does he think he's too smart to need a lawyer?" Paul asked.

"Possibly. He's definitely not short on arrogance. Or maybe he was afraid his assigned counsel would be a woman. Anyway, the problem that last time was John Hershey, his selected target. He was on board right up until the end. But then he fell apart when it came to the actual killing. Hershey found out that torture in real life is actually a little different from a video game. According to Bradford, he couldn't take Tracy's muffled screams of agony and he bolted, leaving Bradford with a hysterical, half-dead woman on his hands. Bradford was so furious that he silenced her screams with a baseball bat to the head and then finished her by strangling her like the rest, leaving her on the table to go after Hershey. But Hershey disappeared and Bradford couldn't track him down at any of the spots where he thought he might have gone, including his house. Then he had the bad luck to come back and discover that there was a regatta taking place at the Heron Way Marina just upriver. There were boats moored all over so he couldn't risk being seen putting the body in the boat. They also blocked his way out to the main branch of the Annisquam. He had to wait three more days for the regatta to finish and for all the participants to clear out so he could transport the body without risk of being seen."

Matt felt warmed by a nasty satisfaction over Bradford's dilemma. "By that point decomposition would have been progressing nicely. This couldn't have gone worse for him if we'd planned it, could it?"

Leigh smiled back with the same apparent satisfaction. "Not at all. Anyway, that took him to last Wednesday morning when we caught him trying to bury the body solo. Once that went south on him and he got away from us, he really went after Hershey."

Paul gave a harsh laugh. "He must have been pretty pissed at that point."

"Very. He'd been seen, he'd lost his latest kill, and his burial ground had been discovered. He knew at that point that he had a very good chance of being caught because of evidence that might be found on any of the remains."

"And because of the fast ID that you'd be able to do on the newest victim. That was going to mean a much more specific Missing Persons search," Kiko said.

"It was all crashing down on him," Leigh agreed. "But as far as he was concerned, the most important thing he needed to do was to make John Hershey pay for all the damage he'd caused and for daring to escape." She lightly touched Matt's arm. "Do you remember what you told me about Orcus being the punisher of broken oaths? Well, he certainly took that role seriously based on what he did to John. The only definite location he had for Hershey was his house, so Bradford bet everything that he'd be back at some point. He broke in and holed up there to wait. On Saturday, Hershey took the chance of coming back for some personal items that he'd need for a long-term escape, and Bradford had him."

Matt's gaze flicked to Leigh to find her eyes steady on him.

"Until we interrupted him," he said in a flatly unemotional tone.

"But you lost him there too," Paul said.

"Yes," Leigh agreed. "In his arrogance, I think he thought he could get away with it. That if he laid low, as long as a connection could not be made back to him, he might be able to regroup and start it all again later."

"That is damned cocky," Paul growled.

"He'd need a new burial ground," Kiko suggested. "He'd have to change his setup."

"All of which he'd have been happy to do. Once he got past the anger, think of the satisfaction he would have felt at having stumped the police again. Too bad that didn't happen." She picked up her coffee again, absently swirling the liquid in the cup. "So that's where we are at this point. The official announcement about Bradford's arrest will be made tonight, and, once he's deemed fit enough, he'll be transferred to a state holding facility to await arraignment. I highly doubt that bail will be set in this case, considering that we're talking about ten deaths now that we know about Luke Simons. Too great a flight risk." She abruptly straightened, as if suddenly remembering something. "Oh! I almost forgot this part. Crime Scene Services called me today after we'd finished with Bradford. They were collecting evidence at the fallout shelter. They found a stash in one of the back rooms—a box that had every purse and wallet of all of the victims as well as all the clothing from the women. Needless to say, this is going to speed up the ID process significantly."

"It will be nice to put some names to our victims, instead of numbers," Kiko said.

"He removed all identification from the men before placing them in the grave?" Juka asked.

"That's our guess. If the victims were found, he wanted to make any potential ID as hard as possible. He felt his identity

was protected as long as the victims were unknown or, preferably, undiscovered."

"So that's it? Now all that's left is building such an airtight
case that there's no chance of him getting away?" Paul asked.

"Yes," Leigh said. "And that's where I need you guys. You
have a lot of remains to catalog. And that evidence is going to
be crucial. I don't want any nasty surprises. I want this to be
open and shut. And for that I need all of you."

"You've got us," Matt said. "No worries there."

"Yeah." Paul grinned. "Remember, we're your team? We're
going to connect every one of his weapons to every injury we've
recorded and we're going to nail this bastard's ass to the wall."
Paul picked up his coffee cup and toasted the group with it. "To
teamwork."

Five paper coffee cups came together over the center of the
table.

Epilogue

Leigh was just leaving the ladies' restroom in the Essex Police Department, makeup bag in hand and her bruise covered as best she could manage with foundation and powder, when one of the Essex officers rushed up to her.

"Trooper Abbott, there's a man outside with the media group who he says he wants to see you. A Dr. Lowell?"

Leigh's eyebrows rose in surprise. "Please, let him through, Officer. He's part of my team on this case."

As the officer hurried away, Leigh made her way through the maze of desks in the bullpen. She found the navy blazer she left draped over the back of one of the chairs and was just pulling it on as Matt entered the room.

"Hey."

She shrugged her shoulders settling the jacket. "What are you doing up here?"

"Ouch. Nice to see you too." At her pointed look, he chuckled. "I just came to wish you good luck. And to let you know the students and I drew up a schedule for examining the rest of the remains. I told them to take tomorrow off to sleep and to zone out, but then they're back in on Thursday and we think we can have everything wrapped up for you inside of a

285

week and a half. Two weeks tops. We'll make sure both you and the ADA get the full report."

Leigh hadn't missed his comment about only the students taking tomorrow off. "What about you? You've had a harder time of it than they have. Are you going to take tomorrow off?"

"Are you?" he retorted pointedly.

He had her there. "No."

"Didn't think so. Me either then. I may give myself a break and ease back a bit on Saturday and Sunday though. I think Dad's forgotten what I look like, he's seen so little of me. It would be nice to take him out on the Charles if the weather co-operates."

She smiled. "You could use the break. We all could." She heard voices and looked toward the far side of the room. Detective Lieutenant Harper, District Attorney Aaron Saxon, and his press officer Sharon Collins had all stepped into the bullpen. In response to Detective Lieutenant Harper's glance in her direction, Leigh raised one hand in acknowledgment.

"They must be ready for us." She turned back to Matt. "So . . . once this is all done, you're back to the charnel house at the Old North Church? That's going to be a nice change of pace after all this."

"I never thought I'd say it, but it's going to be a bit dull after the past week," Matt said wryly.

Leigh gave a short, cynical laugh. "Maybe dull's not a bad thing." Her name was called, drawing her attention back across the room. "Sorry, it looks like we're about to get started. Are you going to stay?"

"For the press conference? Nah . . . this is your area, not mine. I don't do the spotlight."

Leigh raised a single eyebrow at him. "Newsflash, Dr. Lowell. Neither do I."

"You're going to do it this time apparently whether you like it or not." Matt opened his mouth as if to say something else, and then snapped it closed again.

Leigh stared at him. "What? Have I forgotten something that I'll need for this?"

"No, no . . . it's nothing case related." He met her eyes and she saw something shift in his gaze—a resolution being made. He suddenly took a step closer, his voice dropping low so the small knot of people on the other side of the room couldn't hear him. "Have dinner with me Friday night."

One brow rose in interest. "Dinner?"

"Dinner. No case, no students, no bones, no blood. Just . . . dinner."

It amused her that he looked a bit anxious. "I'd like that. It would certainly be a nice change after the last week. I'll be wrapping up the details of this case over the next few days, but by then I think they'll let me have an evening off."

A slow grin split his face. Leigh accurately read his expression of relief and realized that this, not his scientific schedule and report, had been the real reason for his trip to the Essex coast.

He stepped forward again, crowding her slightly, but she didn't move, allowing him into her space. "Do you like Italian? There's this great little Italian place in the Back Bay that stocks the best wines. I know the owner. He'll give us a nice quiet table in a dark corner."

Her smile spread to match his. "Sounds wonderful. I'll call you and we can set up—". She stopped abruptly, hearing her name called again. "Damn. Time to start. I hate these things." She stepped back and tugged on the lapels of her blazer with uncharacteristic nervousness. "Do I look okay?"

The heat that filled his eyes caught her off guard, as did the hand that rose to feather the lightest of touches over the shadow that marred her jaw even through the makeup. "Beautiful," he said huskily. Then his hand dropped and he stepped back. When he spoke again, his tone was matter of fact and she found that she preferred the previous intimacy. "Knock 'em dead, Trooper." Turning, he strode from the room.

Her eyes stayed fixed on him as he disappeared through the doorway and she thought about dinner with him. *Possibilities,* she thought. *Definite possibilities.*

Then she turned to join the legal and law enforcement team as, together, they walked out the front door of the police department to face the media throng that waited for them.

ABOUT THE AUTHORS

A scientist specializing in infectious diseases, **Jen J. Danna** works as part of a dynamic research group at a cutting-edge Canadian university. However, her true passion lies in indulging her love of the mysterious through her writing. Together with her partner, **Ann Vanderlaan**, a retired research scientist herself, she crafts suspenseful crime fiction with a realistic scientific edge.

Ann lives near Austin, Texas, with her three rescued pit bull companions. Jen lives near Toronto, Ontario, with her husband and two daughters, and is a member of the Crime Writers of Canada. You can reach her at jenjdanna@gmail.com or through her website and blog at www.jenjdanna.com.